The Adventures of
Sir Gawain

The Adventures of Sir Gawain

Table of Contents

Sir Gawain and the Green Knight
Translated by Jessie Weston

Preface

The poem of which the following pages offer a prose rendering is contained in a MS., believed to be unique, of the Cottonian Collection, Nero A.X., preserved in the British Museum. The MS. is of the end of the fourteenth century, but it is possible that the composition of the poem is somewhat earlier; the subject-matter is certainly of very old date. There has been a considerable divergence of opinion among scholars on the question of authorship, but the view now generally accepted is that it is the work of the same hand as *Pearl*, another poem of considerable merit contained in the same MS.

Our poem, or, to speak more correctly, metrical romance, contains over 2500 lines, and is composed in staves of varying length, ending in five short rhyming lines, technically known as a bob and a wheel,–the lines forming the body of the stave being not rhyming, but alliterative. The dialect in which it is written has been decided to be West Midland, probably Lancashire, and is by no means easy to understand. Indeed, it is the real difficulty and obscurity of the language, which, in spite of careful and scholarly editing, will always place the poem in its original form outside the range of any but professed students of mediæval literature, which has encouraged me to make an attempt to render it more accessible to the general public, by giving it a form that shall be easily intelligible, and at the same time preserve as closely as possible the style of the author.

For that style, in spite of a certain roughness, unavoidable at a period in which the language was still in a partially developed and amorphous stage, is really charming. The author has a keen eye for effect; a talent for description, detailed without becoming wearisome; a genuine love of Nature and sympathy with her varying moods; and a real refinement and elevation of feeling which enable him to deal with a risqué: situation with an absence of coarseness, not, unfortunately, to be always met with in a mediæval writer. Standards of taste vary with the age, but even judged by that of our own day the author of *Sir Gawain and the Green Knight* comes not all too badly out of the ordeal!

The Adventures of Sir Gawain

The story with which the poem deals, too, has claims upon our interest. I have shown elsewhere that the beheading challenge is an incident of very early occurrence in heroic legend, and that the particular form given to it in the English poem is especially interesting, corresponding as it does to the variations of the story as preserved in the oldest known version, that of the old Irish *Fled Bricrend*.

But in no other version is the incident coupled with that of a temptation and testing of the hero's honour and chastity, such as meets us here. At first sight one is inclined to assign the episode of the lady of the castle to the class of stories of which the oldest version is preserved in Biblical record–the story of Joseph and Potiphar's wife; a *motif* not unseldom employed by mediæval writers, and which notably occurs in what we may call the *Launfal* group of stories. But there are certain points which may make us hesitate as to whether in its first conception the tale was really one of this class.

It must be noted that here the lady is acting throughout with the knowledge and consent of the husband, an important point of difference. In the second place, it is very doubtful whether her entire attitude was not a ruse. From the Green Knight's words to Gawain when he finally reveals himself, "I wot we shall soon make peace with my wife, who was thy bitter enemy," her conduct hardly seems to have been prompted by real passion.

In my Studies on the *Legend of Sir Gawain*, already referred to, I have suggested that the character of the lady here is, perhaps, a reminiscence of that of the Queen of the Magic Castle or Isle, daughter or niece of an enchanter, who at an early stage of Gawain's story was undoubtedly his love. I think it not impossible that she was an integral part of the tale as first told, and her *rôle* here was determined by that which she originally played. In most versions of the story she has dropped out altogether. It is, of course, possible that, there being but a confused reminiscence of the original tale, her share may have been modified by the influence of the *Launfal* group; but I should prefer to explain the episode on the whole as a somewhat distorted survival of an original feature.

But in any case we may be thankful for this, that the author of the most important English metrical romance dealing with Arthurian legend faithfully adheres to the original conception of Gawain's character, as drawn before the monkish lovers of edification laid their ruthless hands on his legend, and turned the model of knightly virtues and courtesy into a mere vulgar libertine.

Brave, chivalrous, loyally faithful to his plighted word, scrupulously heedful of his own and others' honour, Gawain stands before us in this poem. We take up Malory or Tennyson, and in spite of their charm of style, in spite of the halo of religious mysticism in which they have striven to enwrap their characters, we lay them down with a feeling of dissatisfaction. How did the Gawain of their imagination, this empty-headed, empty-hearted worldling, cruel murderer, and treacherous friend, ever come to be the typical English hero? For such Gawain certainly was, even more than Arthur himself. Then we turn back to these faded pages, and read the quaintly earnest words in which the old writer reveals the hidden meaning of that mystic symbol, the pentangle, and vindicates Gawain's title to claim it as his badge—and we smile, perhaps, but we cease to wonder at the widespread popularity of King Arthur's famous nephew, or at the immense body of romance that claims him as its hero.

Scholars know all this, of course; they can read the poem for themselves in its original rough and intricate phraseology; perhaps they will be shocked at an attempt to handle it in simpler form. But this little book is not for them, and if to those to whom the tale would otherwise be a sealed treasure these pages bring some new knowledge of the way in which our forefathers looked on the characters of the Arthurian legend, the tales they told of them (unconsciously betraying the while how they themselves lived and thought and spoke)—if by that means they gain a keener appreciation of our national heroes, a wider knowledge of our national literature,—then the spirit of the long-dead poet will doubtless not be the slowest to pardon my handling of what was his masterpiece, as it is, in M. Gaston Paris' words, "The jewel of English mediæval literature."

BOURNEMOUTH, June 1898

Sir Gawain and the Green Knight

After the siege and the assault of Troy, when that burg was destroyed and burnt to ashes, and the traitor tried for his treason, the noble Æneas and his kin sailed forth to become princes and patrons of well-nigh all the Western Isles. Thus Romulus built Rome (and gave to the city his own name, which it bears even to this day); and Ticius turned him to Tuscany; and Langobard raised him up dwellings in Lombardy; and Felix Brutus sailed far over the French flood, and founded the kingdom of Britain, wherein have been war and waste and wonder, and bliss and bale, ofttimes since.

And in that kingdom of Britain have been wrought more gallant deeds than in any other; but of all British kings Arthur was the most valiant, as I have heard tell, therefore will I set forth a wondrous adventure that fell out in his time. And if ye will listen to me, but for a little while, I will tell it even as it stands in story stiff and strong, fixed in the letter, as it hath long been known in the land.

*

King Arthur lay at Camelot upon a Christmas-tide, with many a gallant lord and lovely lady, and all the noble brotherhood of the Round Table. There they held rich revels with gay talk and jest; one while they would ride forth to joust and tourney, and again back to the court to make carols; 2 for there was the feast holden fifteen days with all the mirth that men could devise, song and glee, glorious to hear, in the daytime, and dancing at night. Halls and chambers were crowded with noble guests, the bravest of knights and the loveliest of ladies, and Arthur himself was the comeliest king that ever held a court. For all this fair folk were in their youth, the fairest and most fortunate under heaven, and the king himself of such fame that it were hard now to name so valiant a hero.

Now the New Year had but newly come in, and on that day a double portion was served on the high table to all the noble guests, and thither came the king with all his knights, when the service in the chapel had been sung to an end. And they greeted each other for the New Year, and gave rich gifts, the one to the other (and they that received them were not wroth, that may ye well believe!), and the maidens laughed and made mirth till it was time to get them to meat. Then they washed and sat them down to the feast in fitting rank and order, and Guinevere the queen, gaily clad, sat on the high daïs. Silken was her seat, with a fair canopy over her head, of rich tapestries of Tars, embroidered, and studded with costly gems; fair she was to look upon, with her shining grey eyes, a fairer woman might no man boast himself of having seen.

But Arthur would not eat till all were served, so full of joy and gladness was he, even as a child; he liked not either to lie long, or to sit long at meat, so worked upon him his young blood and his wild brain. And another custom he had also, that came of his nobility, that he would never eat upon an high day till he had been advised of some knightly deed, or some strange and marvellous tale, of his ancestors, or of arms, or of other ventures. Or till some stranger knight should seek of him leave to joust with one of the Round Table, that they might set their lives in jeopardy, one against another, as fortune might favour them. Such was the king's custom when he sat in hall at each high feast with his noble knights, therefore on that New Year tide, he abode, fair of face, on the throne, and made much mirth withal.

Thus the king sat before the high tables, and spake of many things; and there good Sir Gawain was seated by Guinevere the queen, and on her other side sat Agravain, à la dure main; 3 both were the king's sister's sons and full gallant knights. And at the end of the table was Bishop Bawdewyn, and Ywain, King Urien's son, sat at the other side alone. These were worthily served on the daïs, and at the lower tables sat many valiant knights. Then they bare the first course with the blast of trumpets and waving of banners, with the sound of drums and pipes, of song and lute, that many a heart was uplifted at the melody. Many were the dainties, and rare the meats, so great was the plenty they might scarce find room on the board to set on the dishes. Each helped himself as he liked best, and to each two were twelve dishes, with great plenty of beer and wine.

Now I will say no more of the service, but that ye may know there was no lack, for there drew near a venture that the folk might well have left their labour to gaze upon. As the sound of the music ceased, and the first course had been fitly served, there came in at the hall door one terrible to behold, of stature greater than any on earth; from neck to loin so strong and thickly made, and with limbs so long and so great that he seemed even as a giant. And yet he was but a man, only the mightiest that might mount a steed; broad of chest and shoulders and slender of waist, and all his features of like fashion; but men marvelled much at his colour, for he rode even as a knight, yet was green all over.

For he was clad all in green, with a straight coat, and a mantle above; all decked and lined with fur was the cloth and the hood that was thrown back from his locks and lay on his shoulders. Hose had he of the same green, and spurs of bright gold with silken fastenings richly worked; and all his vesture was verily green. Around his waist and his saddle were bands with fair stones set upon silken work, 'twere too long to tell of all the trifles that were embroidered thereon–birds and insects in gay gauds of green and gold. All the trappings of his steed were of metal of like enamel, even the stirrups that he stood in stained of the same, and stirrups and saddle-bow alike gleamed and shone with green stones. Even the steed on which he rode was of the same hue, a green horse, great and strong, and hard to hold, with broidered bridle, meet for the rider.

The knight was thus gaily dressed in green, his hair falling around his shoulders; on his breast hung a beard, as thick and green as a bush, and the beard and the hair of his head were clipped all round above his elbows. The lower part of his sleeves were fastened with clasps in the same wise as a king's mantle. The horse's mane was crisp and plaited with many a knot folded in with gold thread about the fair green, here a twist of the hair, here another of gold. The tail was twined in like manner, and both were bound about with a band of bright green set with many a precious stone; then they were tied aloft in a cunning knot, whereon rang many bells of burnished gold. Such a steed might no other ride, nor had such ever been looked upon in that hall ere that time; and all who saw that knight spake and said that a man might scarce abide his stroke.

The knight bore no helm nor hauberk, neither gorget nor breast-plate, neither shaft nor buckler to smite nor to shield, but in one hand he had a holly-bough, that is greenest when the groves are bare, and in his other an axe, huge and uncomely, a cruel weapon in fashion, if one would picture it. The head was an ell-yard long, the metal all of green steel and gold, the blade burnished bright, with a broad edge, as well shapen to shear as a sharp razor. The steel was set into a strong staff, all bound round with iron, even to the end, and engraved with green in cunning work. A lace was twined about it, that looped at the head, and all adown the handle it was clasped with tassels on buttons of bright green richly broidered.

The knight rideth through the entrance of the hall, driving straight to the high daïs, and greeted no man, but looked ever upwards; and the first words he spake were, "Where is the ruler of this folk? I would gladly look upon that hero, and have speech with him." He cast his eyes on the knights, and mustered them up and down, striving ever to see who of them was of most renown.

Then was there great gazing to behold that chief, for each man marvelled what it might mean that a knight and his steed should have even such a hue as the green grass; and that seemed even greener than green enamel on bright gold. All looked on him as he stood, and drew near unto him wondering greatly what he might be; for many marvels had they seen, but none such as this, and phantasm and faërie did the folk deem it. Therefore were the gallant knights slow to answer, and gazed astounded, and sat stone still in a deep silence through that goodly hall, as if a slumber were fallen upon them. I deem it was not all for doubt, but some for courtesy that they might give ear unto his errand.

Then Arthur beheld this adventurer before his high daïs, and knightly he greeted him, for fearful was he never. "Sir," he said, "thou art welcome to this place–lord of this hall am I, and men call me Arthur. Light thee down, and tarry awhile, and what thy will is, that shall we learn after."

"Nay," quoth the stranger, "so help me He that sitteth on high, 'twas not mine errand to tarry any while in this dwelling; but the praise of this thy folk and thy city is lifted up on high, and thy warriors are holden for the best and the most valiant of those who ride mail-clad to the fight. The wisest and the worthiest of this world are they, and well proven in all knightly sports. And here, as I have heard tell, is fairest courtesy, therefore have I come hither as at this time. Ye may be sure by the branch that I bear here that I come in peace, seeking no strife. For had I willed to journey in warlike guise I have at home both hauberk and helm, shield and shining spear, and other weapons to mine hand, but since I seek no war my raiment is that of peace. But if thou be as bold as all men tell thou wilt freely grant me the boon I ask."

And Arthur answered, "Sir Knight, if thou cravest battle here thou shalt not fail for lack of a foe."

And the knight answered, "Nay, I ask no fight, in faith here on the benches are but beardless children, were I clad in armour on my steed there is no man here might match me. Therefore I ask in this court but a Christmas jest, for that it is Yule-tide, and New Year, and there are here many fain for sport. If any one in this hall holds himself so hardy, 4 so bold both of blood and brain, as to dare strike me one stroke for another, I will give him as a gift this axe, which is heavy enough, in sooth, to handle as he may list, and I will abide the first blow, unarmed as I sit. If any knight be so bold as to prove my words let him come swiftly to me here, and take this weapon, I quit claim to it, he may keep it as his own, and I will abide his stroke, firm on the floor. Then shalt thou give me the right to deal him another, the respite of a year and a day shall he have. Now haste, and let see whether any here dare say aught."

Now if the knights had been astounded at the first, yet stiller were they all, high and low, when they had heard his words. The knight on his steed straightened himself in the saddle, and rolled his eyes fiercely round the hall, red they gleamed under his green and bushy brows. He frowned and twisted his beard, waiting to see who should rise, and when none answered

11

he cried aloud in mockery, "What, is this Arthur's hall, and these the knights whose renown hath run through many realms? Where are now your pride and your conquests, your wrath, and anger, and mighty words? Now are the praise and the renown of the Round Table overthrown by one man's speech, since all keep silence for dread ere ever they have seen a blow!"

With that he laughed so loudly that the blood rushed to the king's fair face for very shame; he waxed wroth, as did all his knights, and sprang to his feet, and drew near to the stranger and said, "Now by heaven foolish is thy asking, and thy folly shall find its fitting answer. I know no man aghast at thy great words. Give me here thine axe and I shall grant thee the boon thou hast asked." Lightly he sprang to him and caught at his hand, and the knight, fierce of aspect, lighted down from his charger.

Then Arthur took the axe and gripped the haft, and swung it round, ready to strike. And the knight stood before him, taller by the head than any in the hall; he stood, and stroked his beard, and drew down his coat, no more dismayed for the king's threats than if one had brought him a drink of wine.

Then Gawain, who sat by the queen, leaned forward to the king and spake, "I beseech ye, my lord, let this venture be mine. Would ye but bid me rise from this seat, and stand by your side, so that my liege lady thought it not ill, then would I come to your counsel before this goodly court. For I think it not seemly when such challenges be made in your hall that ye yourself should undertake it, while there are many bold knights who sit beside ye, none are there, methinks, of readier will under heaven, or more valiant in open field. I am the weakest, I wot, and the feeblest of wit, and it will be the less loss of my life if ye seek sooth. For save that ye are mine uncle naught is there in me to praise, no virtue is there in my body save your blood, and since this challenge is such folly that it beseems ye not to take it, and I have asked it from ye first, let it fall to me, and if I bear myself ungallantly then let all this court blame me."

Then they all spake with one voice that the king should leave this venture and grant it to Gawain.

Then Arthur commanded the knight to rise, and he rose up quickly and knelt down before the king, and caught hold of the weapon; and the king loosed his hold of it, and lifted up his hand, and gave him his blessing, and bade him be strong both of heart and hand. "Keep thee well, nephew," quoth Arthur, "that thou give him but the one blow, and if thou redest him rightly I trow thou shalt well abide the stroke he may give thee after."

Gawain stepped to the stranger, axe in hand, and he, never fearing, awaited his coming. Then the Green Knight spake to Sir Gawain, "Make we our covenant ere we go further. First, I ask thee, knight, what is thy name? Tell me truly, that I may know thee."

"In faith," quoth the good knight, "Gawain am I, who give thee this buffet, let what may come of it; and at this time twelvemonth will I take another at thine hand with whatsoever weapon thou wilt, and none other."

Then the other answered again, "Sir Gawain, so may I thrive as I am fain to take this buffet at thine hand," and he quoth further, "Sir Gawain, it liketh me well that I shall take at thy fist that which I have asked here, and thou hast readily and truly rehearsed all the covenant that I asked of the king, save that thou shalt swear me, by thy troth, to seek me thyself wherever thou hopest that I may be found, and win thee such reward as thou dealest me to-day, before this folk."

"Where shall I seek thee?" quoth Gawain. "Where is thy place? By Him that made me, I wot never where thou dwellest, nor know I thee, knight, thy court, nor thy name. But teach me truly all that pertaineth thereto, and tell me thy name, and I shall use all my wit to win my way thither, and that I swear thee for sooth, and by my sure troth."

"That is enough in the New Year, it needs no more," quoth the Green Knight to the gallant Gawain, "if I tell thee truly when I have taken the blow, and thou hast smitten me; then will I teach thee of my house and home, and mine own name, then mayest thou ask thy road and keep covenant. And if I waste no words then farest thou the better, for thou canst dwell in thy land, and seek no further. But take now thy toll, and let see how thy strikest."

"Gladly will I," quoth Gawain, handling his axe.

Then the Green Knight swiftly made him ready, he bowed down his head, and laid his long locks on the crown that his bare neck might be seen. Gawain gripped his axe and raised it on high, the left foot he set forward on the floor, and let the blow fall lightly on the bare neck. The sharp edge of the blade sundered the bones, smote through the neck, and clave it in two, so that the edge of the steel bit on the ground, and the fair head fell to the earth that many struck it with their feet as it rolled forth. The blood spurted forth, and glistened on the green raiment, but the knight neither faltered nor fell; he started forward with out-stretched hand, and caught the head, and lifted it up; then he turned to his steed, and took hold of the bride, set his foot in the stirrup, and mounted. His head he held by the hair, in his hand. Then he seated himself in his saddle as if naught ailed him, and he were not headless. He turned his steed about, the grim corpse bleeding freely the while, and they who looked upon him doubted them much for the covenant.

For he held up the head in his hand, and turned the face towards them that sat on the high daïs, and it lifted up the eyelids and looked upon them and spake as ye shall hear. "Look, Gawain, that thou art ready to go as thou hast promised, and seek leally till thou find me, even as thou hast sworn in this hall in the hearing of these knights. Come thou, I charge thee, to the Green Chapel, such a stroke as thou hast dealt thou hast deserved, and it shall be promptly paid thee on New Year's morn. Many men know me as the knight of the Green Chapel, and if thou askest, thou shalt not fail to find me. Therefore it behoves thee to come, or to yield thee as recreant."

With that he turned his bridle, and galloped out at the hall door, his head in his hands, so that the sparks flew from beneath his horse's hoofs. Whither he went none knew, no more than they wist whence he had come; and the king and Gawain they gazed and laughed, for in sooth this had proved a greater marvel than any they had known aforetime.

Though Arthur the king was astonished at his heart, yet he let no sign of it be seen, but spake in courteous wise to the fair queen: "Dear lady, be not dismayed, such craft is well suited to Christmas-tide when we seek jesting, laughter and song, and fair carols of knights and ladies. But now I may well get me to meat, for I have seen a marvel I may not forget." Then he looked on Sir Gawain, and said gaily, "Now, fair nephew, hang up thine axe, since it has hewn enough," and they hung it on the dossal above the daïs, where all men might look on it for a marvel, and by its true token tell of the wonder. Then the twain sat them down together, the king and the good knight, and men served them with a double portion, as was the share of the noblest, with all manner of meat and of minstrelsy. And they spent that day in gladness, but Sir Gawain must well bethink him of the heavy venture to which he had set his hand. *****

This beginning of adventures had Arthur at the New Year; for he yearned to hear gallant tales, though his words were few when he sat at the feast. But now had they stern work on hand. Gawain was glad to begin the jest in the hall, but ye need have no marvel if the end be heavy. For though a man be merry in mind when he has well drunk, yet a year runs full swiftly, and the beginning but rarely matches the end.

For Yule was now over-past, and the year after, each season in its turn following the other. For after Christmas comes crabbed Lent, that will have fish for flesh and simpler cheer. But then the weather of the world chides with winter; the cold withdraws itself, the clouds uplift, and the rain falls in warm showers on the fair plains. Then the flowers come forth, meadows and grove are clad in green, the birds make ready to build, and sing sweetly for solace of the soft summer that follows thereafter. The blossoms bud and blow in the hedgerows rich and rank, and noble notes enough are heard in the fair woods.

After the season of summer, with the soft winds, when zephyr breathes lightly on seeds and herbs, joyous indeed is the growth that waxes thereout when the dew drips from the leaves beneath the blissful glance of the bright sun. But then comes harvest and hardens the grain, warning it to wax ripe ere the winter. The drought drives the dust on high, flying over the face of the land; the angry wind of the welkin wrestles with the sun; the leaves fall from the trees and light upon the ground, and all brown are the groves that but now were green, and ripe is the fruit that once was flower. So the year passes into many yesterdays, and winter comes again, as it needs no sage to tell us.

When the Michaelmas moon was come in with warnings of winter, Sir Gawain bethought him full oft of his perilous journey. Yet till All Hallows Day he lingered with Arthur, and on that day they made a great feast for the hero's sake, with much revel and richness of the Round Table. Courteous knights and comely ladies, all were in sorrow for the love of that knight, and though they spake no word of it, many were joyless for his sake.

And after meat, sadly Sir Gawain turned to his uncle, and spake of his journey, and said, "Liege lord of my life, leave from you I crave. Ye know well how the matter stands without more words, to-morrow am I bound to set forth in search of the Green Knight."

Then came together all the noblest knights, Ywain and Erec, and many another. Sir Dodinel le Sauvage, the Duke of Clarence, Launcelot and Lionel, and Lucan the Good, Sir Bors and Sir Bedivere, valiant knights both, and many another hero, with Sir Mador de la Porte, and they all drew near, heavy at heart, to take counsel with Sir Gawain. Much sorrow and weeping was there in the hall to think that so worthy a knight as Gawain should wend his way to seek a deadly blow, and should no more wield his sword in fight. But the knight made ever good cheer, and said, "Nay, wherefore should I shrink? What may a man do but prove his fate?"

He dwelt there all that day, and on the morn he arose and asked betimes for his armour; and they brought it unto him on this wise: first, a rich carpet was stretched on the floor6 (and brightly did the gold gear glitter upon it), then the knight stepped on to it, and handled the steel; clad he was in a doublet of silk, with a close hood, lined fairly throughout. Then they set the steel shoes upon his feet, and wrapped his legs with greaves, with polished knee-caps, fastened with knots of gold. Then they cased his thighs in cuisses closed with thongs, and brought him the byrny of bright steel rings sewn upon a fair stuff. Well burnished braces they set on each arm with good elbow-pieces, and gloves of mail, and all the goodly gear that should shield him in his need. And they cast over all a rich surcoat, and set the golden spurs on his heels, and girt him with a trusty sword fastened with a silken bawdrick. When he was thus clad his harness was costly, for the least loop or latchet gleamed with gold. So armed as he was he hearkened Mass and made his offering at the high altar. Then he came to the king, and the knights of his court, and courteously took leave of lords and ladies, and they kissed him, and commended him to Christ.

With that was Gringalet ready, girt with a saddle that gleamed gaily with many golden fringes, enriched and decked anew for the venture. The bridle was all barred about with bright gold buttons, and all the covertures and trappings of the steed, the crupper and the rich skirts, accorded with the saddle; spread fair with the rich red gold that glittered and gleamed in the rays of the sun.

Then the knight called for his helmet, which was well lined throughout, and set it high on his head, and hasped it behind. He wore a light kerchief over the vintail, that was broidered and studded with fair gems on a broad silken ribbon, with birds of gay colour, and many a turtle and true-lover's knot interlaced thickly, even as many a maiden had wrought diligently for seven winter long. But the circlet which crowned his helmet was yet more precious, being adorned with a device in diamonds. Then they brought him his shield, which was of bright red, with the pentangle painted thereon in gleaming gold.7 And why that noble prince bare the pentangle I am minded to tell you, though my tale tarry thereby. It is a sign that Solomon set ere-while, as betokening truth; for it is a figure with five points and

16

each line overlaps the other, and nowhere hath it beginning or end, so that in English it is called "the endless knot." And therefore was it well suiting to this knight and to his arms, since Gawain was faithful in five and five-fold, for pure was he as gold, void of all villainy and endowed with all virtues. Therefore he bare the pentangle on shield and surcoat as truest of heroes and gentlest of knights.

For first he was faultless in his five senses; and his five fingers never failed him; and all his trust upon earth was in the five wounds that Christ bare on the cross, as the Creed tells. And wherever this knight found himself in stress of battle he deemed well that he drew his strength from the five joys which the Queen of Heaven had of her Child. And for this cause did he bear an image of Our Lady on the one half of his shield, that whenever he looked upon it he might not lack for aid. And the fifth five that the hero used were frankness and fellowship above all, purity and courtesy that never failed him, and compassion that surpasses all; and in these five virtues was that hero wrapped and clothed. And all these, five-fold, were linked one in the other, so that they had no end, and were fixed on five points that never failed, neither at any side were they joined or sundered, nor could ye find beginning or end. And therefore on his shield was the knot shapen, red-gold upon red, which is the pure pentangle. Now was Sir Gawain ready, and he took his lance in hand, and bade them all Farewell, he deemed it had been for ever.

Then he smote the steed with his spurs, and sprang on his way, so that sparks flew from the stones after him. All that saw him were grieved at heart, and said one to the other, "By Christ, 'tis great pity that one of such noble life should be lost! I'faith, 'twere not easy to find his equal upon earth. The king had done better to have wrought more warily. Yonder knight should have been made a duke; a gallant leader of men is he, and such a fate had beseemed him better than to be hewn in pieces at the will of an elfish man, for mere pride. Who ever knew a king to take such counsel as to risk his knights on a Christmas jest?" Many were the tears that flowed from their eyes when that goodly knight rode from the hall. He made no delaying, but went his way swiftly, and rode many a wild road, as I heard say in the book.

So rode Sir Gawain through the realm of Logres, on an errand that he held for no jest. Often he lay companionless at night, and must lack the fare that he liked. No comrade had he save his steed, and none save God with whom to take counsel. At length he drew nigh to North Wales, and left the isles of Anglesey on his left hand, crossing over the fords by the foreland over at Holyhead, till he came into the wilderness of Wirral8, where but few dwell who love God and man of true heart. And ever he asked, as he fared, of all whom he met, if they had heard any tidings of a Green Knight in the country thereabout, or of a Green Chapel? And all answered him, Nay, never in their lives had they seen any man of such a hue. And the knight wended his way by many a strange road and many a rugged path, and the fashion of his countenance changed full often ere he saw the Green Chapel.

Many a cliff did he climb in that unknown land, where afar from his friends he rode as a stranger. Never did he come to a stream or a ford but he found a foe before him, and that one so marvellous, so foul and fell, that it behoved him to fight. So many wonders did that knight behold, that it were too long to tell the tenth part of them. Sometimes he fought with dragons and wolves; sometimes with wild men that dwelt in the rocks; another while with bulls, and bears, and wild boars, or with giants of the high moorland that drew near to him. Had he not been a doughty knight, enduring, and of well-proved valour, and a servant of God, doubtless he had been slain, for he was oft in danger of death. Yet he cared not so much for the strife, what he deemed worse was when the cold clear water was shed from the clouds, and froze ere it fell on the fallow ground. More nights than enough he slept in his harness on the bare rocks, near slain with the sleet, while the stream leapt bubbling from the crest of the hills, and hung in hard icicles over his head.

Thus in peril and pain, and many a hardship, the knight rode alone till Christmas Eve, and in that tide he made his prayer to the Blessed Virgin that she would guide his steps and lead him to some dwelling. On that morning he rode by a hill, and came into a thick forest, wild and drear; on each side were high hills, and thick woods below them of great hoar oaks, a hundred together, of hazel and hawthorn with their trailing boughs intertwined, and rough ragged moss spreading everywhere. On the bare twigs the birds chirped piteously, for pain of the cold. The knight upon Gringalet rode lonely beneath them, through marsh and mire, much troubled at heart lest he should fail to see the service of the Lord, who on that self-same night was born of a maiden for the cure of our grief; and therefore he said, sighing, "I beseech Thee, Lord, and Mary Thy gentle Mother, for some shelter where I may hear Mass, and Thy mattins at morn. This I ask meekly, and thereto I pray my Paternoster, Ave, and Credo."

Thus he rode praying, and lamenting his misdeeds, and he crossed himself, and said, "May the Cross of Christ speed me."

Now that knight had crossed himself but thrice ere he was aware in the wood of a dwelling within a moat, above a lawn, on a mound surrounded by many mighty trees that stood round the moat. 'Twas the fairest castle that ever a knight owned9; built in a meadow with a park all about it, and a spiked palisade, closely driven, that enclosed the trees for more than two miles. The knight was ware of the hold from the side, as it shone through the oaks. Then he lifted off his helmet, and thanked Christ and S. Julian that they had courteously granted his prayer, and hearkened to his cry. "Now," quoth the knight, "I beseech ye, grant me fair hostel." Then he pricked Gringalet with his golden spurs, and rode gaily towards the great gate, and came swiftly to the bridge end.

The bridge was drawn up and the gates close shut; the walls were strong and thick, so that they might fear no tempest. The knight on his charger abode on the bank of the deep double ditch that surrounded the castle. The walls were set deep in the water, and rose aloft to a wondrous height; they were of hard hewn stone up to the corbels, which were adorned beneath the battlements with fair carvings, and turrets set in between with many a loophole; a better barbican Sir Gawain had never looked upon. And within he beheld the high hall, with its tower and many windows with carven cornices, and chalk-white chimneys on the turreted roofs that shone fair in the sun. And everywhere, thickly scattered on the castle battlements, were pinnacles, so many that it seemed as if it were all wrought out of paper, so white was it.

The knight on his steed deemed it fair enough, if he might come to be sheltered within it to lodge there while that the Holy-day lasted. He called aloud, and soon there came a porter of kindly countenance, who stood on the wall and greeted this knight and asked his errand.

"Good sir," quoth Gawain, "wilt thou go mine errand to the high lord of the castle, and crave for me lodging?"

"Yea, by S. Peter," quoth the porter. "In sooth I trow that ye be welcome to dwell here so long as it may like ye."

Then he went, and came again swiftly, and many folk with him to receive the knight. They let down the great drawbridge, and came forth and knelt on their knees on the cold earth to give him worthy welcome. They held wide open the great gates, and courteously he bid them rise, and rode over the bridge. Then men came to him and held his stirrup while he dismounted, and took and stabled his steed. There came down knights and squires to bring the guest with joy to the hall. When he raised his helmet there were many to take it from his hand, fain to serve him, and they took from him sword and shield.

Sir Gawain gave good greeting to the noble and the mighty men who came to do him honour. Clad in his shining armour they led him to the hall, where a great fire burnt brightly on the floor; and the lord of the household came forth from his chamber to meet the hero fitly. He spake to the knight, and said: "Ye are welcome to do here as it likes ye. All that is here is your own to have at your will and disposal."

"Gramercy!" quote Gawain, "may Christ requite ye."

As friends that were fain each embraced the other; and Gawain looked on the knight who greeted him so kindly, and thought 'twas a bold warrior that owned that burg.

Of mighty stature he was, and of high age; broad and flowing was his beard, and of a bright hue. He was stalwart of limb, and strong in his stride, his face fiery red, and his speech free: in sooth he seemed one well fitted to be a leader of valiant men.

Then the lord led Sir Gawain to a chamber, and commanded folk to wait upon him, and at his bidding there came men enough who brought the guest to a fair bower. The bedding was noble, with curtains of pure silk wrought with gold, and wondrous coverings of fair cloth all embroidered. The curtains ran on ropes with rings of red gold, and the walls were hung with carpets of Orient, and the same spread on the floor. There with mirthful speeches they took from the guest his byrny and all his shining armour, and brought him rich robes of the choicest in its stead. They were long and flowing, and became him well, and when he was clad in them all who looked on the hero thought that surely God had never made a fairer knight: he seemed as if he might be a prince without peer in the field where men strive in battle.

Then before the hearth-place, whereon the fire burned, they made ready a chair for Gawain, hung about with cloth and fair cushions; and there they cast around him a mantle of brown samite, richly embroidered and furred within with costly skins of ermine, with a hood of the same, and he seated himself in that rich seat, and warmed himself at the fire, and was cheered at heart. And while he sat thus the serving men set up a table on trestles, and covered it with a fair white cloth, and set thereon salt-cellar, and napkin, and silver spoons; and the knight washed at his will, and set him down to meat.

The folk served him courteously with many dishes seasoned of the best, a double portion. All kinds of fish were there, some baked in bread, some broiled on the embers, some sodden, some stewed and savoured with spices, with all sorts of cunning devices to his taste. And often he called it a feast, when they spake gaily to him all together, and said, "Now take ye this penance, and it shall be for your amendment." Much mirth thereof did Sir Gawain make.

Then they questioned that prince courteously of whence he came; and he told them that he was of the court of Arthur, who is the rich royal King of the Round Table, and that it was Gawain himself who was within their walls, and would keep Christmas with them, as the chance had fallen out. And when the lord of the castle heard those tidings he laughed aloud for gladness, and all men in that keep were joyful that they should be in the company of him to whom belonged all fame, and valour, and courtesy, and whose honour was praised above that of all men on earth. Each said softly to his fellow, "Now shall we see courteous bearing, and the manner of speech befitting courts. What charm lieth in gentle speech shall we learn without asking, since here we have welcomed the fine father of courtesy. God has surely shewn us His grace since He sends us such a guest as Gawain! When men shall sit and sing, blithe for Christ's birth, this knight shall bring us to the knowledge of fair manners, and it may be that hearing him we may learn the cunning speech of love."

By the time the knight had risen from dinner it was near nightfall. Then chaplains took their way to the chapel, and rang loudly, even as they should, for the solemn evensong of the high feast. Thither went the lord, and the lady also, and entered with her maidens into a comely closet, and thither also went Gawain. Then the lord took him by the sleeve and led him to a seat, and called him by his name, and told him he was of all men in the world the most welcome. And Sir Gawain thanked him truly, and each kissed the other, and they sat gravely together throughout the service.

Then was the lady fain to look upon that knight; and she came forth from her closet with many fair maidens. The fairest of ladies was she in face, and figure, and colouring, fairer even than Guinevere, so the knight thought. She came through the chancel to greet the hero, another lady held her by the left hand, older than she, and seemingly of high estate, with many nobles about her. But unlike to look upon were those ladies, for if the younger were fair, the elder was yellow. Rich red were the cheeks of the one, rough and wrinkled those of the other; the kerchiefs of the one were broidered with many glistening pearls, her throat and neck bare, and whiter than the snow that lies on the hills; the neck of the other was swathed in a gorget, with a white wimple over her black chin. Her forehead was wrapped in silk with many folds, worked with knots, so that naught of her was seen save her black brows, her eyes, her nose and her lips, and those were bleared, and ill to look upon. A worshipful lady in sooth one might call her! In figure was she short and broad, and thickly made—far fairer to behold was she whom she led by the hand.

When Gawain beheld that fair lady, who looked at him graciously, with leave of the lord he went towards them, and, bowing low, he greeted the elder, but the younger and fairer he took lightly in his arms, and kissed her courteously, and greeted her in knightly wise. Then she hailed him as friend, and he quickly prayed to be counted as her servant, if she so willed. Then they took him between them, and talking, led him to the chamber, to the hearth, and bade them bring spices, and they brought them in plenty with the good wine that was wont to be drunk at such seasons. Then the lord sprang to his feet and bade them make merry, and took off his hood, and hung it on a spear, and bade him win the worship thereof who should make most mirth that Christmas-tide. "And I shall try, by my faith, to fool it with the best, by the help of my friends, ere I lose my raiment." Thus with gay words the lord made trial to gladden Gawain with jests that night, till it was time to bid them light the tapers, and Sir Gawain took leave of them and gat him to rest.

In the morn when all men call to mind how Christ our Lord was born on earth to die for us, there is joy, for His sake, in all dwellings of the world; and so was there here on that day. For high feast was held, with many dainties and cunningly cooked messes. On the daïs sat gallant men, clad in their best. The ancient dame sat on the high seat, with the lord of the castle beside her. Gawain and the fair lady sat together, even in the midst of the board, when the feast was served; and so throughout all the hall each sat in his degree, and was served in order. There was meat, there was mirth, there was much joy, so that to tell thereof would take me too long, though peradventure I might strive to declare it. But Gawain and that fair lady had much joy of each other's company through her sweet words and courteous converse. And there was music made before each prince, trumpets and drums, and merry piping; each man hearkened his minstrel, and they too hearkened theirs.

So they held high feast that day and the next, and the third day thereafter, and the joy on S. John's Day was fair to hearken, for 'twas the last of the feast and the guests would depart in the grey of the morning. Therefore they awoke early, and drank wine, and danced fair carols, and at last, when it was late, each man took his leave to wend early on his way. Gawain would bid his host farewell, but the lord took him by the hand, and led him to his own chamber beside the hearth, and there he thanked him for the favour he had shown him in honouring his dwelling at that high season, and gladdening his castle with his fair countenance. "I wis, sir, that while I live I shall be held the worthier that Gawain has been my guest at God's own feast."

"Gramercy, sir," quoth Gawain, "in good faith, all the honour is yours, may the High King give it you, and I am but at your will to work your behest, inasmuch as I am beholden to you in great and small by rights."

Then the lord did his best to persuade the knight to tarry with him, but Gawain answered that he might in no wise do so. Then the host asked him courteously what stern behest had driven him at the holy season from the king's court, to fare all alone, ere yet the feast was ended?

"Forsooth," quoth the knight, "ye say but the truth: 'tis a high quest and a pressing that hath brought me afield, for I am summoned myself to a certain place, and I know not whither in the world I may wend to find it; so help me Christ, I would give all the kingdom of Logres an I might find it by New Year's morn. Therefore, sir, I make request of you that ye tell me truly if ye ever heard word of the Green Chapel, where it may be found, and the Green Knight that keeps it. For I am pledged by solemn compact sworn between us to meet that knight at the New Year if so I were on life; and of that same New Year it wants but little—I'faith, I would look on that hero more joyfully than on any other fair sight! Therefore, by your will, it behoves me to leave you, for I have but barely three days, and I would as fain fall dead as fail of mine errand."

Then the lord quoth, laughing, "Now must ye needs stay, for I will show you your goal, the Green Chapel, ere your term be at an end, have ye no fear! But ye can take your ease, friend, in your bed, till the fourth day, and go forth on the first of the year and come to that place at mid-morn to do as ye will. Dwell here till New Year's Day, and then rise and set forth, and ye shall be set in the way; 'tis not two miles hence."

Then was Gawain glad, and he laughed gaily. "Now I thank you for this above all else. Now my quest is achieved I will dwell here at your will, and otherwise do as ye shall ask."

Then the lord took him, and set him beside him, and bade the ladies be fetched for their greater pleasure, tho' between themselves they had solace. The lord, for gladness, made merry jest, even as one who wist not what to do for joy; and he cried aloud to the knight, "Ye have promised to do the thing I bid ye: will ye hold to this behest, here, at once?"

"Yea, forsooth," said that true knight, "while I abide in your burg I am bound by your behest."

"Ye have travelled from far," said the host, "and since then ye have waked with me, ye are not well refreshed by rest and sleep, as I know. Ye shall therefore abide in your chamber, and lie at your ease tomorrow at Mass-tide, and go to meat when ye will with my wife, who shall sit with you, and comfort you with her company till I return; and I shall rise early and go forth to the chase." And Gawain agreed to all this courteously.

"Sir knight," quoth the host, "we shall make a covenant. Whatsoever I win in the wood shall be yours, and whatever may fall to your share, that shall ye exchange for it. Let us swear, friend, to make this exchange, however our hap may be, for worse or for better."

"I grant ye your will," quoth Gawain the good; "if ye list so to do, it liketh me well."

"Bring hither the wine-cup, the bargain is made," so said the lord of that castle. They laughed each one, and drank of the wine, and made merry, these lords and ladies, as it pleased them. Then with gay talk and merry jest they arose, and stood, and spoke softly, and kissed courteously, and took leave of each other. With burning torches, and many a serving-man, was each led to his couch; yet ere they gat them to bed the old lord oft repeated their covenant, for he knew well how to make sport.

*

Full early, ere daylight, the folk rose up; the guests who would depart called their grooms, and they made them ready, and saddled the steeds, tightened up the girths, and trussed up their mails. The knights, all arrayed for riding, leapt up lightly, and took their bridles, and each rode his way as pleased him best.

The lord of the land was not the last. Ready for the chase, with many of his men, he ate a sop hastily when he had heard Mass, and then with blast of the bugle fared forth to the field.10 He and his nobles were to horse ere daylight glimmered upon the earth.

Then the huntsmen coupled their hounds, unclosed the kennel door, and called them out. They blew three blasts gaily on the bugles, the hounds bayed fiercely, and they that would go a-hunting checked and chastised them. A hundred hunters there were of the best, so I have heard tell. Then the trackers gat them to the trysting-place and uncoupled the hounds, and forest rang again with their gay blasts.

At the first sound of the hunt the game quaked for fear, and fled, trembling, along the vale. They betook them to the heights, but the liers in wait turned them back with loud cries; the harts they let pass them, and the stags with their spreading antlers, for the lord had forbidden that they should be slain, but the hinds and the does they turned back, and drave down into the valleys. Then might ye see much shooting of arrows. As the deer fled under the boughs a broad whistling shaft smote and wounded each sorely, so that, wounded and bleeding, they fell dying on the banks. The hounds followed swiftly on their tracks, and hunters, blowing the horn, sped after them with ringing shouts as if the cliffs burst asunder. What game escaped those that shot was run down at the outer ring. Thus were they driven on the hills, and harassed at the waters, so well did the men know their work, and the greyhounds were so great and swift that they ran them down as fast as the hunters could slay them. Thus the lord passed the day in mirth and joyfulness, even to nightfall.

So the lord roamed the woods, and Gawain, that good night, lay ever a-bed, curtained about, under the costly coverlet, while the daylight gleamed on the walls. And as he lay half slumbering, he heard a little sound at the door, and he raised his head, and caught back a corner of the curtain, and waited to see what it might be. It was the lovely lady, the lord's wife; she shut the door softly behind her, and turned towards the bed; and Gawain was shamed, laid him down softly and made as if he slept. And she came lightly to the bedside, within the curtain, and sat herself down beside him, to wait till he wakened. The knight lay there awhile, and marvelled within himself what her coming might betoken; and he said to himself, "'Twere more seemly if I asked her what hath brought her hither." Then he made feint to waken, and turned towards her, and opened his eyes as one astonished, and crossed himself; and she looked on him laughing, with her cheeks red and white, lovely to behold, and small smiling lips.

"Good morrow, Sir Gawain," said that fair lady; "ye are but a careless sleeper, since one can enter thus. Now are ye taken unawares, and lest ye escape me I shall bind you in your bed; of that be ye assured!" Laughing, she spake these words.

"Good morrow, fair lady," quoth Gawain blithely. "I will do your will, as it likes me well. For I yield me readily, and pray your grace, and that is best, by my faith, since I needs must do so." Thus he jested again, laughing. "But an ye would, fair lady, grant me this grace that ye pray your prisoner to rise. I would get me from bed, and array me better, then could I talk with ye in more comfort."

"Nay, forsooth, fair sir," quoth the lady, "ye shall not rise, I will rede ye better. I shall keep ye here, since ye can do no other, and talk with my knight whom I have captured. For I know well that ye are Sir Gawain, whom all the world worships, wheresoever ye may ride. Your honour and your courtesy are praised by lords and ladies, by all who live. Now ye are here and we are alone, my lord and his men are afield; the serving men in their beds, and my maidens also, and the door shut upon us. And since in this hour I have him that all men love, I shall use my time well with speech, while it lasts. Ye are welcome to my company, for it behoves me in sooth to be your servant."

"In good faith," quoth Gawain, "I think me that I am not him of whom ye speak, for unworthy am I of such service as ye here proffer. In sooth, I were glad if I might set myself by word or service to your pleasure; a pure joy would it be to me!"

"In good faith, Sir Gawain," quoth the gay lady, "the praise and the prowess that pleases all ladies I lack them not, nor hold them light; yet are there ladies enough who would liever now have the knight in their hold, as I have ye here, to dally with your courteous words, to bring them comfort and to ease their cares, than much of the treasure and the gold that are theirs. And now, through the grace of Him who upholds the heavens, I have wholly in my power that which they all desire!"

Thus the lady, fair to look upon, made him great cheer, and Sir Gawain, with modest words, answered her again: "Madam," he quoth, "may Mary requite ye, for in good faith I have found in ye a noble frankness. Much courtesy have other folk shown me, but the honour they have done me is naught to the worship of yourself, who knoweth but good."

"By Mary," quoth the lady, "I think otherwise; for were I worth all the women alive, and had I the wealth of the world in my hand, and might choose me a lord to my liking, then, for all that I have seen in ye, Sir Knight, of beauty and courtesy and blithe semblance, and for all that I have hearkened and hold for true, there should be no knight on earth to be chosen before ye!"

"Well I wot," quoth Sir Gawain, "that ye have chosen a better; but I am proud that ye should so prize me, and as your servant do I hold ye my sovereign, and your knight am I, and may Christ reward ye."

So they talked of many matters till mid-morn was past, and ever the lady made as though she loved him, and the knight turned her speech aside. For though she were the brightest of maidens, yet had he forborne to shew her love for the danger that awaited him, and the blow that must be given without delay.

Then the lady prayed her leave from him, and he granted it readily. And she gave [the text reads "have"] him good-day, with laughing glance, but he must needs marvel at her words:

"Now He that speeds fair speech reward ye this disport; but that ye be Gawain my mind misdoubts me greatly."

"Wherefore?" quoth the knight quickly, fearing lest he had lacked in some courtesy.

And the lady spake: "So true a knight as Gawain is holden, and one so perfect in courtesy, would never have tarried so long with a lady but he would of his courtesy have craved a kiss at parting."

Then quoth Gawain, "I wot I will do even as it may please ye, and kiss at your commandment, as a true knight should who forbears to ask for fear of displeasure."

At that she came near and bent down and kissed the knight, and each commended the other to Christ, and she went forth from the chamber softly.

Then Sir Gawain arose and called his chamberlain and chose his garments, and when he was ready he gat him forth to Mass, and then went to meat, and made merry all day till the rising of the moon, and never had a knight fairer lodging than had he with those two noble ladies, the elder and the younger.

And even the lord of the land chased the hinds through holt and heath till eventide, and then with much blowing of bugles and baying of hounds they bore the game homeward; and by the time daylight was done all the folk had returned to that fair castle. And when the lord and Sir Gawain met together, then were they both well pleased. The lord commanded them all to assemble in the great hall, and the ladies to descend with their maidens, and there, before them all, he bade the men fetch in the spoil of the day's hunting, and he called unto Gawain, and counted the tale of the beasts, and showed them unto him, and said, "What think ye of this game, Sir Knight? Have I deserved of ye thanks for my woodcraft?"

"Yea, I wis," quoth the other, "here is the fairest spoil I have seen this seven year in the winter season."

"And all this do I give ye, Gawain," quoth the host, "for by accord of covenant ye may claim it as your own."

"That is sooth," quoth the other, "I grant you that same; and I have fairly won this within walls, and with as good will do I yield it to ye." With that he clasped his hands round the lord's neck and kissed him as courteously as he might. "Take ye here my spoils, no more have I won; ye should have it freely, though it were greater than this."

"'Tis good," said the host, "gramercy thereof. Yet were I fain to know where ye won this same favour, and if it were by your own wit?"

"Nay," answered Gawain, "that was not in the bond. Ask me no more: ye have taken what was yours by right, be content with that."

They laughed and jested together, and sat them down to supper, where they were served with many dainties; and after supper they sat by the hearth, and wine was served out to them; and oft in their jesting they promised to observe on the morrow the same covenant that they had made before, and whatever chance might betide to exchange their spoil, be it much or little, when they met at night. Thus they renewed their bargain before the whole court, and then the night-drink was served, and each courteously took leave of the other and gat him to bed.

By the time the cock had crowed thrice the lord of the castle had left his bed; Mass was sung and meat fitly served. The folk were forth to the wood ere the day broke, with hound and horn they rode over the plain, and uncoupled their dogs among the thorns. Soon they struck on the scent, and the hunt cheered on the hounds who were first to seize it, urging them with shouts. The others hastened to the cry, forty at once, and there rose such a clamour from the pack that the rocks rang again. The huntsmen spurred them on with shouting and blasts of the horn; and the hounds drew together to a thicket betwixt the water and a high crag in the cliff beneath the hillside. There where the rough rock fell ruggedly they, the huntsmen, fared to the finding, and cast about round the hill and the thicket behind them. The knights wist well what beast was within, and would drive him

28

forth with the bloodhounds. And as they beat the bushes, suddenly over the beaters there rushed forth a wondrous great and fierce boar, long since had he left the herd to roam by himself. Grunting, he cast many to the ground, and fled forth at his best speed, without more mischief. The men hallooed loudly and cried, "Hay! Hay!" and blew the horns to urge on the hounds, and rode swiftly after the boar. Many a time did he turn to bay and tare the hounds, and they yelped, and howled shrilly. Then the men made ready their arrows and shot at him, but the points were turned on his thick hide, and the barbs would not bite upon him, for the shafts shivered in pieces, and the head but leapt again wherever it hit.

But when the boar felt the stroke of the arrows he waxed mad with rage, and turned on the hunters and tare many, so that, affrightened, they fled before him. But the lord on a swift steed pursued him, blowing his bugle; as a gallant knight he rode through the woodland chasing the boar till the sun grew low.

So did the hunters this day, while Sir Gawain lay in his bed lapped in rich gear; and the lady forgat not to salute him, for early was she at his side, to cheer his mood.

She came to the bedside and looked on the knight, and Gawain gave her fit greeting, and she greeted him again with ready words, and sat her by his side and laughed, and with a sweet look she spoke to him:

"Sir, if ye be Gawain, I think it a wonder that ye be so stern and cold, and care not for the courtesies of friendship, but if one teach ye to know them ye cast the lesson out of your mind. Ye have soon forgotten what I taught ye yesterday, by all the truest tokens that I knew!"

"What is that?" quoth the knight. "I trow I know not. If it be sooth that ye say, then is the blame mine own."

"But I taught ye of kissing, " quoth the fair lady. "Wherever a fair countenance is shown him, it behoves a courteous knight quickly to claim a kiss."

"Nay, my dear," said Sir Gawain, "cease that speech; that durst I not do lest I were denied, for if I were forbidden I wot I were wrong did I further entreat."

"I' faith," quoth the lady merrily, "ye may not be forbid, ye are strong enough to constrain by strength an ye will, were any so discourteous as to give ye denial."

"Yea, by Heaven," said Gawain, "ye speak well; but threats profit little in the land where I dwell, and so with a gift that is given not of good will!

I am at your commandment to kiss when ye like, to take or to leave as ye list."

Then the lady bent her down and kissed him courteously.

And as they spake together she said, "I would learn somewhat from ye, an ye would not be wroth, for young ye bare and fair, and so courteous and knightly as ye are known to be, the head of all chivalry, and versed in all wisdom of love and war—'tis ever told of true knights how they adventured their lives for their true love, and endured hardships for her favours, and avenged her with valour, and eased her sorrows, and brought joy to her bower; and ye are the fairest knight of your time, and your fame and your honour are everywhere, yet I have sat by ye here twice, and never a word have I heard of love! Ye who are so courteous and skilled in such love ought surely to teach one so young and unskilled some little craft of true love! Why are ye so unlearned who art otherwise so famous? Or is it that ye deemed me unworthy to hearken to your teaching? For shame, Sir Knight! I come hither alone and sit at your side to learn of ye some skill; teach me of your wit, while my lord is from home."

"In good faith," quoth Gawain, "great is my joy and my profit that so fair a lady as ye are should deign to come hither, and trouble ye with so poor a man, and make sport with your knight with kindly countenance, it pleaseth me much. But that I, in my turn, should take it upon me to tell of love and such like matters to ye who know more by half, or a hundred fold, of such craft than I do, or ever shall in all my lifetime, by my troth 'twere folly indeed! I will work your will to the best of my might as I am bounden, and evermore will I be your servant, so help me Christ!"

Then often with guile she questioned that knight that she might win him to woo her, but he defended himself so fairly that none might in any wise blame him, and naught but bliss and harmless jesting was there between them. They laughed and talked together till at last she kissed him, and craved her leave of him, and went her way.

Then the knight arose and went forth to Mass, and afterward dinner was served and he sat and spake with the ladies all day. But the lord of the castle rode ever over the land chasing the wild boar, that fled through the thickets, slaying the best of his hounds and breaking their backs in sunder; till at last he was so weary he might run no longer, but made for a hole in a mound by a rock. He got the mound at his back and faced the hounds, whetting his white tusks and foaming at the mouth. The huntsmen stood aloof, fearing to draw nigh him; so many of them had been already wounded that they were loth to be torn with his tusks, so fierce he was and mad with rage. At length the lord himself came up, and saw the beast at bay, and the men standing aloof. Then quickly he sprang to the ground and drew out a bright blade, and waded through the stream to the boar.

When the beast was aware of the knight with weapon in hand, he set up his bristles and snorted loudly, and many feared for their lord lest he should be slain. Then the boar leapt upon the knight so that beast and man were one atop of the other in the water; but the boar had the worst of it, for the man had marked, even as he sprang, and set the point of his brand to the beast's chest, and drove it up to the hilt, so that the heart was split in twain, and the boar fell snarling, and was swept down by the water to where a hundred hounds seized on him, and the men drew him to shore for the dogs to slay.

Then was there loud blowing of horns and baying of hounds, the huntsmen smote off the boar's head, and hung the carcase by the four feet to a stout pole, and so went on their way homewards. The head they bore before the lord himself, who had slain the beast at the ford by force of his strong hand.

It seemed him o'er long ere he saw Sir Gawain in the hall, and he called, and the guest came to take that which fell to his share. And when he saw Gawain the lord laughed aloud, and bade them call the ladies and the household together, and he showed them the game, and told them the tale, how they hunted the wild boar through the woods, and of his length and breadth and height; and Sir Gawain commended his deeds and praised him for his valour, well proven, for so mighty a beast had he never seen before.

Then they handled the huge head, and the lord said aloud, "Now, Gawain, this game is your own by sure covenant, as ye right well know."

"'Tis sooth," quoth the knight, "and as truly will I give ye all I have gained." He took the host round the neck, and kissed him courteously twice. "Now are we quits," he said, "this eventide, of all the covenants that we made since I came hither."

And the lord answered, "By S. Giles, ye are the best I know; ye will be rich in a short space if ye drive such bargains!"

Then they set up the tables on trestles, and covered them with fair cloths, and lit waxen tapers on the walls. The knights sat and were served in the hall, and much game and glee was there round the hearth, with many songs, both at supper and after; song of Christmas, and new carols, with all the mirth one may think of. And ever that lovely lady sat by the knight, and with still stolen looks made such feint of pleasing him, that Gawain marvelled much, and was wroth with himself, but he could not for his courtesy return her fair glances, but dealt with her cunningly, however she might strive to wrest the thing.

When they had tarried in the hall so long as it seemed them good, they turned to the inner chamber and the wide hearthplace, and there they drank wine, and the host proffered to renew the covenant for New Year's Eve; but the knight craved leave to depart on the morrow, for it was nigh to the term when he must fulfil his pledge. But the lord would withhold him from so doing, and prayed him to tarry, and said,

"As I am a true knight I swear my troth that ye shall come to the Green Chapel to achieve your task on New Year's morn, long before prime. Therefore abide ye in your bed, and I will hunt in this wood, and hold ye to the covenant to exchange with me against all the spoil I may bring hither. For twice have I tried ye, and found ye true, and the morrow shall be the third time and the best. Make we merry now while we may, and think on joy, for misfortune may take a man whensoever it wills."

Then Gawain granted his request, and they brought them drink, and they gat them with lights to bed.

Sir Gawain lay and slept softly, but the lord, who was keen on woodcraft, was afoot early. After Mass he and his men ate a morsel, and he asked for his steed; all the knights who should ride with him were already mounted before the hall gates.

'Twas a fair frosty morning, for the sun rose red in ruddy vapour, and the welkin was clear of clouds. The hunters scattered them by a forest side, and the rocks rang again with the blast of their horns. Some came on the scent of a fox, and a hound gave tongue; the huntsmen shouted, and the pack followed in a crowd on the trail. The fox ran before them, and when they saw him they pursued him with noise and much shouting, and he wound and turned through many a thick grove, often cowering and hearkening in a hedge. At last by a little ditch he leapt out of a spinney, stole away slily by a copse path, and so out of the wood and away from the hounds. But he went, ere he wist, to a chosen tryst, and three started forth on him at once, so he must needs double back, and betake him to the wood again.

Then was it joyful to hearken to the hounds; when all the pack had met together and had sight of their game they made as loud a din as if all the lofty cliffs had fallen clattering together. The huntsmen shouted and threatened, and followed close upon him so that he might scarce escape, but Reynard was wily, and he turned and doubled upon them, and led the lord and his men over the hills, now on the slopes, now in the vales, while the knight at home slept through the cold morning beneath his costly curtains.

But the fair lady of the castle rose betimes, and clad herself in a rich mantle that reached even to the ground, left her throat and her fair neck bare, and was bordered and lined with costly furs. On her head she wore no golden circlet, but a network of precious stones, that gleamed and shone through her tresses in clusters of twenty together. Thus she came into the chamber, closed the door after her, and set open a window, and called to him gaily, "Sir Knight, how may ye sleep? The morning is so fair."

Sir Gawain was deep in slumber, and in his dream he vexed him much for the destiny that should befall him on the morrow, when he should meet the knight at the Green Chapel, and abide his blow; but when the lady spake he heard her, and came to himself, and roused from his dream and answered swiftly. The lady came laughing, and kissed him courteously, and he welcomed her fittingly with a cheerful countenance. He saw her so glorious and gaily dressed, so faultless of features and complexion, that it warmed his heart to look upon her.

They spake to each other smiling, and all was bliss and good cheer between them. They exchanged fair words, and much happiness was therein, yet was there a gulf between them, and she might win no more of her knight, for that gallant prince watched well his words–he would neither take her love, nor frankly refuse it. He cared for his courtesy, lest he be deemed churlish, and yet more for his honour lest he be traitor to his host. "God forbid," quoth he to himself, "that it should so befall." Thus with courteous words did he set aside all the special speeches that came from her lips.

Then spake the lady to the knight, "Ye deserve blame if ye hold not that lady who sits beside ye above all else in the world, if ye have not already a love whom ye hold dearer, and like better, and have sworn such firm faith to that lady that ye care not to loose it–and that am I now fain to believe. And now I pray ye straitly that ye tell me that in truth, and hide it not."

And the knight answered, "By S. John" (and he smiled as he spake) "no such love have I, nor do I think to have yet awhile."

"That is the worst word I may hear," quoth the lady, "but in sooth I have mine answer; kiss me now courteously, and I will go hence; I can but mourn as a maiden that loves much."

Sighing, she stooped down and kissed him, and then she rose up and spake as she stood, "Now, dear, at our parting do me this grace: give me some gift, if it were but thy glove, that I may bethink me of my knight, and lessen my mourning."

"Now, I wis," quoth the knight, "I would that I had here the most precious thing that I possess on earth that I might leave ye as love-token, great or small, for ye have deserved forsooth more reward than I might give ye. But it is not to your honour to have at this time a glove for reward as gift from Gawain, and I am here on a strange errand, and have no man with me, nor mails with goodly things–that mislikes me much, lady, at this time; but each man must fare as he is taken, if for sorrow and ill."

"Nay, knight highly honoured," quoth that lovesome lady, "though I have naught of yours, yet shall ye have somewhat of mine." With that she reached him a ring of red gold with a sparkling stone therein, that shone even as the sun (wit ye well, it was worth many marks); but the knight refused it, and spake readily,

"I will take no gift, lady, at this time. I have none to give, and none will I take."

She prayed him to take it, but he refused her prayer, and sware in sooth that he would not have it.

The lady was sorely vexed, and said, "If ye refuse my ring as too costly, that ye will not be so highly beholden to me, I will give you my girdle 11 as a lesser gift." With that she loosened a lace that was fastened at her side, knit upon her kirtle under her mantle. It was wrought of green silk, and gold, only braided by the fingers, and that she offered to the knight, and besought him though it were of little worth that he would take it, and he said nay, he would touch neither gold nor gear ere God give him grace to achieve the adventure for which he had come hither. "And therefore, I pray ye, displease ye not, and ask me no longer, for I may not grant it. I am dearly beholden to ye for the favour ye have shown me, and ever, in heat and cold, will I be your true servant."

"Now," said the lady, "ye refuse this silk, for it is simple in itself, and so it seems, indeed; lo, it is small to look upon and less in cost, but whoso knew the virtue that is knit therein he would, peradventure, value it more highly. For whatever knight is girded with this green lace, while he bears it knotted about him there is no man under heaven can overcome him, for he may not be slain for any magic on earth."

Then Gawain bethought him, and it came into his heart that this were a jewel for the jeopardy that awaited him when he came to the Green Chapel to seek the return blow–could he so order it that he should escape unslain, 'twere a craft worth trying. Then he bare with her chiding, and let her say her say, and she pressed the girdle on him and prayed him to take it, and he granted her prayer, and she gave it him with good will, and besought him for her sake never to reveal it but to hide it loyally from her lord; and the knight agreed that never should any man know it, save they two alone. He thanked her often and heartily, and she kissed him for the third time.

Then she took her leave of him, and when she was gone Sir Gawain arose, and clad him in rich attire, and took the girdle, and knotted it round him, and hid it beneath his robes. Then he took his way to the chapel, and sought out a priest privily and prayed him to teach him better how his soul might be saved when he should go hence; and there he shrived him, and showed his misdeeds, both great and small, and besought mercy and craved absolution; and the priest assoiled him, and set him as clean as if Doomsday had been on the morrow. And afterwards Sir Gawain made him merry with the ladies, with carols, and all kinds of joy, as never he did but that one day, even to nightfall; and all the men marvelled at him, and said that never since he came thither had he been so merry.

Meanwhile the lord of the castle was abroad chasing the fox; awhile he lost him, and as he rode through a spinny he heard the hounds near at hand, and Reynard came creeping through a thick grove, with all the pack at his heels. Then the lord drew out his shining brand, and cast it at the beast, and the fox swerved aside for the sharp edge, and would have doubled back, but a hound was on him ere he might turn, and right before the horse's feet they all fell on him, and worried him fiercely, snarling the while.

Then the lord leapt from his saddle, and caught the fox from the jaws, and held it aloft over his head, and hallooed loudly, and many brave hounds bayed as they beheld it; and the hunters hied them thither, blowing their horns; all that bare bugles blew them at once, and all the others shouted. 'Twas the merriest meeting that ever men heard, the clamour that was raised at the death of the fox. They rewarded the hounds, stroking them and rubbing their heads, and took Reynard and stripped him of his coat; then blowing their horns, they turned them homewards, for it was nigh nightfall.

The lord was gladsome at his return, and found a bright fire on the hearth, and the knight beside it, the good Sir Gawain, who was in joyous mood for the pleasure he had had with the ladies. He wore a robe of blue, that reached even to the ground, and a surcoat richly furred, that became him well. A hood like to the surcoat fell on his shoulders, and all alike were done about with fur. He met the host in the midst of the floor, and jesting, he greeted him, and said, "Now shall I be first to fulfil our covenant which we made together when there was no lack of wine." Then he embraced the knight, and kissed him thrice, as solemnly as he might.

"Of a sooth," quoth the other, "ye have good luck in the matter of this covenant, if ye made a good exchange!"

"Yea, it matters naught of the exchange," quoth Gawain, "since what I owe is swiftly paid."

"Marry," said the other, "mine is behind, for I have hunted all this day, and naught have I got but this foul fox-skin, and that is but poor payment for three such kisses as ye have here given me."

"Enough," quoth Sir Gawain, "I thank ye, by the Rood."

Then the lord told them of his hunting, and how the fox had been slain.

With mirth and minstrelsy, and dainties at their will, they made them as merry as a folk well might till 'twas time for them to sever, for at last they must needs betake them to their beds. Then the knight took his leave of the lord, and thanked him fairly.

"For the fair sojourn that I have had here at this high feast may the High King give ye honour. I give ye myself, as one of your servants, if ye so like; for I must needs, as you know, go hence with the morn, and ye will give me, as ye promised, a guide to show me the way to the Green Chapel, an God will suffer me on New Year's Day to deal the doom of my weird."

"By my faith," quoth the host, "all that ever I promised, that shall I keep with good will." Then he gave him a servant to set him in the way, and lead him by the downs, that he should have no need to ford the stream, and should fare by the shortest road through the groves; and Gawain thanked the lord for the honour done him. Then he would take leave of the ladies, and courteously he kissed them, and spake, praying them to receive his thanks, and they made like reply; then with many sighs they commended him to Christ, and he departed courteously from that folk. Each man that he met he thanked him for his service and his solace, and the pains he had been at to do his will; and each found it as hard to part from the knight as if he had ever dwelt with him.

Then they led him with torches to his chamber, and brought him to his bed to rest. That he slept soundly I may not say, for the morrow gave him much to think on. Let him rest awhile, for he was near that which he sought, and if ye will but listen to me I will tell ye how it fared with him thereafter. *****

Now the New Year drew nigh, and the night passed, and the day chased the darkness, as is God's will; but wild weather wakened therewith. The clouds cast the cold to the earth, with enough of the north to slay them that lacked clothing. The snow drave smartly, and the whistling wind blew from the heights, and made great drifts in the valleys. The knight, lying in his bed, listened, for though his eyes were shut, he might sleep but little, and hearkened every cock that crew.

He arose ere the day broke, by the light of a lamp that burned in his chamber, and called to his chamberlain, bidding him bring his armour and saddle his steed. The other gat him up, and fetched his garments, and robed Sir Gawain.

First he clad him in his clothes to keep off the cold, and then in his harness, which was well and fairly kept. Both hauberk and plates were well burnished, the rings of the rich byrny freed from rust, and all as fresh as at first, so that the knight was fain to thank them. Then he did on each piece, and bade them bring his steed, while he put the fairest raiment on himself; his coat with its fair cognizance, adorned with precious stones upon velvet, with broidered seams, and all furred within with costly skins. And he left not the lace, the lady's gift, that Gawain forgot not, for his own good. When he had girded on his sword he wrapped the gift twice about him, swathed around his waist. The girdle of green silk set gaily and well upon the royal red cloth, rich to behold, but the knight ware it not for pride of the pendants, polished though they were with fair gold that gleamed brightly on the ends, but to save himself from sword and knife, when it behoved him to abide his hurt without question. With that the hero went forth, and thanked that kindly folk full often.

Then was Gringalet ready, that was great and strong, and had been well cared for and tended in every wise; in fair condition was that proud steed, and fit for a journey. Then Gawain went to him, and looked on his coat, and said by his sooth, "There is a folk in this place that thinketh on honour; much joy may they have, and the lord who maintains them, and may all good betide that lovely lady all her life long. Since they for charity cherish a guest, and hold honour in their hands, may He who holds the heaven on high requite them, and also ye all. And if I might live anywhere on earth, I would give ye full reward, readily, if so I might." Then he set foot in the stirrup and bestrode his steed, and his squire gave him his shield, which he laid on his shoulder. Then he smote Gringalet with his golden spurs, and the steed pranced on the stones and would stand no longer.

By that his man was mounted, who bare his spear and lance, and Gawain quoth, "I commend this castle to Christ, may He give it ever good fortune." Then the drawbridge was let down, and the broad gates unbarred and opened on both sides; the knight crossed himself, and passed through the gateway, and praised the porter, who knelt before the prince, and gave him good-day, and commended him to God. Thus the knight went on his way with the one man who should guide him to that dread place where he should receive rueful payment.

The two went by hedges where the boughs were bare, and climbed the cliffs where the cold clings. Naught fell from the heavens, but 'twas ill beneath them; mist brooded over the moor and hung on the mountains; each hill had a cap, a great cloak, of mist. The streams foamed and bubbled between their banks, dashing sparkling on the shores where they shelved downwards. Rugged and dangerous was the way through the woods, till it was time for the sun-rising. Then were they on a high hill; the snow lay white beside them, and the man who rode with Gawain drew rein by his master.

"Sir," he said, "I have brought ye hither, and now ye are not far from the place that ye have sought so specially. But I will tell ye for sooth, since I know ye well, and ye are such a knight as I well love, would ye follow my counsel ye would fare the better. The place whither ye go is accounted full perilous, for he who liveth in that waste is the worst on earth, for he is strong and fierce, and loveth to deal mighty blows; taller is he than any man on earth, and greater of frame than any four in Arthur's court, or in any other. And this is his custom at the Green Chapel; there may no man pass by that place, however proud his arms, but he does him to death by force of his hand, for he is a discourteous knight, and shews no mercy. Be he churl or chaplain who rides by that chapel, monk or mass priest, or any man else, he thinks it as pleasant to slay them as to pass alive himself. Therefore, I tell ye, as sooth as ye sit in saddle, if ye come there and that knight know it, ye shall be slain, though ye had twenty lives; trow me that truly! He has dwelt here full long and seen many a combat; ye may not defend ye against his blows. Therefore, good Sir Gawain, let the man be, and get ye away some other road; for God's sake seek ye another land, and there may Christ speed ye! And I will hie me home again, and I promise ye further that I will swear by God and the saints, or any other oath ye please, that I will keep counsel faithfully, and never let any wit the tale that ye fled for fear of any man."

"Gramercy," quoth Gawain, but ill-pleased. "Good fortune be his who wishes me good, and that thou wouldst keep faith with me I will believe; but didst thou keep it never so truly, an I passed here and fled for fear as thou sayest, then were I a coward knight, and might not be held guiltless. So I will to the chapel let chance what may, and talk with that man, even as I may list, whether for weal or for woe as fate may have it. Fierce though he may be in fight, yet God knoweth well how to save His servants."

"Well," quoth the other, "now that ye have said so much that ye will take your own harm on yourself, and ye be pleased to lose your life, I will neither let nor keep ye. Have here your helm and the spear in your hand, and ride down this same road beside the rock till ye come to the bottom of the valley, and there look a little to the left hand, and ye shall see in that vale the chapel, and the grim man who keeps it. Now fare ye well, noble Gawain; for all the gold on earth I would not go with ye nor bear ye fellowship one step further." With that the man turned his bridle into the wood, smote the horse with his spurs as hard as he could, and galloped off, leaving the knight alone.

Quoth Gawain, "I will neither greet nor groan, but commend myself to God, and yield me to His will."

Then the knight spurred Gringalet, and rode adown the path close in by a bank beside a grove. So he rode through the rough thicket, right into the dale, and there he halted, for it seemed him wild enough. No sign of a chapel could he see, but high and burnt banks on either side and rough rugged crags with great stones above. An ill-looking place he thought it.

Then he drew in his horse and looked around to seek the chapel, but he saw none and thought it strange. Then he saw as it were a mound on a level space of land by a bank beside the stream where it ran swiftly, the water bubbled within as if boiling. The knight turned his steed to the mound, and lighted down and tied the rein to the branch of a linden; and he turned to the mound and walked round it, questioning with himself what it might be. It had a hole at the end and at either side, and was overgrown with clumps of grass, and it was hollow within as an old cave or the crevice of a crag; he knew not what it might be.

"Ah," quoth Gawain, "can this be the Green Chapel? Here might the devil say his mattins at midnight! Now I wis there is wizardry here. 'Tis an ugly oratory, all overgrown with grass, and 'twould well beseem that fellow in green to say his devotions on devil's wise. Now feel I in five wits, 'tis the foul fiend himself who hath set me this tryst, to destroy me here! This is a chapel of mischance: ill-luck betide it, 'tis the cursedest kirk that ever I came in!"

Helmet on head and lance in hand, he came up to the rough dwelling, when he heard over the high hill beyond the brook, as it were in a bank, a wondrous fierce noise, that rang in the cliff as if it would cleave asunder. 'Twas as if one ground a scythe on a grindstone, it whirred and whetted like water on a mill-wheel and rushed and rang, terrible to hear.

"By God," quoth Gawain, "I trow that gear is preparing for the knight who will meet me here. Alas! naught may help me, yet should my life be forfeit, I fear not a jot!" With that he called aloud. "Who waiteth in this place to give me tryst? Now is Gawain come hither: if any man will aught of him let him hasten hither now or never."

"Stay," quoth one on the bank above his head, "and ye shall speedily have that which I promised ye." Yet for a while the noise of whetting went on ere he appeared, and then he came forth from a cave in the crag with a fell weapon, a Danish axe newly dight, wherewith to deal the blow. An evil head it had, four feet large, no less, sharply ground, and bound to the handle by the lace that gleamed brightly. And the knight himself was all green as before, face and foot, locks and beard, but now he was afoot. When he came to the water he would not wade it, but sprang over with the pole of his axe, and strode boldly over the brent that was white with snow.

Sir Gawain went to meet him, but he made no low bow. The other said, "Now, fair sir, one may trust thee to keep tryst. Thou art welcome, Gawain, to my place. Thou hast timed thy coming as befits a true man. Thou knowest the covenant set between us: at this time twelve months agone thou didst take that which fell to thee, and I at this New Year will readily requite thee. We are in this valley, verily alone, here are no knights to sever us, do what we will. Have off thy helm from thine head, and have here thy pay; make me no more talking than I did then when thou didst strike off my head with one blow."

"Nay," quoth Gawain, "by God that gave me life, I shall make no moan whatever befall me, but make thou ready for the blow and I shall stand still and say never a word to thee, do as thou wilt."

With that he bent his head and shewed his neck all bare, and made as if he had no fear, for he would not be thought a-dread.

Then the Green Knight made him ready, and grasped his grim weapon to smite Gawain. With all his force he bore it aloft with a mighty feint of slaying him: had it fallen as straight as he aimed he who was ever doughty of deed had been slain by the blow. But Gawain swerved aside as the axe came gliding down to slay him as he stood, and shrank a little with the shoulders, for the sharp iron. The other heaved up the blade and rebuked the prince with many proud words:

"Thou art not Gawain," he said, "who is held so valiant, that never feared he man by hill or vale, but thou shrinkest for fear ere thou feelest hurt. Such cowardice did I never hear of Gawain! Neither did I flinch from thy blow, or make strife in King Arthur's hall. My head fell to my feet, and yet I fled not; but thou didst wax faint of heart ere any harm befell. Wherefore must I be deemed the braver knight."

Quoth Gawain, "I shrank once, but so will I no more, though an my head fall on the stones I cannot replace it. But haste, Sir Knight, by thy faith, and bring me to the point, deal me my destiny, and do it out of hand, for I will stand thee a stroke and move no more till thine axe have hit me—my troth on it."

"Have at thee, then," quoth the other, and heaved aloft the axe with fierce mien, as if he were mad. He struck at him fiercely but wounded him not, withholding his hand ere it might strike him.

Gawain abode the stroke, and flinched in no limb, but stood still as a stone or the stump of a tree that is fast rooted in the rocky ground with a hundred roots.

Then spake gaily the man in green, "So now thou hast thine heart whole it behoves me to smite. Hold aside thy hood that Arthur gave thee, and keep thy neck thus bent lest it cover it again."

Then Gawain said angrily, "Why talk on thus? Thou dost threaten too long. I hope thy heart misgives thee."

"For sooth," quoth the other, "so fiercely thou speakest I will no longer let thine errand wait its reward." Then he braced himself to strike, frowning with lips and brow, 'twas no marvel that it pleased but ill him who hoped for no rescue. He lifted the axe lightly and let it fall with the edge of the blade on the bare neck. Though he struck swiftly it hurt him no more than on the one side where it severed the skin. The sharp blade cut into the flesh so that the blood ran over his shoulder to the ground. And when the knight saw the blood staining the snow, he sprang forth, swift-foot, more than a spear's length, seized his helmet and set it on his head, cast his shield over his shoulder, drew out his bright sword, and spake boldly (never since he was born was he half so blithe), "Stop, Sir Knight, bid me no more blows. I have stood a stroke here without flinching, and if thou give me another, I shall requite thee, and give thee as good again. By the covenant made betwixt us in Arthur's hall but one blow falls to me here. Halt, therefore."

Then the Green Knight drew off from him and leaned on his axe, setting the shaft on the ground, and looked on Gawain as he stood all armed and faced him fearlessly–at heart it pleased him well. Then he spake merrily in a loud voice, and said to the knight, "Bold sir, be not so fierce, no man here hath done thee wrong, nor will do, save by covenant, as we made at Arthur's court. I promised thee a blow and thou hast it–hold thyself well paid! I release thee of all other claims. If I had been so minded I might perchance have given thee a rougher buffet. First I menaced thee with a feigned one, and hurt thee not for the covenant that we made in the first night, and which thou didst hold truly. All the gain didst thou give me as a true man should. The other feint I proffered thee for the morrow: my fair wife kissed thee, and thou didst give me her kisses–for both those days I gave thee two blows without scathe–true man, true return. But the third time thou didst fail, and therefore hadst thou that blow. For 'tis my weed thou wearest, that same woven girdle, my own wife wrought it, that do I wot for sooth. Now know I well thy kisses, and thy conversation, and the wooing of my wife, for 'twas mine own doing. I sent her to try thee, and in sooth I think thou art the most faultless knight that ever trode earth. As a pearl among white peas is of more worth than they, so is Gawain, i' faith, by other knights. But thou didst lack a little, Sir Knight, and wast wanting in loyalty, yet that was for no evil work, nor for wooing neither, but because thou lovedst thy life–therefore I blame thee the less."

Then the other stood a great while, still sorely angered and vexed within himself; all the blood flew to his face, and he shrank for shame as the Green Knight spake; and the first words he said were, "Cursed be ye, cowardice and covetousness, for in ye is the destruction of virtue." Then he loosed the girdle, and gave it to the knight. "Lo, take there the falsity, may foul befall it! For fear of thy blow cowardice bade me make friends with covetousness and forsake the customs of largess and loyalty, which befit all knights. Now am I faulty and false and have been afeared: from treachery and untruth come sorrow and care. I avow to thee, Sir Knight, that I have ill done; do then thy will. I shall be more wary hereafter."

Then the other laughed and said gaily, "I wot I am whole of the hurt I had, and thou hast made such free confession of thy misdeeds, and hast so borne the penance of mine axe edge, that I hold thee absolved from that sin, and purged as clean as if thou hadst never sinned since thou wast born. And this girdle that is wrought with gold and green, like my raiment, do I give thee, Sir Gawain, that thou mayest think upon this chance when thou goest forth among princes of renown, and keep this for a token of the adventure of the Green Chapel, as it chanced between chivalrous knights. And thou shalt come again with me to my dwelling and pass the rest of this feast in gladness." Then the lord laid hold of him, and said, "I wot we shall soon make peace with my wife, who was thy bitter enemy."

"Nay, forsooth," said Sir Gawain, and seized his helmet and took it off swiftly, and thanked the knight: "I have fared ill, may bliss betide thee, and may He who rules all things reward thee swiftly. Commend me to that courteous lady, thy fair wife, and to the other my honoured ladies, who have beguiled their knight with skilful craft. But 'tis no marvel if one be made a fool and brought to sorrow by women's wiles, for so was Adam beguiled by one, and Solomon by many, and Samson all too soon, for Delilah dealt him his doom; and David thereafter was wedded with Bathsheba, which brought him much sorrow–if one might love a woman and believe her not, 'twere great gain! And since all they were beguiled by women, methinks 'tis the less blame to me that I was misled! But as for thy girdle, that will I take with good will, not for gain of the gold, nor for samite, nor silk, nor the costly pendants, neither for weal nor for worship, but in sign of my frailty. I shall look upon it when I ride in renown and remind myself of the fault and faintness of the flesh; and so when pride uplifts me for prowess of arms, the sight of this lace shall humble my heart. But one thing would I pray, if it displease thee not: since thou art lord of yonder land wherein I have dwelt, tell me what thy rightful name may be, and I will ask no more."

The Adventures of Sir Gawain

"That will I truly," quoth the other. "Bernlak de Hautdesert am I called in this land. Morgain le Fay dwelleth in mine house 12, and through knowledge of clerkly craft hath she taken many. For long time was she the mistress of Merlin, who knew well all you knights of the court. Morgain the goddess is she called therefore, and there is none so haughty but she can bring him low. She sent me in this guise to yon fair hall to test the truth of the renown that is spread abroad of the valour of the Round Table. She taught me this marvel to betray your wits, to vex Guinevere and fright her to death by the man who spake with his head in his hand at the high table. That is she who is at home, that ancient lady, she is even thine aunt, Arthur's half-sister, the daughter of the Duchess of Tintagel, who afterward married King Uther. Therefore I bid thee, knight, come to thine aunt, and make merry in thine house; my folk love thee, and I wish thee as well as any man on earth, by my faith, for thy true dealing."

But Sir Gawain said nay, he would in no wise do so; so they embraced and kissed, and commended each other to the Prince of Paradise, and parted right there, on the cold ground. Gawain on his steed rode swiftly to the king's hall, and the Green Knight got him whithersoever he would.

Sir Gawain who had thus won grace of his life, rode through wild ways on Gringalet; oft he lodged in a house, and oft without, and many adventures did he have and came off victor full often, as at this time I cannot relate in tale. The hurt that he had in his neck was healed, he bare the shining girdle as a baldric bound by his side, and made fast with a knot 'neath his left arm, in token that he was taken in a fault—and thus he came in safety again to the court.

Then joy awakened in that dwelling when the king knew that the good Sir Gawain was come, for he deemed it gain. King Arthur kissed the knight, and the queen also, and many valiant knights sought to embrace him. They asked him how he had fared, and he told them all that had chanced to him—the adventure of the chapel, the fashion of the knight, the love of the lady—at last of the lace. He showed them the wound in the neck which he won for his disloyalty at the hand of the knight, the blood flew to his face for shame as he told the tale.

"Lo, lady," he quoth, and handled the lace, "this is the bond of the blame that I bear in my neck, this is the harm and the loss I have suffered, the cowardice and covetousness in which I was caught, the token of my covenant in which I was taken. And I must needs wear it so long as I live,

44

for none may hide his harm, but undone it may not be, for if it hath clung to thee once, it may never be severed."

Then the king comforted the knight, and the court laughed loudly at the tale, and all made accord that the lords and the ladies who belonged to the Round Table, each hero among them, should wear bound about him a baldric of bright green for the sake of Sir Gawain.13 And to this was agreed all the honour of the Round Table, and he who ware it was honoured the more thereafter, as it is testified in the best book of romance. That in Arthur's days this adventure befell, the book of Brutus bears witness. For since that bold knight came hither first, and the siege and the assault were ceased at Troy, I wis

Many a venture herebefore
 Hath fallen such as this:
May He that bare the crown of thorn
 Bring us unto His bliss.

Amen.

Gawain and the Lady of Avalon
by George Augustus Simcox

Came tidings unto Caerleon,
   Where Arthur kept Shrovetide,
How, far away in Avalon,
   A scaly dragon's pride,
With visage like a woman's, wan,
   Wasted the country-side.

Arthur let cry through all his land,
   "Who curses me for wrong?"
Then flowed there in on every hand
   The stream of loyal song,
"If right could make a king's throne stand,
   Then Arthur's would stand long."

When Arthur's praise was duly sung,
   A way-worn maiden came,
And said, with duteous faltering tongue,
   "Ye are not much to blame,
My liege, for we were very young,
   Though ye forgat our game.

"We played at guessing thoughts," she said.
   "Ye did not guess aright.
Ye sware to give me one to wed,
   To be my lord and knight.
Now twenty years, methinks, are fled,
   And ye forget our plight."

The dew was on her raven hair
   And her blue glistering eye;
No dust on foot or ankle bare,
   Though all the land was dry;
And every knight was ready there
   To wed with her or die.

"But I," she said, "am dowerless,
   And comfortless of men,
And sojourn in the wilderness,

The Adventures of Sir Gawain

And in the dragon's den."
Pale looks were plentiful, I guess,
    About the Table then.

Lancelot looked in her pleading face,
    And sighed, "If I were free;"
Quoth Tristram as he left the place,
    "His answer serves for me."
Galahad said something of God's grace;
    She said, "I choose not thee."

Geraint bowed over Enid's veil;
    His visage was more white.
Lamorack buckled up his mail,
    And looked into the night.
Gawain, whose face was always pale,
    Seemed ruddy in the light.

She laid her little hand in his,
    He chose to let it stay;
She put her rosy cheek to his,
    He did not turn away;
She put her cherry lips to his,
    Which were as dim as clay.

He spake, as soon as it was time,
    Of pleasant ways of love,
That rules the sweetly-ordered chime
    Of stars and saints above,
And bade the minstrels sing the rhyme
    Of the true turtle-dove;

And bade them call the holy priest
    To knit the twain in one.
She said, "I keep my marriage-feast
    Not here, at Avalon."
None knew why all men as she ceased
    Trembled in Caerleon.

The Adventures of Sir Gawain

"Where shall we find a priest to wait
  And bless the marriage-bed?
And if your house be desolate,
  How shall your guests be fed?
And who will guide them to our gate?"
  The courteous bridegroom said.

"The dragon's scales of woven glass
  Will light my banquet well;
Iscariot will sing the mass,
  And Pilate toll the bell;
And all my marriage guests will pass
  Over the mouth of hell.

"I go to the great wilderness,
  And to the dragon's lair,
Where the great hills are harbourless,
  And the sharp rocks are bare;
And if thou pity my distress,
  Then thou wilt meet me there.

"But sit thou with thy master here
  For three days yet," saith she;
"Then shalt thou ride in desert drear,
  Three days alone to me;
The seventh day with lordly cheer
  Our marriage-feast shall be."

She kissed Sir Gawain on the mouth,
  He kissed her on the hand;
Then she departed to the south,
  Between the sea and sand,
Leaving behind a bitter drouth
  In all King Arthur's land.

Thereat the King was full of woe,
  The princes of dismay.
A bolder man had feared to go,

The Adventures of Sir Gawain

But Gawain feared to stay,
And parted in a storm of snow,
  Alone, on the third day.

The seventh day, by Grammarie,
  And by the dragon's power,
He saw beside a leaden sea
  A rosy granite tower,
That fronted to a sunny lea,
  Blood-red with wild windflower.

Thereon went many quick and dead,
  And some who do not die;
Each wore a garland on the head,
  Each laughed within the eye.
No flower was bent beneath their tread,
  No dewy leaf brushed dry.

They passed within the granite gate,
  And there was room for all;
Gawain could see his lady wait,
  In green and purple pall.
As he lit down, the cloud of fate
  Went up from Arthur's hall.

Beneath Gawain his feet seemed lame,
  He stumbled and he fell;
There lived for him a subtle flame
  In every crushed wind-bell.
She said, "No marvel, for ye came
  Over the mouth of hell."

He saw an altar to the west,
  He saw the incense sink,
And in the bag on the priest's breast
  He heard the silver chink.
One stood to serve in purple vest,
  Whose hands were washed in ink.

The Adventures of Sir Gawain

Black serpents round the altar ran,
   But Judas chanted well,
And sweetly rang his sacristan
   The silver sacring bell;
And so the marriage rite began,
   Over the pit of hell.

Sweet gusts of music from below
   Lifted the lady's veil;
Soft sudden flakes of rosy snow
   Flecked the black serpent's mail.
'Mid happy faces all aglow
   The bridegroom's face was pale.

The altar sank beneath the floor,
   Arose the marriage feast,
Sweeter and merrier and more
   The melody increased;
None started as grim graveworms tore
   The sacristan and priest.

In shifting many-coloured light,
   Too bright to look upon,
You saw the guests, you saw the knight,
   Where that wild radiance shone;
You did not see the lady bright
   Who reigns in Avalon.

Yet all, as though beneath her eye,
   Were busy to rejoice;
And now the music mounted high
   To glorify her choice,
Who felt the dragon sliding by,
   And heard the lady's voice.

A moment not a guest was seen
   Within the marriage room;
A moment, and the magic sheen

The Adventures of Sir Gawain

Faded in magic gloom,
Through which, half seen, the fairy queen
  Scattered a sweet perfume.

Gawain bent low for courtesie,
  And thanked her for her grace;
He laid his hand upon her knee
  And looked into her face,
And wondered if he did not see
  The dragon in her place.

The lady his weak hand hath ta'en,
  And bidden him be of cheer;
He asked her, "Is the dragon slain?"
  She said, "He is not here.
The dragon will not waste again
  In Arthur's golden year."

Arose a happy fairy sound,
  As of a little well
By the first break of spring unbound;
  Cool flowers began to swell
From underneath the burning ground,
  To veil the mouth of hell.

The moon above the misty lea
  Hung like a globe of fire,
Whereby Gawain a hag might see
  In ghastly gay attire,
Whose wrinkled face flushed horribly
  With jubilant desire.

He knew her, for she held the hand
  He gave to one more fair;
He knew her by the magic band
  His lady used to wear,
With jewels from an unknown land
  Bound in her raven hair.

The Adventures of Sir Gawain

Fondly she lisped, "My honey knight,
   It needs not to rehearse
Wherefore I lifted up the blight,
   And took away the curse,
Because ye took me in God's sight
   For better and for worse.

"Though thou be very fair to see,
   And I a loathly crone,
Yet what is that to thee and me
   Before King Arthur's throne?
And when I hunger after thee,
   I hunger for mine own."

Gawain, the knight of courtesie,
   Bowed down his stately head,
And said, "Sweet wife, most certainly
   We in God's sight are wed,"
As he drew back the canopy
   Over the bridal bed.

Full still he lay till break of day
   In counterfeited bliss,
Nor turned his loyal cheek away
   From any loathly kiss,
And saw the while the lightnings play,
   And heard her serpents hiss.

There lay beside Gawain at morn
   A maiden undefiled,
As rosy as the blooming thorn
   When eves in May are mild;
As tender as the babe unborn,
   To life scarce reconciled.

Her brow was veiled with woven brass,
   And bonds were on the hands,
Which held an emerald hourglass

The Adventures of Sir Gawain

Wherein few golden sands;
Her feet seemed quivering to pass
  Into untravelled lands.

She kissed her husband thick and fast
  On lip and brow and cheek,
Her captive arms round him she cast,
  And then she tried to speak,
Until the love came out at last,
  Although the voice was weak.

"Wilt have by day a lovely may,
  By night a loathly crone,
That other men may see and say,
  His bride becomes a throne;
Or have me foul for them by day,
  And fair for thee alone?"

He thought, "Whate'er my choice may be,
  I cannot choose but ill,
For she by slight of Grammarie
  Would fool my simple skill."
He said, "This is too hard for me,
  Use your own gentle will."

Oh, sweetly smiled the lady then,
  And sweetly laughed the lea,
Sweet roses veiled the dragon's den;
  "Henceforth my face shall be
Fair when I will for other men,
  And all day long for thee!"

She laughed, "'Tis well ye did not play
  When Arthur lost the game,
For you have guessed aright to-day
  The wish of every dame."
"Yet," said Gawain, "I cannot say
  My lady's lovesome name."

The Adventures of Sir Gawain

The colours of the dragon's mail
  Flashed in the dewy grass;
The lady's face flushed red and pale,
  "And I had hoped, alas!
That thou shouldst rend the brazen veil,
  And loose the bonds of glass.

"Ah! woe is me, it may not be,
  And I have loved thee so;
But henceforth thou shalt never see
  My footprints where I go,
To wake the flowers upon the lea,
  And kiss away the snow."

He smiled farewell, her colour rose;
  She cried aloud, "For shame!
I sojourn seven years with those
  Who do not ask my name.
Hence with thee and thy painted shows;
  Hence by the road ye came!

"Go home and boast in Caerleon,
  Below thy courtly breath,
About the bonny bride ye won,
  For whom hell hungereth!
But come no more to Avalon,
  For that will be thy death."

Low fell the veil of woven brass,
  On heavy eyelids bound;
On folded hands the bonds of glass
  Clanked softly without sound;
And so Gawain beheld her pass
  Over the dewy ground.

Sir Gawaine's Quest for the White Hart

by Sir Thomas Malory

Then was the high feast made ready, and the king was wedded at Camelot unto Dame Guenever in the church of Saint Stephen's, with great solemnity. And as every man was set after his degree, Merlin went to all the knights of the Round Table, and bade them sit still, that none of them remove. For ye shall see a strange and a marvellous adventure. Right so as they sat there came running in a white hart into the hall, and a white brachet next him, and thirty couple of black running hounds came after with a great cry, and the hart went about the Table Round as he went by other boards. The white brachet bit him by the buttock and pulled out a piece, wherethrough the hart leapt a great leap and overthrew a knight that sat at the board side; and therewith the knight arose and took up the brachet, and so went forth out of the hall, and took his horse and rode his way with the brachet. Right so anon came in a lady on a white palfrey, and cried aloud to King Arthur, Sir, suffer me not to have this despite, for the brachet was mine that the knight led away. I may not do therewith, said the king.

With this there came a knight riding all armed on a great horse, and took the lady away with him with force, and ever she cried and made great dole. When she was gone the king was glad, for she made such a noise. Nay, said Merlin, ye may not leave these adventures so lightly; for these adventures must be brought again or else it would be disworship to you and to your feast. I will, said the king, that all be done by your advice. Then, said Merlin, let call Sir Gawaine, for he must bring again the white hart. Also, sir, ye must let call Sir Tor, for he must bring again the brachet and the knight, or else slay him. Also let call King Pellinore, for he must bring again the lady and the knight, or else slay him. And these three knights shall do marvellous adventures or they come again. Then were they called all three as it rehearseth afore, and each of them took his charge, and armed them surely. But Sir Gawaine had the first request, and therefore we will begin at him.

*

The Adventures of Sir Gawain

SIR GAWAINE rode more than a pace, and Gaheris his brother that rode with him instead of a squire to do him service. So as they rode they saw two knights fight on horseback passing sore, so Sir Gawaine and his brother rode betwixt them, and asked them for what cause they fought so. The one knight answered and said, We fight for a simple matter, for we two be two brethren born and begotten of one man and of one woman. Alas, said Sir Gawaine, why do ye so? Sir, said the elder, there came a white hart this way this day, and many hounds chased him, and a white brachet was alway next him, and we understood it was adventure made for the high feast of King Arthur, and therefore I would have gone after to have won me worship; and here my younger brother said he would go after the hart, for he was better knight than I: and for this cause we fell at debate, and so we thought to prove which of us both was better knight. This is a simple cause, said Sir Gawaine; uncouth men ye should debate withal, and not brother with brother; therefore but if you will do by my counsel I will have ado with you, that is ye shall yield you unto me, and that ye go unto King Arthur and yield you unto his grace. Sir knight, said the two brethren, we are forfoughten and much blood have we lost through our wilfulness, and therefore we would be loath to have ado with you. Then do as I will have you, said Sir Gawaine. We will agree to fulfil your will; but by whom shall we say that we be thither sent? Ye may say, By the knight that followeth the quest of the hart that was white. Now what is your name? said Gawaine. Sorlouse of the Forest, said the elder. And my name is, said the younger, Brian of the Forest. And so they departed and went to the king's court, and Sir Gawaine on his quest.

And as Gawaine followed the hart by the cry of the hounds, even afore him there was a great river, and the hart swam over; and as Sir Gawaine would follow after, there stood a knight over the other side, and said, Sir knight, come not over after this hart but if thou wilt joust with me. I will not fail as for that, said Sir Gawaine, to follow the quest that I am in, and so made his horse to swim over the water. And anon they gat their spears and ran together full hard; but Sir Gawaine smote him off his horse, and then he turned his horse and bade him yield him. Nay, said the knight, not so, though thou have the better of me on horseback. I pray thee, valiant knight, alight afoot, and match we together with swords. What is your name? said Sir Gawaine. Allardin of the Isles, said the other. Then either dressed their shields and smote together, but Sir Gawaine smote him so hard through the helm that it went to the brains, and the knight fell down dead. Ah! said Gaheris, that was a mighty stroke of a young knight.

Then Gawaine and Gaheris rode more than a pace after the white hart, and let slip at the hart three couple of greyhounds, and so they chased the hart into a castle, and in the chief place of the castle they slew the hart; Sir Gawaine and Gaheris followed after. Right so there came a knight out of a chamber with a sword drawn in his hand and slew two of the greyhounds, even in the sight of Sir Gawaine, and the remnant he chased them with his sword out of the castle. And when he came again, he said, O my white hart, me repenteth that thou art dead, for my sovereign lady gave thee to me, and evil have I kept thee, and thy death shall be dear bought an I live. And anon he went into his chamber and armed him, and came out fiercely, and there met he with Sir Gawaine. Why have ye slain my hounds? said Sir Gawaine, for they did but their kind, and liefer I had ye had wroken your anger upon me than upon a dumb beast. Thou sayest truth, said the knight, I have avenged me on thy hounds, and so I will on thee or thou go. Then Sir Gawaine alighted afoot and dressed his shield, and struck together mightily, and clave their shields, and stoned their helms, and brake their hauberks that the blood ran down to their feet.

At the last Sir Gawaine smote the knight so hard that he fell to the earth, and then he cried mercy, and yielded him, and besought him as he was a knight and gentleman, to save his life. Thou shalt die, said Sir Gawaine, for slaying of my hounds. I will make amends, said the knight, unto my power. Sir Gawaine would no mercy have, but unlaced his helm to have stricken off his head. Right so came his lady out of a chamber and fell over him, and so he smote off her head by misadventure. Alas, said Gaheris, that is foully and shamefully done, that shame shall never from you; also ye should give mercy unto them that ask mercy, for a knight without mercy is without worship. Sir Gawaine was so stonied of the death of this fair lady that he wist not what he did, and said unto the knight, Arise, I will give thee mercy. Nay, nay, said the knight, I take no force of mercy now, for thou hast slain my love and my lady that I loved best of all earthly things. Me sore repenteth it, said Sir Gawaine, for I thought to strike unto thee; but now thou shalt go unto King Arthur and tell him of thine adventures, and how thou art overcome by the knight that went in the quest of the white hart. I take no force, said the knight, whether I live or I die; but so for dread of death he swore to go unto King Arthur, and he made him to bear one greyhound before him on his horse, and another behind him. What is your name? said Sir Gawaine, or we depart. My name is, said the knight, Ablamar of the Marsh. So he departed toward Camelot.

And Sir Gawaine went into the castle, and made him ready to lie there all night, and would have unarmed him. What will ye do, said Gaheris, will ye unarm you in this country? Ye may think ye have many enemies here. They had not sooner said that word but there came four knights well armed, and assailed Sir Gawaine hard, and said unto him, Thou new-made knight, thou hast shamed thy knighthood, for a knight without mercy is dishonoured. Also thou hast slain a fair lady to thy great shame to the world's end, and doubt thou not thou shalt have great need of mercy or thou depart from us. And therewith one of them smote Sir Gawaine a great stroke that nigh he fell to the earth, and Gaheris smote him again sore, and so they were on the one side and on the other, that Sir Gawaine and Gaheris were in jeopardy of their lives; and one with a bow, an archer, smote Sir Gawaine through the arm that it grieved him wonderly sore. And as they should have been slain, there came four fair ladies, and besought the knights of grace for Sir Gawaine; and goodly at request of the ladies they gave Sir Gawaine and Gaheris their lives, and made them to yield them as prisoners. Then Gawaine and Gaheris made great dole. Alas! said Sir Gawaine, mine arm grieveth me sore, I am like to be maimed; and so made his complaint piteously.

Early on the morrow there came to Sir Gawaine one of the four ladies that had heard all his complaint, and said, Sir knight, what cheer? Not good, said he. It is your own default, said the lady, for ye have done a passing foul deed in the slaying of the lady, the which will be great villainy unto you. But be ye not of King Arthur's kin? said the lady. Yes truly, said Sir Gawaine. What is your name? said the lady, ye must tell it me or ye pass. My name is Gawaine, the King Lot of Orkney's son, and my mother is King Arthur's sister. Ah! then are ye nephew unto King Arthur, said the lady, and I shall so speak for you that ye shall have conduct to go to King Arthur for his love. And so she departed and told the four knights how their prisoner was King Arthur's nephew, and his name is Sir Gawaine, King Lot's son of Orkney. And they gave him the hart's head because it was in his quest. Then anon they delivered Sir Gawaine under this promise, that he should bear the dead lady with him in this manner; the head of her was hanged about his neck, and the whole body of her lay before him on his horse's mane. Right so rode he forth unto Camelot. And anon as he was come, Merlin desired of King Arthur that Sir Gawaine should be sworn to tell of all his adventures, and how he slew the lady, and how he would give no mercy unto the knight, wherethrough the lady was slain. Then the king and the queen were greatly displeased with Sir Gawaine for the slaying of the lady. And there by ordinance of the queen there was set a quest of ladies on Sir Gawaine, and they judged him for ever while he lived to be with all ladies, and to fight for their quarrels; and that ever he should be courteous, and never to refuse mercy to him that asketh mercy. Thus was Gawaine sworn upon the Four Evangelists that he should never be against lady nor gentlewoman, but if he fought for a lady and his adversary fought for another. And thus endeth the adventure of Sir Gawaine that he did at the marriage of King Arthur

Amen.

Sir Gawain Meets Sir Prianius

Sir Gawain took his horse and rode away from his fellows to seek some adventure. Soon he saw an armed knight walking his horse by a wood's side, with his shield laced to his shoulder, and no attendant with him save a page, bearing a mighty spear; and on his shield were blazoned three gold griffins. When Sir Gawain spied him, he put his spear in rest, and riding straight to him, asked who he was. "A Tuscan," said he; "and they mayest prove me when thou wilt, for thou shalt be my prisoner ere we part."

Then said Sir Gawain, "Thou vauntest thee greatly, and speakest proud words; yet I counsel thee, for all thy boastings, look to thyself the best thou canst."

At that they took their spears and ran at each other with all the might they had, and smote each other through their shields into their shoulders; and then drawing swords smote with great strokes, till the fire sprang out of their helms. Then was Sir Gawain enraged, and with his good sword Galotine struck his enemy through shield and hauberk, and splintered into pieces all the precious stones of it, and made so huge a wound that men might see both lungs and liver. At that the Tuscan, groaning loudly, rushed on to Sir Gawain, and gave him a deep slanting stroke, and made a mighty wound and cut a great vein asunder, so that he bled fast. Then he cried out, "Bind thy wound quickly up, Sir knight, for thou be-bloodest all thy horse and thy fair armour, and all the surgeons of the world shall never staunch thy blood; for so shall it be to whomsoever is hurt with this good sword."

Then answered Sir Gawain, "It grieveth me but little, and thy boastful words give me no fear, for thou shalt suffer greater grief and sorrow ere we part; but tell me quickly who can staunch this blood."

"That can I do," said the strange knight, "and will, if thou wilt aid and succour me to become christened, and to believe on God, which now I do require of thee upon thy manhood."

"I am content," said Sir Gawain; "and may God help me to grant all thy wishes. But tell me first, what soughtest thou thus here alone, and of what land art thou?"

"Sir," said the knight, "my name is Prianius, and my father is a great prince, who hath rebelled against Rome. He is descended from Alexander and Hector, and of our lineage also were Joshua and Maccabaeus. I am of right the king of Alexandria, and Africa, and all the outer isles, yet I would believe in the Lord thou worshippest, and for thy labour I will give thee treasure enough. I was so proud in heart that I thought none my equal, but now have I encountered with thee, who hast given me my fill of fighting; wherefore, I pray thee, Sir knight, tell me of thyself."

"I am no knight," said Sir Gawain; "I have been brought up many years in the wardrobe of the noble prince King Arthur, to mind his armour and array."

"Ah," said Prianius, "if his varlets be so keen and fierce, his knights must be passing good! Now, for the love of heaven, whether thou be knight or knave, tell me thy name."

"By heaven!" said Gawain, "now will I tell thee the truth. My name is Sir Gawain, and I am a knight of the Round Table."

"Now am I better pleased," said Prianius, "than if thou hadst given me all the province of Paris the rich. I had rather have been torn by wild horses than that any varlet should have won such victory over me as thou hast done. But now, Sir knight, I warn thee that close by is the Duke of Lorraine, with sixty thousand good men of war; and we had both best flee at once, for he will find us else, and we be sorely wounded and never likely to recover. And let my page be careful that he blow no horn, for hard by are a hundred knights, my servants; and if they seize thee, no ransom of gold or silver would acquit thee."

Then Sir Gawain rode over a river to save himself, and Sir Prianius after him, and so they both fled till they came to his companions who were in the meadow, where they spent the night. When Sir Whishard saw Sir Gawain so hurt, he ran to him weeping, and asked him who it was had wounded him; and Sir Gawain told him how he had fought with that man—pointing to Prianius—who had salves to heal them both. "But I can tell ye other tidings," said he—"that soon we must encounter many enemies, for a great army is close to us in our front."

Then Prianius and Sir Gawain alighted and let their horses graze while they unarmed, and when they took their armour and their clothing off, the hot blood ran down freshly from their wounds till it was piteous to see. But Prianius took from his page a vial filled from the four rivers that flow out of Paradise, and anointed both their wounds with a certain balm, and washed them with that water, and within an hour afterwards they were both as sound and whole as ever they had been. Then, at the sound of a trumpet, all the knights were assembled to council; and after much talking, Prianius said, "Cease your words, for I warn you in yonder wood ye shall find knights out of number, who will put out cattle for a decoy to lead you on; and ye are not seven hundred!"

"Nevertheless," said Sir Gawain, "let us at once encounter them, and see what they can do; and may the best have the victory."

Then they saw suddenly an earl named Sir Ethelwold, and the Duke of Duchmen come leaping out of ambush of the woods in front, with many a thousand after them, and all rode straight down to the battle. And Sir Gawain, full of ardour and courage, comforted his knights, saying, "They all are ours." Then the seven hundred knights, in one close company, set spurs to their horses and began to gallop, and fiercely met their enemies. And then were men and horses slain and overthrown on every side, and in and out amidst them all, the knights of the Round Table pressed and thrust, and smote down to the earth all who withstood them, till at length the whole of them turned back and fled.

"By heaven!" said Sir Gawain, "this gladdeneth well my heart, for now behold them as they flee! they are full seventy thousand less in number than they were an hour ago!"

Thus was the battle quickly ended, and a great host of high lords and knights of Lombardy and Saracens left dead upon the field. Then Sir Gawain and his company collected a great plenty of cattle, and of gold and silver, and all kind of treasure, and returned to King Arthur, where he still kept the siege.

"Now God be thanked," cried he; "but who is he that standeth yonder by himself, and seemeth not a prisoner?"

"Sir," said Sir Gawain, "he is a good man with his weapons, and hath matched me; but cometh hither to be made a Christian. Had it not been for his warnings, we none of us should have been here this day. I pray thee, therefore, let him be baptized, for there can be few nobler men, or better knights."

So Prianius was christened, and made a duke and knight of the Round Table.

Sir Gawain and the Maid with the Narrow Sleeves

Now it happened that as Sir Gawain was riding one day through the country he encountered a troop of knights, followed by a squire, who led a Spanish charger, and about whose neck was hung a shield. Gawain rode up to the squire and said, "Tell me, what is yonder troop that hath ridden by?"

The squire answered, "Sir, Meliance of Lis, a brave and hardy knight."

"Is it to him you belong?" Sir Gawain asked.

"Nay, sir," said the squire, "my master is Teudaves, a knight as worthy as this one."

"Teudaves I know," said Gawain. "Whither fareth he? Tell me the truth."

"He proceedeth to a tourney, sir, which this Meliance of Lis hath undertaken against Thiébault of Tintagel. If you will take my advice you will throw yourself into the castle, and take part against the outsiders."

"Was it not," cried Gawain, "in the house of this Thiébault that Meliance of Lis was nurtured?"

"Aye, sir, so God save me!" said the squire. "His father loved Thiébault and trusted him so much that on his death-bed he committed to his care his little son, whom Thiébault cherished and protected, until the time came when the youth petitioned his daughter to give him her love; but she replied that she would never do that until he should be made a knight. The youth, being ardent, forthwith had himself knighted, and then returned to the maiden. 'Nay,' answered the girl to his renewed suit, 'it shall never be, until in my presence you shall have achieved such feats of arms that I will know my love hath cost you somewhat; for those things which come suddenly are not so sweet as those we earn. If you wish my love, take a tournament of my father. I desire to be certain that my love would be well placed in case I were to grant it.' What she suggested he performed, for love hath such lordship over lovers that those who are under his power would never dare refuse whatever it pleased him to enjoin. And you, sir, sluggish will you be if you do not enter the castle, for they will need you greatly, if you might help them."

The Adventures of Sir Gawain

To which Sir Gawain answered, "Brother, go thy way, it would be wise of you, and let my affairs be." So the squire departed, and Gawain rode towards Tintagel, for there was no other way by which he could pass.

Now Thiébault had summoned all his kith and kin, who had come, high and low, old and young; but he could not get the permission of his council to joust with his master, for the councillors feared lest he should utterly ruin their castle. Therefore the gates had been walled up with stones and mortar, leaving as the only approach one small postern, which had a gate made of copper, as much as a cart could haul. Sir Gawain rode to the gate, behind the troop that bore his harness, for there was no other road within seven leagues. He found the postern shut and so he turned into a close below the tower, that was fenced with a palisade. He dismounted under an oak and hung up his shields. Thither came the folk from the castle, most of them sorry that the tourney had been abandoned; in the fortress was an aged nobleman, great in land and lineage, whose word no one disputed. A long way off the troop had been pointed out to him, and before they rode into the close he went to Thiébault, and said, "Sir, so God save me, I have seen two companions of King Arthur, worthy men, who ride this way; I advise you to tourney with good hope, for we have brave knights, and servants, and archers, who will slay their horses, and I am certain they will joust before this gate; if their pride shall bring them the gain will be ours, and theirs will be the loss and the shame."

As a result of this counsel Thiébault allowed those who wished to take their arms and sally forth. The knights were right glad, and their squires ran after their horses, while the dames and the damsels climbed high places to see the tourney. Below, in the meadow, they saw the arms of Sir Gawain, and at first thought that there were two knights, because two shields hung from the tree. They cried out that they were fortunate to see two such knights arm. So some thought; but others exclaimed, "Fair Lord God, this knight hath arms and steeds sufficient for two; if he hath no companion, what will he do with two shields? Never was seen a knight who carried two shields at one and the same time. It is very strange if one man means to bear two shields."

While the ladies talked and the knights went forth from the castle the elder daughter of Thiébault mounted to the tower, she on account of whom the tournament had been undertaken, and with her her younger sister, whose sleeves were so quaint that she was called the Maid with the Narrow Sleeves, for she wore them tight. Dames and damsels climbed the

64

tower with them, and the tourney was joined in front of the castle. None bore himself so well as Meliance of Lis, by the testimony of his fair friend, who said to those about her, "Ladies, never did I see a knight who delighted me as doth Meliance of Lis. Is it not a pleasure to see such a knight? That man must have a good seat and be skillful in the use of lance and shield who beareth himself so excellently."

Thereupon her sister, who sat by her side, said that she saw a fairer knight. The elder maiden was angry and rose to strike her sister. But the ladies interfered, and held her back, so that she missed her blow, which greatly incensed her.

In the tournament many lances were shivered, shields pierced, and knights unhorsed; and it went hard with the knight who met Meliance of Lis, for there was none he did not throw on the hard ground. If his lance broke, he dealt great blows with his sword; and he bore himself better than any other knight on either side, to the great joy of his fair friend, who could not resist exclaiming, "Ladies, it is wonderful! Behold the best bachelor knight of whom minstrel hath ever sung or whom eyes have ever seen, the fairest and bravest of all those in the tourney!"

Then the little girl cried, "I see a handsomer one, and 'tis like, a better!"

The elder sister grew hot. "Ha, girl, you were malapert when you were so unlucky as to blame one whom I praised! Take that, to teach you better another time!" So saying, she slapped her sister, so hard that she left on the little girl's cheek the print of her five fingers. But the ladies who sat near scolded her and took her away.

After that they fell to talking of Sir Gawain. One of the damsels said, "The knight beneath yonder tree, why doth he delay to take arms?" A second damsel, who was ruder, exclaimed, "He hath sworn to keep the peace." And a third added, "He is a merchant. Don't tell me that he desireth to joust; he bringeth horses to market." "He is a money-changer," said a fourth. "The goods he hath he meaneth to sell to poor bachelors. Trust me, he hath money or raiment in those chests."

"You have wicked tongues!" cried the little girl. "And you lie! Do you think a merchant would bear such huge lances? You tire me to death, talking such nonsense! By the faith that I owe the Holy Spirit, he seemeth to me a knight rather than a merchant or a money-changer. He is a knight, and he looketh like one!"

The ladies all cried with one voice, "Fair sweet friend, if he looketh so, it doth not follow that he is so. He putteth it on because he wisheth to cheat the tariff. But in spite of all his cleverness he is a fool, for he will be taken up and hung for a cheat."

Now Gawain heard all that the ladies said about him, and he was ashamed and annoyed. But he thought, and thought rightly, that he lay under an accusation of treason, and that it was his duty to keep his pledge or forever disgrace himself and his line. It was for this reason that he took no part in the tourney, lest, if he fought, he should be wounded or taken prisoner.

Meliance of Lis called for great lances, to strike harder blows. Until night fell the tourney continued before the gate; the man who took any booty carried it to some place where he thought it would be safe. Then the ladies saw a squire, tall and strong, who held a piece of a lance and bore on his neck a steel cap. One of the ladies, who was foolish, called to him, saying, "Sir squire, so God help me, it is foolish of you to make prize of that tester, those arms and croup-piece. If you do a squire's duty you deserve a squire's wage. Below, in yonder meadow, is a man who hath riches he cannot defend. Unwise is he who misseth his gain while he hath the power to take it. He seemeth the most debonair of knights, and yet he would not stir if one plucked his beard. If you are wise, take the armor and the treasure, none will hinder you."

The squire went into the meadow and struck one of Gawain's horses, crying, "Vassal, are you sick that all day long you gape here and have done nothing, neither pierced shield nor shivered lance?"

Sir Gawain answered, "Pray, what is it to you why I tarry? You shall know, but not now. Get you gone about your business."

The squire withdrew, for Gawain was not the type of man to whom he would dare say anything unpleasant.

The tourney ended, after many knights had been killed and many horses captured. The outsiders had had the best, and the people of the castle gained by the intermission. At parting they all agreed that on the morrow with songs they would meet again and continue the encounter. So for that night they separated and those who had sallied forth returned to the castle, followed by Sir Gawain. At the gate he met the nobleman who had advised his lord to engage in the tourney. This man accosted him pleasantly, and said, "Fair sir, in this castle your hostel is ready. If it pleaseth you, remain here, for if you should go on it would be long before you arrived at a lodging; therefore I urge you to stay."

"I will tarry, your mercy!" said Gawain. "I have heard worse words."

The Adventures of Sir Gawain

The man led the guest to his house, talking of this and that, and asked him why on that day he had not borne arms. Sir Gawain explained how he had been accused of treason and was bound to be on his guard against prison and wounds until he could free himself from the reproach that was cast upon him, for it would be to the dishonor of himself and his friends if he should fail to appear at the time appointed.

The nobleman praised him, and said that if this was the reason he had done right. With that he led Gawain to his house, where they dismounted. The people of the castle blamed him, wondering how his lord would take it; while the elder daughter of Thiébault did her best to make trouble for Gawain, on account of her sister, with whom she was angry. "Sir," she said to her father, "on this day you have suffered no loss, but made a gain, greater than you think; you have only to go and take it. The man who hath brought it will not dare to defend it, for he is wily. Lances and shields he bringeth, with palfreys and chargers, and maketh himself resemble a knight to cheat the customs, so that he may pass free when he cometh to sell his wares. Render him his deserts. He is with Garin, the son of Bertan, who hath taken him to lodge at his house. I just saw him pass."

Thiébault took his horse, for he himself wished to go there. The little girl, who saw him leave, went out secretly by a back gate and straight down the hill to the house of Garin, who had two fair daughters. When these saw their little lady they should have been glad, and glad they were, each took her by a hand and led her into the house, kissing her eyes and lips.

In the meantime Garin and his son Herman had left the house and were going up to the castle to speak to their lord. Midway there they met Thiébault and saluted him. He asked whither Garin was going and said he had intended to pay him a visit. "By my faith," said the nobleman, "that will not displease me, and at my house you shall see the fairest of knights."

"It is even he whom I seek," said Thiébault, "to arrest him. He is a merchant who selleth horses and pretendeth to be a knight."

"Alas," said Garin, "'tis a churlish speech I hear you make! I am your man and you are my master, but on the spot I renounce your homage, and in the name of all my line now defy you, rather than suffer you to disgrace my house."

"Indeed," answered Thiébault, "I have no wish to do any such thing. Neither you nor your house shall ever receive aught but honor from me; not but what I have been counseled so to proceed."

"Your great mercy!" exclaimed the nobleman. "It will be my honor if you will visit my guest."

So side by side they went on until they reached the house. When Sir Gawain saw them, he rose out of courtesy, and said, "Welcome!" The two saluted him and took their seats beside him. Then the nobleman, who was the lord of that country, asked why he had taken no part in the tourney, and Gawain narrated how a knight had accused him of treason and how he was on his way to defend himself in a royal court. "Doubtless," answered the lord, "that is sufficient excuse. But where is the battle to be held?"

"Sir, before the king of Cavalon, whither I am journeying."

"And I," said the nobleman, "will guide you. Since you must needs pass through a poor country, I will provide you with food and packbeasts to carry it."

Gawain answered that he had no need to accept anything, for if it could be bought he would have food and lodging wherever he went.

With these words Thiébault took leave. As he departed, from the opposite direction he saw come his little daughter, who embraced Gawain's leg, and said, "Fair sir, listen! I have come to complain of my sister, who hath beaten me. So please you, do me justice!"

Gawain made no answer, for he did not know what she meant. He put his hand on her head, while the girl pulled him, saying, "To you, fair sir, I complain of my sister. I do not love her, since to-day she hath done me great shame for your sake."

"Fair one, what have I to do with that? How can I do you justice against your sister?"

Thiébault, who had taken leave, heard his child's entreaty, and said, "Girl, who bade you come here and complain to this knight?"

Gawain asked, "Fair sweet sir, is this maid your daughter?"

"Aye; but never mind what she says. A girl is a silly creature."

"Certes," said Gawain, "I should be churlish if I did not do what she desires. Tell me, my sweet child and fair, in what manner I can justify you against your sister."

"If it pleaseth you, for love of me, bear arms in the tourney."

"Tell me, dear friend," said Gawain, "have you ever before made petition to any knight?"

"No, sir."

"Never mind her," exclaimed her father. "Pay no heed to her folly."

Sir Gawain answered, "Sir, so aid me the Lord God, for so little a girl, she hath spoken very well, and I will not refuse her. To-morrow, if she wisheth, I will be her knight."

"Your mercy, fair sweet sir!" cried the child, who was overjoyed, and bowed down to his feet.

Without more words they parted. Thiébault carried his daughter back on the neck of his palfrey. As they rode up the hill be asked her what the quarrel had been about, and she told him the story from beginning to end, saying, "Sir, I was vexed with my sister, who declared that Meliance of Lis was the best of all the knights; and I, who had seen this knight in the meadow, could not help saying that I had seen a fairer, whereupon my sister called me a silly girl and beat me. Fie on me, if I take it from her! I would cut off both my braids close to my head, which would be a great loss, if to-morrow in the tourney this knight would conquer Meliance of Lis, and put an end to the fuss of madam, my sister! She talked so much that she tired all the ladies; but a little rain will hush a great wind."

"Fair child," said her father, "I command and allow you, in courtesy, to send him some love-token, a sleeve or a wimple."

The child, who was simple, answered, "With pleasure since you bid me. But my sleeves are so small, I should not like to send them. Most likely he would not care for them."

"Daughter, say no more," said Thiébault. "I will think about it. I am very glad." So saying, he took her in his arms, and had great joy of embracing and kissing her, until he came in front of his palace. But when his elder daughter saw him approach, with the child before him, she was vexed, and exclaimed, "Sir, whence cometh my sister, the Maid with the Narrow Sleeves? She is full of her tricks; she hath been quick about it; where did you find her?"

"And you," he answered, "what is it to you? Hush, for she is better than you are. You pulled her hair and beat her, which grieveth me. You acted rudely; you were discourteous."

When she heard her father's rebuke, the maid was greatly abashed.

Thiébault had brought from his chests a piece of red samite, and he bade his people cut out and make a sleeve, wide and long. Then he called his daughter and said, "Child, to-morrow rise betimes and visit the knight before he leaveth his hostel. For love's sake you will give him this new sleeve, which he will wear in the tourney when he goeth thither."

The Adventures of Sir Gawain

The girl answered that so soon as ever she saw the clear dawn she would dress herself and go. With that her father went his way, while she, in great glee, charged her companions that they should not let her oversleep but should wake her when day broke, if they would have her love them. They did as she wished, and when it dawned caused her to wake and dress. All alone she went to the house where Sir Gawain lodged, but, early though it was, the knights had risen and gone to the monastery to hear mass sung. She waited until they had offered long orisons and listened to the service, as much as was right. When they returned the child rose to greet Sir Gawain, and cried, "Sir, on this day may God save and honor you! For love of me, wear the sleeve which I carry in my hand."

"With pleasure," he answered; "friend, your mercy!"

After that the knights were not slow to take arms, and came pouring out of the town, while the damsels again went up to the walls and the dames of the castle saw the troops of brave and hardy knights approach.

They rode with loose rein, and in front was Meliance of Lis, who went so fast that he left the rest in the rear, two rods and more. When his maiden saw her friend she could not keep quiet, but cried, "Ladies, yonder comes the man who hath the lordship of chivalry!"

As swiftly as his horse would carry him Sir Gawain charged Meliance of Lis, who did not evade the blow, but met it boldly, and shivered his lance. On his part Sir Gawain smote so hard that he grieved Meliance, whom he flung on the field; the steed he grasped by the rein and gave to a varlet, bidding him take it to the lady on whose account he had entered the tourney, and say that his master had sent her the first spoil he had made that day. The youth took the charger, saddled as it was, and led it towards the girl, who was sitting at the window of the tower, whence she had watched the joust, and when she saw the encounter she cried to her sister, "Sister, there lies Meliance of Lis, whom you praised so highly! A wise man ought to give praise where it is due. You see, I was right yesterday when I said I saw a better knight."

Thus she teased her sister, who grew angry, and cried, "Child, hold your tongue! If you say another word, I will slap you so that you will not have a foot to stand on!" "Oh, sister," answered the little girl, "remember God! You ought not to beat me because I told you the truth. I saw him tumble as well as you; I think he will not be able to get up. Be as cross as you please, I must say that there is not a lady here who did not see him fall flat on the ground."

The Adventures of Sir Gawain

Her sister would have struck her, had she been able, but the ladies around would not allow it.

With that came the squire, who held the rein in his right hand. He saw the girl sitting at the window and presented the steed. She thanked him a hundred times, and bade the steed be taken in charge. The squire returned to tell his master, who seemed the lord of the tournament, for there was no knight so gallant that he did not cast from the saddle, if he reached him with the lance. On that day he captured four steeds. The first he sent to the little girl, the second to the wife of the nobleman who had been so kind, and the third and fourth to his own daughters.

The tourney was over and the knights entered the city. On both sides the honor belonged to Sir Gawain. It was not yet noon when he returned from the encounter; the city was full of knights, who ran after him, asking who he was and of what land. At the gate of his hostel he was met by the damsel, who did naught but grasp his stirrup, salute him, and cry, "A thousand mercies, fair sweet sir!" He answered frankly, "Friend, before I am recreant to your service, may I be aged and bald! I shall never be so remote, but a message will bring me. If I know your need, I shall come at the first summons, whatever business be mine!"

While they talked her father came and wished Sir Gawain to stay with him for that night; but first he begged, that if his guest pleased, he would tell his name. Sir Gawain answered, "Sir, I am called Gawain. My name was never concealed, nor have I ever told it before it hath been asked."

When Thiébault knew that the knight was Sir Gawain his heart was full of joy, and he exclaimed, "Sir, be pleased to lodge with me, and accept my service. Hitherto I have done you little worship, and never did I set eyes on a knight whom so much I longed to honor."

In spite of urging, Sir Gawain refused to stay. The little girl, who was good and clever, clasped his foot and kissed it, commending him to God. Sir Gawain asked why she had done that, and the girl replied that she had kissed his foot in order that he should remember her wherever he went. He answered, "Doubt it not, fair sweet friend! I shall never forget you, after I have parted hence."

With that Sir Gawain took leave of his host and the others, who one and all commended him to God. That night he slept in an abbey, and had all that was necessary.

Sir Gawain and the Lady of Lys

Hearken to me and ye shall hear how the good King Arthur and his knights went forth to the wood for archery, and how at vesper-tide they gat them homeward right joyfully.

The knights rode gaily ahead, holding converse the one with the other, and behind them came the king, on a tall and prancing steed. He ware no robe of state, but a short coat, which became him right well.

Behind all his men he rode, pensive and frowning, as one lost in thought. And as he thus lagged behind Sir Gawain looked back, and saw the king riding alone and pensive, and he bade his comrades draw rein and wait for their lord. And as the king came anigh he drew his steed beside him, and stretched out his hand, laughing, and laid hold on the bridle, and said, "Sire, tell us, for the love of God, of what ye may now be thinking? Sire, your thoughts should be of naught but good, for there is no prince in this world equal to ye in valour or in honour, therefore should ye be very joyful!"

The king made answer courteously, "Fair nephew, an I may be joyful I will tell ye truly that whereon I thought. There is no king living on earth who hath had such good and such great service from his men as I; it seemeth to me now right and fitting that I should give to them that which they have deserved for the toil they have suffered for me, whereby I be come to such high estate. Fair nephew, I bethought me that my riches would avail little if through sloth I failed to reward the good service of these my knights, who have made me everywhere to be obeyed and honoured. Now without delay will I tell ye that I am minded to hold, at Pentecost, a far greater court than is my wont, and to give to each and all such gifts as shall be well pleasing to them, so that each may be glad and joyful, and ever hereafter of good will towards me."

Swiftly, and before all the others, Sir Gawain made answer, "Fair Sire, blessed be the thought into which ye have fallen, for 'tis so fair and so good that neither kaiser nor king nor count might think a better."

And the king asked, "Nephew, tell me straightway where do ye counsel that this my court be held?"

"Sire, at Carnarvon; there let all your knighthood assemble, for there is not in all your kingdom a fairer place, nor nobler halls, and it lieth in the marches of Wales, and of the land of Britain."

The king and all his company rode back joyfully, and that selfsame night did the king Arthur give command that all the knights and all the barons throughout the land should be summoned by letter to come to him at Pentecost.

That great knighthood came thither, that famous knighthood came thither, even so have I heard, and assembled for this court at Carnarvon.

Ah God! from what far-off lands did they come. Thither were come the men of Ireland, and of Scotland, of Iceland, of Wales, and of Galvoie (a land where many a man goeth astray). From Logres they came, and from Escavalon; men of Norway, Bretons, Danes, and they of Orcanie. Never was so great a knighthood assembled at any court as that which the good king Arthur summoned to him.

The day of the Holy Feast, when he had worn his crown at the high procession, knights and barons conducted him with joy to his palace; and therewith Kay, the seneschal, bade them sound the trumpets and bring water. First the king washed, and thereafter sat down aloft, on the high daïs, so that all who sat there at meat might see him. Four hundred knights, save three, sat themselves down at the Round Table; at the second were seated the thirty peers. Crowded were the ranks of the other knights who were seated throughout the hall, as was fitting, on daïs, and at tables on the ground. Then quickly Kay the seneschal bare the first meat, and the service was made throughout the hall, in joyful wise, as befitted such high festivity.

Now as the king ate, he looked towards the Round Table, even as one who would take knowledge of all, and by hap his eye fell on the seat of a knight good and true, which was void and lacking its rightful lord. Then so great a pity and tenderness took him that the tears rose from his heart to his eyes, and thence welled forth, and he sighed a great and piteous sigh when he remembered him of that knight. He took a knife which Yones held (nephew was he to king Ydier, and carved before Arthur), and, frowning and thoughtful, smote the blade through the bread which lay on the board. Then he rested his head on the one hand, even as one whose thoughts are troubled by anger or grief, and unheeding, ran the palm of the other adown the sharp knife, so that he was somewhat wounded. At sight of the blood he bethought himself, and left hold of the knife and taking the napkin, wrapped it swiftly around his hand, so that they who ate in the hall below might not see. And with that he fell once more into thought and bowed down his head, and as he mused the tears came again to his eyes.

When Sir Gawain beheld this he marvelled much, and therein was he right, for to all who were in the hall it seemed but folly. Then he rose up straightway, and passed between the ranks till that he came before the daïs, and saw that the king was again lost in thought. He hasted not to speak till that he saw him raise his head, but so soon as he lifted up his face Sir Gawain spake right courteously; "Sire, Sire, 'tis neither right nor fitting that ye should have such wrath or displeasure as should make ye thus moody in the sight of so many high and noble barons as ye may see here around ye; rather should their solace and their company please and rejoice ye."

"Gawain, will ye that I tell ye whence came the thought which has made me thus sad and silent?"

"Yea, Sire, that do I pray of ye."

"Fair nephew, know of a truth that I will tell ye willingly, in the hearing of all these good knights. My thoughts were of ye, and of many another whom I see here, of the wickedness of which ye are full, and of the envy and the treason long time hid, and now made manifest." With that the king held his peace, and said no more.

Sir Gawain grew crimson with anger and shame, and throughout the palace all held their peace, for much they marvelled that the king spake thus evilly to his nephew, calling him in the hearing of all a traitor proven, and all were wroth therefor. Then he to whom the ill words were said answered as best he might, "Sire, that was an ugly word; for your honour bethink ye of what ye have said in the hearing of all who be here within."

"Gawain," answered the king, "'tis no empty word, thus of a truth do I repeat it, and Ywain may well take heed and know that I thought of him but now, when I sat silent and pensive, here within have I not one single comrade whom I do not accuse of treason and too great felony!"

With that I know not how many sprang to their feet, and a great clamour filled the hall. "Lords," cried Tor fis Ares, "I conjure ye by the oath which ye and I alike sware to king Arthur that ye restrain yourselves, and act as is befitting; he accuses ye all of treason—these be right evil tidings!" In like wise also spake Sir Ywain. "Ah God," quoth Sir Gawain, "with what joy was all this great court summoned and assembled, and in what grief shall it be broken up!"

The king heard, and, sighing, spake, "Gawain, I have spoken but the truth!"

"Fair Sire, for the love of God, and for honesty, tell us after what manner and in what fashion we be felon and traitorous?"

Quoth the king, "An ye will I will tell ye; now hearken. Ye know of a truth that aforetime there reigned in this land a folk who built castles and cities, strong towers and fortresses, and the great Chastel Orguellous did they fortify against us. When we heard tell thereof ye, my knights, delayed not to go thither, not with my will! There did I lose so many of my folk that the thought thereof yet grieveth my heart; the greater part were slain, but some among them were made captive. They took one of my companions, three years long have they held him in prison, and thereof have I great grief at heart. Here within do I see no better knight; he was beyond measure valiant, fair of face and form, and very wise was he in counsel. But now, when all this great lordship was set down here to meat, I beheld that knight's seat void and lacking its lord, and for sorrow and grief was my heart heavy and troubled when I saw him not in his place in your ranks; it lacked but little that I were distraught. Therefore, my lords, do I arraign ye all of treason; Giflet fis Do is he named that good and gentle knight, three whole years have gone by since he was imprisoned in that tower, and ye be all traitors who have left your comrade three years and have not sought for or freed him! Yea, and I who have blamed ye, I be even more the traitor in that I ever ware crown, or made joy, or held high feast before I knew if he might be restored to me, or where he now may be, whether dead or living! Now on this have I set my heart,—by the faith I owe to that Heavenly Lord who hath bestowed on me earthly honour, and kingdom, and lands, that for no hap that may befall me will I delay to set forth in search of him, be it in never so distant a land. For verily I tell ye all that the king who loseth so good a knight by wrongful deed or by sloth, he hath right neither to lands nor to honour, nor should he live a day longer, an he deliver not that knight who for his honour suffered toil and was made captive. In the ears of ye all do I make a vow that I will lie not more than one night in any place till that I know whether he be dead, or may be freed."

Then all cried with one voice, "Shame upon him, Sire, who will not plead guilty to this treason, for ye speak with right and reason; by overmuch sloth have we delayed to ride forth and seek him far hence, even at the Chastel Orguellous."

"Lords," quoth the king, "I tell ye here and at once that I shall set forth to-morrow, but by the faith that I owe to Saint Germain I must needs proceed with wisdom, for here is force of no avail."

"True, fair Sire," answered Sir Gawain. "Know for sooth that the roads 'twixt here and the Chastel Orguellous be passing hard and difficult; 'tis a good fifteen days ere ye be come thither; longer days have ye never ridden! 'Tis best that one tell ye the truth! And when ye be come thither, fair Sire, then shall ye have each day battle, as I know right well, one knight against the other, a hundred against a hundred, that shall ye find truly. Now take good counsel for the journey, what folk ye may best take with ye."

"Lords," said the king, "now let us to meat, and afterward will I see by aid of your counsel whom I take with me, and whom I leave to guard my land and my folk."

With that all in the palace, great and small, ate as quickly as might be; and so soon as the king saw that 'twas time and place to speak he bade remove the cloths, which they did without delay. Thereafter they brought water, and bare round the wine in cups of fine gold. Then, it seemeth me, there sprang to their feet at once more than three thousand knights, who cried the king mercy, and prayed that he would take them with him on this adventure, for right willingly would they go.

"Lords," quoth the king, "they whom my barons elect, those will I take, and the others shall remain to keep my kingdom in peace."

Then first, before all others, spake king Urien, a very wise knight was he. "My Lord king, ye have no need to take with ye too great a force; take with ye rather a few, but good, men, so to my thinking will ye more swiftly free Giflet, our good comrade, from his prison. Take with ye the best of your knights, 'twill be for your greater honour, and your foes will be the more speedily vanquished; knight against knight must ye fight there, and I think me that such of their men shall there be worsted that they shall that same day yield ye Giflet the good and valiant knight. Have no doubt for the when or how, but bid them make ready. I can but praise the folk who shall go with ye."

Then quoth the king, "What say ye, Lords? I await your counsel!"

King Ydier spake. "Sire, none of us should give ye praise, or speak other than the best he knoweth. Shamed be he who should give ye counsel

wherein ye may find no honour. I know full well that the more part of your
folk would gladly go with ye, but if ye take them, Sire, 'twill not be for
your honour, but believe king Urien, for he hath given good counsel so I
tell ye of a truth."

"Certes," saith Sir Gawain, "he would be false and foolish who should
give other rede!" And all said, "Let it be as the king will; let him take
those whom he please, and leave the others in the land."

"Ye have said well," said the king; "now go ye to your lodging, and
prepare to depart, and I will cause to be made ready a pennon of silk for
each of those whom I shall lead with me." As he said, so it was done, and
all betook them to their lodging.

The king forthwith sent the pennons, and bade them without fail be
armed and ahorse at dawn.

What more shall I tell ye? At sunrise were all the knights armed, even
as the king commanded, all they who had received the pennons came
together ahorse before the hall.

Now will I tell ye their names: there were Sir Gawain, king Ydier,
Guengasoains, Kay, and Lucains, the butler. The sixth was Tors. Then
Saigremors, and Mabonagrain, who was nephew unto king Urien. Eight
have I now named unto ye, counting the kinsman of king Urien. The
ninth was Lancelot du Lac; the tenth Ider, son of Nut; the Laid Hardi, the
eleventh; with Doon l'Aiglain have we twelve, all very courteous knights.
Galegantins the Galois, and the brave Carados Briefbras, who was a right
cheery comrade, made fourteen, and the fifteenth was the good Taulas de
Rogemont: so many were they, nor more, nor less.

All ready armed were they before the hall the while they awaited the
king, ere he came forth armed from his chamber. Then he mounted his
steed, and I tell ye that, to my knowledge, was never king so richly armed
afore, nor ever hereafter shall there be such. The queen bare him company
even to the entrance of the palace, then she turned her back.

Then the king bade his companions march, and they began to move as
swiftly as might be on the highway, but so great a folk convoyed them that
hardly might they depart or go forth from the burg. And when the king
had ridden three miles he drew rein in the midst of a meadow, and there
he bade farewell to his folk, who, sad and sorrowful, gat them back to the
burg. And the king and his fifteen comrades rode on their way; they passed
even through the land of Britain, so I think me, and hasted them much to
ride quickly.

The Adventures of Sir Gawain

One day the king, fasting, came forth from a very great forest, on to a heath of broom; the sun was hot, and burning, and the country over large and waste. The king was so wearied by the heat, in that he rode fasting, that he had much need of rest, could he but find a fitting spot. By chance they found a great tree, where they drew bridle; beneath was a spring, and for heat and for weariness they bared their heads and their hands, and washed their faces and their mouths. I know well that one and all had much need of food, but they had naught with them, and all were sore vexed for the king, who suffered over much from the fast.

Sir Gawain gazed into the plain, far below, 'neath the forest, and he showed unto the seneschal a house of thatch, well fenced about; "Kay," quoth he, "methinks under that roof there must be folk!"

"'Tis true," said Kay; "I will go and see if I may find victual, and ye shall await me here." With that he departed from them, and went straightway to the house; within he found an old woman, but nothing of what he sought; food was there none.

The crone spake and said, "Sir, so God help me, for twenty miles round about are naught but waste lands, know that well, save only that the king of Meliolant has built there below 'neath the trees a forest lodge. He cometh thither ofttimes privately with his hounds. There, Sir, will ye be well lodged, an ye find him; from that tree yonder may ye see the house on the hill."

The seneschal straightway went even as the crone had said, and he saw the dwelling, right well enclosed with orchards, vineyards and meadows. Ponds were there, lands, and fish-tanks, all well fenced about. In the midst was a tower; ye might ask no better, no defence was lacking to it. Beholding it the seneschal stayed not, but passed the roadway, and the gate, and the chief drawbridge, and thus came to the foot of the tower. There did he dismount, but he found no living soul of whom he might ask concerning the dwelling and who might be within. Then he entered a hall, very high and long and wide. On a great hearth he saw a goodly fire alight, but he found no man save a dwarf, who was roasting a fat peacock ('twere hard to find a better!), well larded, on a spit of apple-wood, which the dwarf knew right well how to turn.

Kay came forward quickly, and the dwarf beheld him with evil countenance. "Dwarf," quoth the seneschal, "tell me if there be any here within save thyself?" But the wretch would not speak a word.

The Adventures of Sir Gawain

Kay would have slain him there and then, if he had not thought to be shamed thereby, but he knew right well that twere too great villainy.

"Miserable hunchback," quoth he, "I see none here in this house save thee and this peacock, which I will now have for my dinner; I will share it as shall seem me good."

"By the King Who lieth not," quoth the dwarf, "ye shall neither eat thereof yourself nor share it with others; I counsel you to quit this hostel, or know ye well, and without doubt, that ye shall be right shamefully thrust out!"

This vexed Kay mightily, and he sprang forward to smite him; with his foot he thrust him against the pillar of the hearth so that the stone thereof became bloody. The dwarf bled freely for the heat, and made loud lament, for he feared lest he should be slain.

Then on the left the seneschal heard a door shut-to sharply, and there came forth a knight, tall and strong, and of proud countenance, and very fair and goodly to look upon; he might not be above thirty years old. He ware a vest of new samite, furred with ermine for warmth; 'twas not long, but wide, and of ample folds. Thus was he well clad and cunningly shod; and I tell ye truly that he ware a fair girdle of golden links; no treasury hath a richer. All uncovered he came forth, in guise of a man greatly wroth, leading two greyhounds by a fair leash of silk which he held in his hand. When he saw that his dwarf bled, he spake, "Ye who be come all armed into this hall, wherefore have ye slain this my servant?"

"A curse upon such a servant," quoth Kay, "from this day on, for in all the world is there not one so evil, so small, or so misshapen!"

Then the knight answered, "By all the saints, but ye say ill, and I challenge ye for it, fair sir."

Quoth the seneschal, "Many a goodly knight have I seen, to the full as noble as ye may be, and ye be evil and vexatious, even if I have smitten this servant who roasted here this peacock, to speak thus concerning the matter."

The knight answered frankly, "Sir, ye speak not courteously, but for God's sake I would ask ye a mere nothing, even that ye vouchsafe to tell me your name."

Kay spake in great wrath, "I will tell ye willingly, so help me God I have told it ere this to five hundred knights better than ye be; know of a truth that my name is Kay."

The Adventures of Sir Gawain

"Certes, sir, I may well believe that ye speak truly; by your speech alone may one quickly know ye. This lad refused ye the peacock; 'tis not the custom of my house that meat be refused to any who may ask for it; ye shall have your share of the peacock, and that right swiftly, so God help me!" With that he seized the spit, and raised it aloft, and with great strength and force smote Sir Kay therewith, so that he well nigh slew him, and know that he smote him on the neck so that he must needs fall, he had no foot so firm that it might keep him upright. And as the peacock burst asunder, the hot blood thereof ran between the links of his hauberk in such wise that Sir Kay bare the mark thereof all the days of his life. Then the knight threw the peacock to his two hounds, and spake, "Sir Kay, rise, that be your share, ye shall have no more; now get out of my sight quickly, I am over wroth when I behold ye!"

With that came quickly two sergeants, fully armed, and led the seneschal forth from the hall. He mounted his steed, and turned him back, passing the bridge and the plain, and came to where the king had dismounted.

Then his comrades asked him, "Seneschal, have ye found nothing of that which ye went to seek?"

"Not I, my lords; 'tis a right evil land here wherein to seek for food; it behoveth us to ride far, for here may we find nor hostelry, nor victual—so hath it been told to me."

Quoth Sir Gawain, laughing, "Certes, he with whom ye spake lives by meat, even as we; without meat might he not dwell in this great and well wooded land."

"By my faith, no," answered Kay, "but I tell ye truly, 'tis so proud a vassal that for naught that we may say will he give us shelter."

The king said, "Then is he right discourteous, and I counsel that we send Gawain to him. Fair nephew, go, and we will wait ye here."

Sir Gawain mounted forthwith. What more shall I tell ye save that he came straight to the dwelling, and when the knight saw him he made marvellous joy of him, and asked his name, and he answered that men called him Gawain, and straightway the knight knew him.

Then he told him his errand, saying, "The king is not far distant, and would fain lodge with ye." This was well pleasing to the knight, and he said, "Fair Sir, go, bring the king hither."

Then Sir Gawain rode swiftly back, and brought Arthur with him to the hostel; but ere they might enter all the waters were set free and the fountains 'gan to play. For joy and in honour of the king the knight had assembled all his folk, and received him with very great honour, and led him into the tower. The hounds were yet there, devouring the flesh of the peacock. The king looked at Taulas, and quoth, "Body of Saint Thomas, these two hounds have fared better than we to-day!" The knight heard, and laughed to himself. Kay saw that, but said naught.

From thence they passed into the hall, and when they had disarmed the meat was made ready, the knight bade bring white napkins, and pasties. After dinner he made them wash their heads, and their necks, and their feet, which were sorely bruised. Then he caused them to rest in fair beds, covered with cloth of samite, and they slept even to the morrow without stirring. But when they were awakened the host had prepared for them a right plenteous meal, this he did of his good will. They sat them down joyfully, and were richly served. I would weary ye if I told all the dishes. The knights made much mirth of the seneschal's burn, for the dwarf would not keep the tale secret from them, but began to speak thereof. Never would it have been known through Kay, if the dwarf had not brought it to mind, for he was over bent on hiding it, and the host even more than he; all that night his comrades mocked and made sport of him even till they betook them to rest.

Next morn, without delay, the king arose at daybreak, and likewise did all the others, and armed themselves. Then the king thanked his host for the good lodging he had given them.

Why should I make long telling thereof? The king saith, "Hide not from me how ye be called."

"Sire, my name is Ydier the fair, and, Sire, this castle is mine own."

Then Ydier prayed the king that of his kindness he would take him with him, but Arthur said he might not lead with him other save those whom he had brought from his own land; and he took leave of the knight since he might no longer abide in his hostelry, and went forth with his companions.

The tale is here over long, but I will shorten it for ye. Two days did they ride without food, for they might not sooner find place where they might win food or seek lodging. Thus must they needs ride till they came to the Orchard of the Sepulchres, where adventures be found oft and perilous. There they ate with the hermits, of whom there were a hundred and more. Here 'tis not fitting to tell of the marvels of the cemetery, so diverse they be, and so great that there is no man living on earth who could think, or believe, that the tale be true. Since 'twas made and established never has the tale been told whence came those graves, nor the custom which the hermits observed; to my mind 'twould take too long did I tell it ye ere the fitting time and place be come. But this will I tell ye of a truth, when the king had sojourned two days, and beheld the Orchard, on the third, after meat, he departed, and took the road once more.

On the morrow he came to a wondrous fair land; small need to seek a richer in meadows, forests, or orchards planted with rare and diverse trees. In the forest ways the grass grew green and tall, reaching even to the horses' girths. Towards even-tide they came to a trodden way, where the tall grass was beaten to earth, and trampled down by horses, even for the length of a bowshot. "A hundred and more have passed this way," quoth the king's men.

Sir Gawain spake to the king, "Fair Sire, follow me gently with these my comrades on this wide road. I will ride on ahead, and seek out, and ask whether there be near at hand hostel where we may lodge this night, for of lodging have we great need. Yet, Sire, I pray that ye leave not the road for word of any."

With that he set spurs to his steed, and rode swiftly on his way; nor had he ridden long ere he was free of the forest, and saw before him a hill, and a company of well-nigh a hundred horsemen, who rode in knightly guise; 'twas on their track he followed.

Sir Gawain pressed on his steed, but when he had crossed the valley and mounted the hill there was never a man in sight. But he saw before him a castle; none so fair had he beheld afore, which stood on the bank of a broad river; 'twould take me over long to tell the fashion thereof, but this and no more will I say, 'twas the fairest ever seen.

Then Sir Gawain looked toward the river, and beheld two maidens, in very fair vesture of purple, bearing pitchers of fine gold, wherein they had drawn water, and he quoth, "Maidens, God save ye, and give ye good speed!" and they answered, as was fitting, "Fair sir, God bless ye!"

"Maidens, by the faith ye owe me answer me, and hide it not, what bear ye in those pitchers?"

Quoth the one, "No need have we to hide aught; 'tis but water, wherewith the good knight shall wash his hands."

"Of a faith," quoth Sir Gawain, "courteously have ye named him; great honour is there in such a name!"

The Adventures of Sir Gawain

The second maiden answered, "Sir, she hath spoken truth; ye will not lightly find a fairer, or a better, knight. See, but now doth he enter within his burg."

Then Sir Gawain hasted, and spake no more with the maidens, but rode over the bridge, and entered the castle by the gateway. Since the hour of his birth never had he seen one so fair, nor, I think me, so long as he live shall he see a fairer. All the way by which he passed was hung with curtains richly wrought, whereat he marvelled strangely. 'Twas closed all along with fair buildings of diverse fashions. In long rows adown the street Sir Gawain beheld rich booths of changers, wherein on many-coloured carpets were set forth vessels of gold and silver (no treasury ever held richer), cups, tankards, and dishes, the fairest ever seen, with money of all lands: esterlins, besants, deniers of Africa, and treasure trove. Every kind of money was there, and much the good knight marvelled thereat.

Stuffs there were too, of all colours, the cost whereof was past his telling. All the doors stood open; but one thing troubled Sir Gawain sore: there was never a living soul to be seen.

Then he said within himself, "Of a sooth, for love and kindness do they bear their lord, who but now hath entered the burg, company to the little castle yonder." Thus he went his way straight to that castle, and came within a goodly hall, both high and wide, and in length equal to a bowshot. On every daïs a linen cloth was spread, and sure never king nor count might eat off fairer or better wrought. All was made ready for meat, and the bread and wine set in readiness on the tables; but never a living soul was there. In a side chamber he beheld on grails of silver more than a hundred boars' heads, with pepper beside them, dressed for the serving. Sir Gawain beheld, and crossed himself with lifted hand, but would no longer abide, finding no man with whom he might have speech.

He turned him again through the castle, thinking to find at the bridgehead the maidens of whom I told but now, whom he had left bearing the water in golden pitchers, but nowhere might he find them, and it vexed him sore that he saw them not, since he thought within himself that they would surely have told him the truth concerning their lord, whom he had seen but now enter the burg.

Much he mused thereon, repenting him that he had not longer spoken with them, but now would he make no more abiding, but set him speedily on his way, to meet the king. Nor did he draw bridle till he came unto him.

"Fair nephew," quoth Arthur, "shall we to-day find hostel where we may take rest, for we have sore need thereof?"

"Fair Sire, be at rest; food shall ye have now," answered Sir Gawain.

"'Tis a good word," quoth Kay; "right gladly will I serve the first course unto the king, and to my comrades after!"

"Kay," saith Sir Gawain "not for all the world might ye guess the marvels I have found!" Then he told unto them the adventure, even as it had fallen out, the while he guided them to the burg. As they rode adown the street the king marvelled greatly at the riches he beheld, and Kay spake a courteous word,

"Castle, he who hence might bear ye
Would do ill an he should spare ye!"

Thus came they all into the inner burg, and, still ahorse, into the great hall, but they found no man to whom they might speak, or to whose care they might give their steeds. Then they said to each other, "'Twere ill to let them fast," and the king spake, "I counsel that after supper we go forth into yonder fair meadow."

This they held for good rede, and dismounted, making fast their steeds to the stag's antlers on the wall. Then they washed their faces and their hands in a bowl of silver, and the king sat himself down first, and his knights after.

With no delay Kay set the first course before the king; 'twas a great boar's head, and he bare it joyfully, and thereafter swiftly served the rest, saying an any found cause for plaint, there was no lack, he could have at his will. "The food hath cost me naught and I give it freely; nay, of a verity we might, an we were so minded, feed our steeds on boars' heads; this is no niggard hostelry! See ye the fair couches in yonder chamber?" And he pointed to an open doorway.

Sir Gawain looked, and saw a shield hanging on the wall, and within the shield yet stood the fragment of a mighty lance, with a silken pennon hanging from it. I tell ye of a truth, so soon as he was ware thereof the blood stirred in his veins; he spake no word, but swiftly as might be he sprang up from meat, casting aside the knife he held, and gat him to his steed, and girthed him tightly, and set his helmet on his head, and sat him down again on a bench near by the daïs, his shield beside him.

The king marvelled greatly, and the knights said the one to the other, "Ha, God, what aileth Sir Gawain?" Each would fain know wherefore he had armed himself thus swiftly; they thought of a surety his head had grown light through over much fasting and the great heat of the day. They were sore dismayed thereat, for they had seen and heard naught that might give occasion for arming, and they might not guess the cause.

The king spake simply, "Fair nephew, say, wherefore have ye ceased to eat? And wherefore thus arm in haste? Ye make us much to marvel; tell me, I pray, doth aught ail ye?"

"Naught, Sire, save that I pray ye to eat quickly, an ye love me!"

"How," quoth Arthur, "without ye, who have fasted even as we? Methinks that were ill done!"

"By God and Saint Thomas, to eat here will profit me naught; ye are wrong, Sire!" Thus answered Sir Gawain, swearing that for naught in the world would he eat in this hostelry, neither might he be joyful or at ease so long as they abode therein. "But I pray ye, Sire, hasten and eat."

Then the king in the hearing of all sware straitly by Him who lieth not, that he would eat naught till that he knew wherefore his nephew had thus donned his helmet.

"Sire," quoth Sir Gawain, "ill and falsely should I have wrought if for the telling of so slight a matter I should make ye fast this day; certes I will tell ye, and lie not. Ye know well how five years agone ye led an army great and strong against the city of Branlant; many a king, many a baron, with twenty thousand men all told, with ye laid siege to the city. Within were many of great valour to aid the lord who held the seignorie of that land. One morn, at break of day, they made a sortie on our host; the cry and clamour were so great that I took no leisure to arm me, but mounted my steed and rode forth, even as I was, to learn the cause of the tumult, bearing with me but shield and lance. Thus I rode forth from the camp, and came straightway on the men of the city, who were hasting to return with their spoil. I followed them, wherein I did foolishly, since I came near to lose my life thereby, for I was wounded by a spear in the shoulder, as ye know, so that I was like to die, and must needs lie sick four months and more ere that I was whole and sound.

"One morning, as I lay in my tent, I bade them raise the hangings around that I might look on the land, and I beheld one of my squires, mounted on the Gringalet, making his way from the stream where he had watered the steed. I called him, and he came to me, and I bade him without delay saddle the good horse, and he did my bidding. I clad me swiftly the while, and bade them bring me my armour secretly, and when I had armed me I mounted, and rode alone out of the camp. Fair Sire, ye followed me, ere I came beyond the tents, praying me straitly to return, but I entreated ye gently that since I had lain overlong sick ye would grant me to go forth into the fields to disport myself, and to test if I were in very truth healed of my wound, promising to return speedily to camp. By this covenant, Sire, ye granted me to ride forth.

"Thus I went my way till I came to a leafy grove, beset with flowers, and abounding in birds, which sang loud and clear. I stayed my steed to hearken, and for the sweetness of the song my heart grew light, and I felt nor pain nor ill. Then I set spurs to my steed, and galloped adown the glade. I found myself hale and strong, and feared no longer for my wound.

"Thus I hearkened to the sweet song of the birds till that I forgat myself, and passed a second grove, and a third, and a fourth, ere that I bethought me of returning. Thus I rode till I came to a clearing fair and wide, where I saw beside a fountain a pavilion, richly fashioned. I rode even to the doorway, and looked within, and there on a couch I beheld so wondrous fair a maiden that I was abashed for her great beauty. Sire, I dismounted, and fastened my steed without the tent and entered and saluted the maiden; but, Sire, first she greeted Sir Gawain ere that she made answer to me.

"Then I asked her wherefore she did thus, and she answered that she held Sir Gawain in honour above all knights, and therefore she first gave him greeting. And when I heard this I spake saying that I was indeed Sir Gawain, and her most true knight, but scarce would the maiden believe me. I must needs unhelm, and from an inner chamber she brought forth a silken ribbon, whereon a Saracen maiden of the queen's household had wrought my semblance. And when she had looked thereon, and beheld me disarmed, and knew of a verity that I was he whom she desired, then she threw her arms around me, and kissed me more than a hundred times, saying that she was mine even as long as she might live.

"Then I took that fair gift right joyfully, and we spake together long, and had our will the one of the other. And this I tell ye that ere we parted I sware to her that other love would I never have. Then when I had armed me again, and mounted my steed, I took leave of the maid right lovingly, and turned me again for the camp, joyful of this my fair adventure.

"Thus I rode swiftly through one grove, but had gone scarce a bowshot beyond when a knight came fast behind me, marvellous well armed, and bearing a lance with a fair pennon. He cried loudly upon me, 'Traitor, ye may go no further; ye must pay dearly for my brother, whom ye slew, and for this my daughter, whom ye have now dishonoured.' Then I answered him, 'Sir Knight, ye might speak more courteously, for I have done ye neither shame nor evil; an I had, I were ready to give ye what amends might seem good to ye and to my lady; treason have I not done.'

"With that I set spurs to my steed, and he likewise, and we came fast the one against the other, and his lance was shivered on my shield, but my blade pierced him through shield and hauberk, so that he fell to the ground sore wounded. Sire, I pray ye eat, for an I tell ye more it may turn to evil." And the king quoth, "Nephew, say on speedily, and delay not."

Then spake Sir Gawain, "Sire, I left the knight lying, and went my way, but ere I had gone far I heard one cry upon me, 'Traitor, stay; ye must pay for my uncle and this my father, whom ye have wrongfully slain, and for my sister, whom ye have dishonoured!' Then I stayed my steed, and prayed him to speak more courteously, for that I was ready to make amends an I had done wrong, but that I was no traitor.

"Then we set ourselves to joust, and I tell ye, Sire, we came so hard together that we were borne both of us to the earth. Then we betook us to our swords, and dealt many a blow the one to the other; but in the end, in that I was scarce healed of my wound, he dealt me more harm than I might deal him; in this I lie not, I was well-nigh worn down, and put to the worse. Then I bethought me, Sire, and prayed him to tell me his name since I was fain to know it; and he told me he was Bran de Lis. Ider de Lis, the good and valiant, was his father, and Melians de Lis his uncle, and he said did I get the better of him, then had I slain the three best knights in any land, yet he deemed well, an God would help him, that he might even avenge the twain; for he quoth, 'I know well that a combat betwixt us may not endure over long, but that one of us must needs be slain.' And I answered, 'Sir, let us do otherwise, for an ye put me to the worse but few will believe the tale, for in this land it were not lightly held that any man may vanquish me. Methinks 'twere better that our combat be fought in the sight of many, who shall bear true witness as to the which of us comes off the better.' Thus, Sire, we made covenant together by token that in what place soever he should find me, whether armed or unarmed, there we should fight. This we sware, the one to the other. By the love I bear ye, Sire, never since that day have I heard aught of him in any land where I might be. Thus was our combat ended, as I tell ye, and of a truth I saw him no more.

The Adventures of Sir Gawain

"But even now, Sire, as I sat at meat, from which I arose in wrath and misease (willingly would I have eaten an I might), this is what chanced: I saw in yonder chamber the selfsame shield which Bran de Lis bare the day we did combat together; full well I remember it, and there it hangeth on the wall. Fair lord king, an God help me 'tis no lie; there in the shield standeth fast my pennon, and a great splinter of my lance; by that token, Sire, Bran de Lis doth haunt this country, since his shield be here. Therefore am I vexed and wrathful, and therefore I arose from meat, since I feared to be taken at a loss; in sooth, I somewhat fear him, for so good a knight I never saw! Sire, now have I told ye the truth, and wherefore I have donned my helmet, ye need press me no further, since not for the kingdom of Logres would I be found unarmed in such place as he may be. Fair Sire, I pray ye hasten, otherwise, an there be long abiding, I may chance to pay over dear for my meat."

Quoth the king, "Fair nephew, sit ye down again, nor have fear of any foe. He cometh not."

But Sir Gawain answered, "Sire, for naught that ye may say will I eat in this hostel!"

"So be it," quoth the king, "an ye will do naught for my prayer." With that all the others betook them to meat in good fellowship.

After no long time they beheld a little brachet, which ran out from a side chamber and came into the hall. A long leash trailed behind it, and round its neck was a collar of gold, wherein were many precious stones, red, and green as ivy leaves. The brachet was white as snow, and smoother than any ermine. I tell ye of a truth 'twas not ugly, but very fair and well shapen, and the king gazed long at it. It barked loudly at the knights on the daïs, and made small joy of them, I tell ye. Then Kay the seneschal coveted it, and spake to the king, "Sire, I will keep this brachet, and take it hence, an ye grant me this gift; 'twill be a comrade for Huden." And the king said, "Take it, seneschal, and bear it hence."

With that the brachet turned tail, and Kay with no delay sprang up and thought to seize it, but the dog would not await him, but fled on through a chamber wrought in marble, and the leash which was long fell about the feet of Kay, who would fain have caught it but might not come at it. Might he set foot on the leash he could have held it, but he failed to catch it.

Thus the chase went from chamber to chamber till five were passed, and the seneschal came into a fair garden set with olive trees and pines, wherein were more folk than in a city. They were playing at diverse games, and making such joy and festivity as 'twere overlong to recount, for that day they were keeping the feast of a saint of that land.

Beneath the shade of a laurel in the midst of an orchard a knight was disarming; tall he was and strong, valiant and proud, and to serve him and honour him the best and most renowned of the folk stood and knelt around waiting on his disarming. The brachet which Kay was chasing stayed not till it came to the knight, and took shelter betwixt his legs, barking loudly at the pursuer.

Kay stayed his steps, abashed at the sight and sound of this folk, and thought to return swiftly, and with no delay; but the knight looked on his people and said, "There is a stranger among us, whoever he may be!" Then beholding Kay, who would turn him again whence he came, he spake, "See him there, take him, and bring him hither!"

This they did swiftly, and brought Kay before him, and when the knight beheld him he said joyfully, "Sir Kay, ye are right welcome as my friend and comrade; where is the king, your master?"

"Sir, he is within, on the daïs, and with him many a valiant knight; they are even now at meat!"

"And is the king's nephew, Gawain, there? Fain would I be assured thereof." And Kay answered, "The best knight in the world is in the king's company; without him would he go nowhither!"

Now when the knight heard this he was like to fly for joy. Half armed as he was he sprang to his feet, and for very gladness stayed not to finish his disarming. A rich mantle had they hung on his shoulders, but the neck was yet unfastened, nor would he tarry to clasp it, for haste and joy. And know that one leg was still shod with iron, which hung downward, half unlaced, nor would he stay to rid himself thereof. Thus he sped in all haste to the hall, and his folk after him, and without slacking speed he ran into the hall, followed by so great a crowd that the king was sore abashed when he heard the tumult.

The knight went forward even to the daïs, and saluted the king courteously, and commanded the folk to bring torches, for 'twas scarce light therein, and they did at his pleasures, and he bade bring other meats, so that Arthur, the valiant and courteous, was well served as befitting a king.

The knight was very joyous, and quoth, "Sire, now hath God done me great honour, for never before might I do ye service; now am I right glad and joyful that ye be lodged here! I have greeted ye in all fair friendship without thought of ill, ye and this goodly company, save one whom as yet I see not!"

With that there entered men bearing torches and tapers, so that the hall, which before was dark and dim, became light and clear. The folk who had come thither that they might look upon the king, of whom they had oft heard tell, made such haste to see him that there was no space to sit down, and all the palace was but a sea of heads.

The lord was sore vexed. He held in his hand a little round staff, short and heavy, and being chafed with anger in that he saw not Sir Gawain, and knew not where he might be, began laying about him to part the crowd, making them by force to mount on the daïs, and sills of the windows, and buttresses of the walls, since he might not drive them from the hall.

When Sir Gawain saw that the folk was thus parted asunder, without delaying he mounted him on his steed. Then first the lord of the castle beheld him, and was sore vexed that he had not come upon him disarmed. Scowling for very anger, he threw his staff aside, and when he had somewhat bethought him he lifted his head, and gat him to Sir Gawain, and laid hold of his bridle, saying, "Fair sir, hearken, are ye ready to keep the covenant ye made with me? It vexeth me that ye are so far quit that I have failed to find ye disarmed, as I fain had done; I had better have been slain the day I made this compact, for then, verily, ye too had died, had I not granted the respite, but now I deem our battle shall last the longer!"

Sir Gawain straightway granted him his battle, and the knight bade bring more torches, for the stars already shone forth. Then they brought them in great plenty, and he told off folk to hold them by the fist full, so that one might see far and near, as clearly as might be. Then the lord of the castle seated himself in the midst of the hall, on a great carpet, which a squire spread swiftly at his bidding, and he bade them bring thither all that was needful to the rightful arming of a knight desirous of battle rather than of aught beside. He donned a greave of iron, and relaced that which hung loose; then he bade them bring armpieces, and he laced them on his arms, and when he had done this he came before the king and said, "Eat joyfully, and be not dismayed; behold me, that I am strong and bold, hale and swift. Your nephew on his part is even as I am; I know not if he hath told ye how the matter be come to this point that the one of us must needs die ere we be parted. 'Twere hard to think this morn that the one of us was so nigh unto his end!"

90

The Adventures of Sir Gawain

Then the king's eyes filled with tears, and the knight, beholding, spake in his pride: "Certes, Sire, I prize ye less than afore; ye are but half-hearted who are thus compassionate for naught; by all the Saints in the calendar, ye be like unto him who crieth out afore he be hurt! Never before did I set eyes on a king who wept, and knew not wherefore! By my faith, this cometh of a cowardly heart!"

He turned him again without further word, and armed him swiftly, and did on his harness, and when he was armed he mounted his steed, and bade bring a lance, stout and strong, with shining blade. Then he hung his shield on his neck by a broidered band, and settled him well in his saddle, and called unto Sir Gawain, and quoth, "Here in this house is the lordship mine by right of heritage, yet would I do no outrage nor take vantage thereof; the rather do I bid and conjure ye to take that part of the hall which seemeth best; now look well where ye will make your stand."

Sir Gawain hearkened, but stirred not, save that he drew somewhat back, and lowered his lance, and his foe, on his part, did likewise. I testify of a truth, and tell ye, that they rode over hard a joust, for as they came together at their horses' full speed the one smote the other so fiercely on the shield that both alike were split asunder, so that the sharp blade passed right through, yet they harmed not the hauberks which clung close and tight. Thus as they sped on the lances bent and brake, yet the steeds stayed not, and the knights who bestrode them were naught dismayed, but when they would have passed each other in their course they came together with such weight of body and shield, and full front of the horses, that they smote each other to the ground, and all four fell on a heap, the good steeds undermost. But the knights lightly sprang to their feet, and threw aside their lances, and drew their good swords, and dealt each the other so mighty a blow on the shining helm that it was well indented. The king and they who looked on were sore anguished and afraid, but the twain, 'twixt whom there was such enmity, ran again on each other in such fashion that, I tell ye and lie not, never was so fierce a mêlée of two knights beheld. They made sparks to spring from the helmet and smote the circlets asunder as those who make no feint to fight. When the good swords smote the shields they made the splinters to fly apace: so eager was each to put the other to the worse that they ceased not nor slackened this the first assault till that both were covered with blood. Then the heat which vexed them mightily made them perforce draw asunder, to recover breath. Too heavy and too sore had been their combat for those who loved them to behold; never day of his life had King Arthur so feared for his nephew.

Now at the head of the master daïs was a door, opening into an inner chamber, and, as the tale telleth, in a little space there came forth a damosel, so fair of face and form that Christendom might not show her peer. She was clad in fair and fitting fashion, in a vesture richly broidered in gold, and had seen, perchance, some twenty summers. She was so fair, so tall and gracious, that no woman born might equal her, and all marvelled at her beauty.

She leant awhile on the head of the daïs, beholding the two knights, who strove hard to slay each the other. They had returned to the onslaught in such pride and wrath that verily I tell ye they might not long endure. Such blows they dealt on helm and shield with their naked blades that they made the splinters fly, and the crimson blood welled from their wounds and streamed through the mail of their hauberk down on to the pavement. Nor was the fight equal, for Sir Gawain had broken the laces of his helm, so that 'twas no longer on his head, but lay on the ground at his feet. Yet he covered himself full well with his shield, as one who was no child in sword play. But his foeman pressed him sore, and oft he smote him with hard and angry blows; Sir Gawain defended himself right valiantly, but it went too ill with him in that he had lost his helm, therefore as much as might be he held himself on the defensive. But once, as he made attack, Bran de Lis smote him so fierce and heavy a blow at his head that, but that it fell first on the shield, it had then and there ended the matter, and all said that without fail he had been a dead man. Bran de Lis spake wrathfully, "Take this blow for mine uncle; ye shall have one anon for my father; if I may, it shall be the last!"

Sir Gawain struck back, but he was sore hindered by the blood which ran down into his eyes ('twas that which vexed him the most); he would fain have drawn him back, but Bran de Lis left him no space, so wrathfully did he run upon him, and Sir Gawain withstood him sturdily, yet so hardly was he pressed that whether he would or no he must needs yield ground.

Then the damosel of whom I spake but now turned her, and ran swiftly into the inner chamber, and in a short space came forth with a little child, whom she set upon the daïs. He wore a little coat of red samite, furred with ermine, cut to his measure; and of his age no fairer child might be seen. His face was oval and fair, his eyes bright and laughing; he was marvellous tall and strong for his age, which might not be more than four years; and by the richness of his clothing 'twas clear that there were those who held him dear.

The knights who fought below still dealt each other such mighty blows that all who beheld them had dole and wrath. I can tell ye each was weak and weary enow, but verily Sir Gawain had yielded ground somewhat, and would fain have wiped away the blood which ran adown his face and into his eyes, but he might in no wise do so, since Bran de Lis held him so close, doing what he might to slay or wound him.

Then without delay the damosel took her child, there where he stood before her, and said very softly, "Fair little son, go quickly to yonder tall knight, 'tis thine uncle, doubt it not, fall at his feet, little son, and kiss them, and pray for God's sake the life of thy father that he slay him not!"

Straightway she set him on the ground, and the child ran, and clasped his uncle by the right leg, and kissed his foot, and said, "My mother prays ye for the love of God, that ye slay not my father, fair sweet uncle; she will die of grief an ye do!"

Great pity fell upon the king when he heard the child speak thus, and all who hearkened and beheld were filled with wrath and anguish. All had compassion on the child, save Bran de Lis alone, for he quoth in wrath and anger, "Get thee hence, son of a light woman!" and he withdrew his foot so swiftly from the child's clasp that, whether he would or no, he fell, and smote face and forehead hard on the stone of the pavement, so that he grazed mouth and face, and lay senseless and bleeding on the floor.

Then King Arthur sprang from the daïs, and caught the child to him, and kissed it twenty times on face and eyes and mouth, and wept for very anger; nor for the blood on the child's face would he cease to caress it, so great love had he towards it, for he thought of a truth that he held again Gawain, whom he now counted for lost. He quoth, "Sir Bran de Lis, this little child is very fair; never in your life did ye do such villainy as to go near to slay so sweet a child, nor ought ye to have denied the request he made, for he asked naught outrageous. Nor will I have him slain, for he is my joy and my solace; henceforward know well that for naught will I leave him in your care!"

Quoth Bran de Lis, "Sire, ye are less courteous than I had heard tell, and ye make overmuch dole and plaint for the life of a single knight; ye should not so be dismayed, this is naught but feebleness of heart."

As Bran de Lis thus spake to the king Sir Gawain wiped off the blood which ran down his face, and bound up his wounds, the while he had respite; the king, who was wise enow, held his foeman the longer in speech that his nephew might be the more refreshed, for the strength and valour of that good knight doubled as midnight passed. For this was the custom of Sir Gawain: when as ever midnight had struck his strength was redoubled and he waxed in force even until noon.

Now so soon as his strength came again, and he saw the king, and his love, and the great folk who beheld them, then a mighty shame overtook him, and he ran in wrath on his foe, and assailed him straitly, but the other yielded not, crying, "Honour to ye that ye thus seek me!"

Then might ye see them smite blows great and fierce, with the swords they wielded, so that they were well nigh beaten down. Sir Bran de Lis smote a mighty blow, thinking to catch Sir Gawain on the head, but that good knight, who knew right well how to cover himself, held his shield in such wise that the stroke fell upon it, and split it adown the midst; so hard had he smitten that the blade entered even to the hilt, and his body following the blow he bent him forwards, and ere he might recover him Sir Gawain smote him full on the helm, so that the laces brake, and it flew off adown the hall, leaving the head bare. And ere Sir Bran de Lis was well aware he followed up the blow with one above the ventaille so that he bled right freely. Now were they again on a par, so that one might scarce tell the which of them had the better. In great pride and wrath they ran each on the other, so that in short space of time they had lost overmuch blood. Mightily each strove to put his foe to the worse, and all who looked upon them waxed strangely pitiful, and would fain have parted them asunder had they dared.

Now might ye have seen that gentle knight, who full oft had made offering of good deeds and alms, right well acquit himself, for so sorely he vexed his foeman that he hacked his shield all to pieces, and he might no longer hold his ground, but whether he would or no he must yield place, and wavered backward adown the hall. Then he smote him again, so that he tottered upon his feet, and Sir Gawain hasted, and threw himself upon him with such weight of body and of shield that he well nigh bare him to earth, so he drave him staggering adown the hall till he fell against a daïs.

When the damosel saw this she tare her child from the king's arms, and ran swiftly, and threw herself right valiantly betwixt the two, so that she came nigh to be cut in pieces, and cried, "Son, pray thy father that he have pity on thy mother, and stay his hand ere he slay my brother, whom I love more than mine own life!" But the child spake no word, but looked up at the glancing sword blades, and laughed blithely. And all were moved to pity and wrath who saw him anon bleeding and now laughing for very joy.

Then Sir Gawain, of right good will, drew himself aback, but he whom he had thus hard pressed drave forward at him, like one reft of his senses, and came nigh to doing him a mischief in that Sir Gawain was off his guard. Then she who held the child sprang swiftly betwixt them, and cried, "Now by God I will see the which of ye twain will slay him, for he shall be cloven asunder ere that I take him hence."

The swords clashed together aloft, but wrought no ill, for neither might come at the other for fear of the child whom they were loth to harm, and for fear of her who held him. And the child laughed gaily at the glancing swords, and stretched up his hands to his own shadow, which he saw on the shining blade, and showed it with his finger to his father when he saw it come anear, and had fain sprung up and caught the blades, sharp though they might be. And many a man wept, and there arose within the hall a great cry, as of one voice, "Good lord king, stay the fight; we will all aid thee thereto, for no man should longer suffer this!"

Then Arthur sprang up swiftly, and seized his sword and shield, and came unto the twain, and parted them asunder, whether they would or no, and said to the knight ye have heard me praise, "Sir, take the amends offered, and I tell ye truly I will add thereto, for I myself will do ye honour, and become your man, for the sake of peace." And all cried with one voice, "Sir, by God and by the True Cross, ye shall not refuse this, for the king has spoken as right valiant man." Then the knight held his hand, hearing that which pleased him.

Thus was peace made, and the battle parted asunder, and Sir Bran de Lis did right sagely, for he spake, "Sire, it were nor right nor reason that ye should become my man, hence will I do ye true homage, but for hostage will I ask the knights of the Round Table, who are the most valiant in the world; also shall your nephew do other amends, even as he promised me, in abbey and nuns, for the repose of my father's soul, and ye shall free one hundred serfs with your own hand." And the king answered, "Know of a truth that all shall be done at my charges."

Then Bran de Lis did homage to the king, and kissed him in all good faith, and then came forward Sir Gawain, and he humbled himself before him, kneeling at his feet, and praying that he would pardon his ill will; and Sir Gawain took him by the hand, and raised him up, and quoth, "I pardon thee all, and henceforth will I be your friend in all good faith and courage, nor will I fail ye for any harm ye may aforetime have done me."

Both were sore faint and feeble, and void of strength by reason of the blood they had lost, so that scarce might they stand on their feet without falling to the ground. They bare them to an inner chamber; never knight nor maiden entered within a fairer, for I tell of a truth there was no good herb in Christendom with which it was not strewn. 'Twas richly garnished, and four great tapers, cunningly placed, gave fitting light. Then leeches searched their wounds and said there was no need for dismay, for neither was wounded to the death, and within fifteen days both might well be healed, and all were joyful at the tidings.

The king and his barons abode the fifteen days at the castle of Lys, nor departed therefrom; in all the world was neither fish nor fowl, fruit nor venison, of which the king might not each day eat in plenty if he so willed. But he was loth to part from Sir Bran de Lis, by reason of the good tales which he told concerning the folk of the Castle Orguellous, whereat the king rejoiced greatly.

"Sire," quoth Bran de Lis, "I myself will go with ye, and we will take with us squires and footmen. My pavilion is large and fair, and by faith, we will carry that too along with us; and also a pack of hounds, the best we may find, for there be thick forests all around, where we may hunt at our will, and go a-shooting too, an it please us, for we shall find great plenty of deer and other game."

Sir Gawain took little heed of all he said, so wholly was he taken up with his lady, and she forgat him not, but was ever at his service, at any hour that might please him; 'twas all gladness, and no ill thought. Nor did Sir Gawain mislike his fair son, whom he caressed right often. Fain would he have tarried long time with them. Nor marvel at that, my masters, for he was there at ease, and he who hath whatsoever he may desire doeth ill methinks to make over haste to change, nor will he make plaint, since he suffereth nor pain nor ill.

But when the fifteen days came to an end, then did the king bid make ready, for he had no mind to tarry longer; well I know 'twas a Tuesday morn that they set them on their way, and with them went that good knight, Sir Bran de Lis.

Sir Gawain and the Lady

Among the knights at King Arthur's court were his nephews, the sons of his sister, Queen Bellicent, and of that King Lot of Orkney, who had joined the league against Arthur in the first years of his reign.

Of each, many tales are told; of Sir Gawain and Sir Gareth to their great renown, but of Sir Mordred to his shame. For Sir Gawain and Sir Gareth were knights of great prowess; but Sir Mordred was a coward and a traitor, envious of other men's fame, and a tale-bearer.

Now Sir Gawain was known as the Ladies' Knight, and this is how he came by the name. It was at Arthur's marriage-feast, when Gawain had just been made knight, that a strange thing befell. There entered the hall a white hart, chased by a hound, and when it had run round the hall, it fled through the doorway again, still followed by the hound. Then, by Merlin's advice, the quest of the hart was given to Gawain as a new-made knight, to follow it and see what adventures it would bring him. So Sir Gawain rode away, taking with him three couples of greyhounds for the pursuit. At the last, the hounds caught the hart, and killed it just as it reached the court-yard of a castle. Then there came forth from the castle a knight, and he was grieved and wroth to see the hart slain, for it was given him by his lady; so, in his anger, he killed two of the hounds. At that moment Sir Gawain entered the court-yard, and an angry man was he when he saw his greyhounds slain. "Sir Knight," said he, "ye would have done better to have taken your vengeance on me rather than on dumb animals which but acted after their kind." "I will be avenged on you also," cried the knight; and the two rushed together, cutting and thrusting that it was wonderful they might so long endure. But at the last the knight grew faint, and crying for mercy, offered to yield to Sir Gawain. "Ye had no mercy on my hounds," said Sir Gawain. "I will make you all the amends in my power," answered the knight. But Sir Gawain would not be turned from his purpose, and unlacing the vanquished knight's helmet, was about to cut off his head, when a lady rushed out from the castle and flung herself on the body of the fallen knight. So it chanced that Sir Gawain's sword descending smote off the lady's head. Then was Sir Gawain grieved and sore ashamed for what he had done, and said to the knight: "I repent for what I have done; and here I give you your life. Go only to Camelot, to

The Adventures of Sir Gawain

King Arthur's court, and tell him ye are sent by the knight who follows the quest of the white hart." "Ye have slain my lady," said the other, "and now I care not what befalls me." So he arose and went to King Arthur's court.

Then Sir Gawain prepared to rest him there for the night; but scarcely had he lain down when there fell upon him four knights, crying: "New-made knight, ye have shamed your knighthood, for a knight without mercy is without honour." Then was Sir Gawain borne to the earth, and would have been slain, but that there came forth from the castle four ladies who besought the knights to spare his life; so they consented and bound him prisoner.

The next morning Sir Gawain was brought again before the knights and their dames; and because he was King Arthur's nephew, the ladies desired that he should be set free, only they required that he should ride again to Camelot, the murdered lady's head hanging from his neck, and her dead body across his saddle-bow; and that when he arrived at the court he should confess his misdeeds.

So Sir Gawain rode sadly back to Camelot, and when he had told his tale, King Arthur was sore displeased. And Queen Guenevere held a court of her ladies to pass sentence on Sir Gawain for his ungentleness. These then decreed that, his life long, he must never refuse to fight for any lady who desired his services, and that ever he should be gentle and courteous and show mercy to all. From that time forth, Sir Gawain never failed in aught that dame or damsel asked of him, and so he won and kept the title of the Ladies' Knight.

The Marriage of Sir Gawaine

PART THE FIRST

King Arthur lives in merry Carleile,
  And seemely is to see;
And there with him queene Guenever,
  That bride soe bright of blee.

And there with him queene Guenever,
  That bride so bright in bowre:
And all his barons about him stoode,
  That were both stiffe and stowre.

The king a royale Christmasse kept,
  With mirth and princelye cheare;
To him repaired many a knighte,
  That came both farre and neare.

And when they were to dinner sette,
  And cups went freely round;
Before them came a faire damsèlle,
  And knelt upon the ground.

A boone, a boone, O kinge Arthùre,
  I beg a boone of thee;
Avenge me of a carlish knighte,
  Who hath shent my love and me.

At Tearne-Wadling his castle stands,
  Near to that lake so fair,
And proudlye rise the battlements,
  And streamers deck the air.

The Adventures of Sir Gawain

Noe gentle knighte, nor ladye gay,
   May pass that castle-walle:
But from that foule discurteous knighte,
   Mishappe will them befalle.

Hee's twyce the size of common men,
   Wi' thewes, and sinewes stronge,
And on his backe he bears a clubbe,
   That is both thicke and longe.

This grimme baròne 'twas our harde happe,
   But yester morne to see;
When to his bowre he bare my love,
   And sore misused mee.

And when I told him, king Arthùre
   As lyttle shold him spare;
Goe tell, sayd hee, that cuckold kinge,
   To meete mee if he dare.

Upp then sterted king Arthùre,
   And sware by hille and dale,
He ne'er wolde quitt that grimme baròne,
   Till he had made him quail.

Goe fetch my sword Excalibar:
   Goe saddle mee my steede;
Nowe, by my faye, that grimme baròne
   Shall rue this ruthfulle deede.

And when he came to Tearne Wadlinge
   Benethe the castle walle:
"Come forth; come forth; thou proude baròne,
   Or yielde thyself my thralle."

The Adventures of Sir Gawain

On magicke grounde that castle stoode,
　And fenc'd with many a spelle:
Noe valiant knighte could tread thereon,
　But straite his courage felle.

Forth then rush'd that carlish knight,
　King Arthur felte the charme:
His sturdy sinewes lost their strengthe,
　Downe sunke his feeble arme.

Nowe yield thee, yield thee, kinge Arthùre,
　Now yield thee, unto mee:
Or fighte with mee, or lose thy lande,
　Noe better termes maye bee,

Unless thou sweare upon the rood,
　And promise on thy faye,
Here to returne to Tearne-Wadling,
　Upon the new-yeare's daye;

And bringe me worde what thing it is
　All women moste desyre;
This is thy ransome, Arthur, he sayes,
　Ile have noe other hyre.

King Arthur then helde up his hande,
　And sware upon his faye,
Then tooke his leave of the grimme barone
　And faste hee rode awaye.

And he rode east, and he rode west,
　And did of all inquyre,
What thing it is all women crave,
　And what they most desyre.

The Adventures of Sir Gawain

Some told him riches, pompe, or state;
  Some rayment fine and brighte;
Some told him mirthe; some flatterye;
  And some a jollye knighte.

In letters all king Arthur wrote,
  And seal'd them with his ringe:
But still his minde was helde in doubte,
  Each tolde a different thinge.

As ruthfulle he rode over a more,
  He saw a ladye sette
Betweene an oke, and a greene holléye,
  All clad in red scarlette.

Her nose was crookt and turnd outwàrde,
  Her chin stoode all awrye;
And where as sholde have been her mouthe,
  Lo! there was set her eye:

Her haires, like serpents, clung aboute
  Her cheekes of deadlye hewe:
A worse-form'd ladye than she was,
  No man mote ever viewe.

To hail the king in seemelye sorte
  This ladye was fulle faine;
But king Arthùre all sore amaz'd,
  No aunswere made againe.

What wight art thou, the ladye sayd,
  That wilt not speake to mee;
Sir, I may chance to ease thy paine,
  Though I be foule to see.

The Adventures of Sir Gawain

If thou wilt ease my paine, he sayd,
   And helpe me in my neede;
Ask what thou wilt, thou grimme ladyè
   And it shall bee thy meede.

O sweare mee this upon the roode,
   And promise on thy faye;
And here the secrette I will telle,
   That shall thy ransome paye.

King Arthur promis'd on his faye,
   And sware upon the roode;
The secrette then the ladye told,
   As lightlye well shee cou'de.

Now this shall be my paye, sir king,
   And this my guerdon bee,
That some yong fair and courtlye knight,
   Thou bringe to marrye mee.

Fast then pricked king Arthùre
   Ore hille, and dale, and downe:
And soone he founde the barone's bowre:
   And soone the grimme baroùne.

He bare his clubbe upon his backe,
   Hee stoode bothe stiffe and stronge;
And, when he had the letters reade,
   Awaye the lettres flunge.

Nowe yielde thee, Arthur, and thy lands,
   All forfeit unto mee;
For this is not thy paye, sir king,
   Nor may thy ransome bee.

Yet hold thy hand, thou proud baròne,
    I praye thee hold thy hand;
And give mee leave to speake once more
    In reskewe of my land.

This morne, as I came over a more,
    I saw a ladye sette
Betwene an oke, and a greene hollèye,
    All clad in red scarlètte.

Shee sayes, all women will have their wille,
    This is their chief desyre;
Now yield, as thou art a barone true,
    That I have payd mine hyre.

An earlye vengeaunce light on her!
    The carlish baron swore:
Shee was my sister tolde thee this,
    And shee's a mishapen whore.

But here I will make mine avowe,
    To do her as ill a turne:
For an ever I may that foule theefe gette,
    In a fyre I will her burne.

PART THE SECONDE

Homewarde pricked king Arthùre,
    And a wearye man was hee;
And soon he mette queene Guenever,
    That bride so bright of blee.

The Adventures of Sir Gawain

What newes! what newes! thou noble king,
  Howe, Arthur, hast thou sped?
Where hast thou hung the carlish knighte?
  And where bestow'd his head?

The carlish knight is safe for mee,
  And free fro mortal harme:
On magicke grounde his castle stands,
  And fenc'd with many a charme.

To bowe to him I was full faine,
  And yielde mee to his hand:
And but for a lothly ladye, there
  I sholde have lost my land.

And nowe this fills my hearte with woe,
  And sorrowe of my life;
I swore a yonge and courtlye knight,
  Sholde marry her to his wife.

Then bespake him sir Gawàine,
  That was ever a gentle knighte:
That lothly ladye I will wed;
  Therefore be merrye and lighte.

Nowe naye, nowe naye, good sir Gawàine;
  My sister's sonne yee bee;
This lothlye ladye's all too grimme,
  And all too foule for yee.

Her nose is crookt and turn'd outwàrde;
  Her chin stands all awrye;
A worse form'd ladye than shee is
  Was never seen with eye.

The Adventures of Sir Gawain

What though her chin stand all awrye,
    And shee be foule to see:
I'll marry her, unkle, for thy sake,
    And I'll thy ransome bee.

Nowe thankes, nowe thankes, good sir Gawàine;
    And a blessing thee betyde!
To-morrow wee'll have knights and squires,
    And wee'll goe fetch thy bride.

And wee'll have hawkes and wee'll have houndes,
    To cover our intent;
And wee'll away to the greene forèst,
    As wee a hunting went.

Sir Lancelot, sir Stephen bolde,
    They rode with them that daye;
And foremoste of the companye
    There rode the stewarde Kaye:

Soe did sir Banier and sir Bore,
    And eke sir Garratte keene;
Sir Tristram too, that gentle knight,
    To the forest freshe and greene.

And when they came to the greene forrèst,
    Beneathe a faire holley tree
There sate that ladye in red scarlètte
    That unseemelye was to see.

Sir Kay beheld that lady's face,
    And looked upon her sweere;
Whoever kisses that ladye, he sayes,
    Of his kisse he stands in feare.

The Adventures of Sir Gawain

Sir Kay beheld that ladye againe,
   And looked upon her snout;
Whoever kisses that ladye, he sayes,
   Of his kisse he stands in doubt.

Peace, brother Kay, sayde sir Gawàine,
   And amend thee of thy life:
For there is a knight amongst us all,
   Must marry her to his wife.

What marry this foule queane, quoth Kay,
   I' the devil's name anone;
Gett mee a wife wherever I maye,
   In sooth shee shall be none.

Then some tooke up their hawkes in haste,
   And some took up their houndes;
And sayd they wolde not marry her,
   For cities, nor for townes.

Then bespake him king Arthùre,
   And sware there by this daye;
For a little foule sighte and mislikìnge,
   Yee shall not say her naye.

Peace, lordinges, peace; sir Gawaine sayd;
   Nor make debate and strife;
This lothlye ladye I will take,
   And marry her to my wife.

Nowe thankes, nowe thankes, good sir Gawaine,
   And a blessinge be thy meede!
For as I am thine owne ladyè,
   Thou never shalt rue this deede.

The Adventures of Sir Gawain

Then up they took that lothly dame,
    And home anone they bringe:
And there sir Gawaine he her wed,
    And married her with a ringe.

And when they were in wed-bed laid,
    And all were done awaye:
"Come turne to mee, mine owne wed-lord
    Come turne to mee I praye."

Sir Gawaine scant could lift his head,
    For sorrowe and for care;
When, lo! instead of that lothelye dame,
    Hee sawe a young ladye faire.

Sweet blushes stayn'd her rud-red cheeke,
    Her eyen were blacke as sloe:
The ripening cherrye swellde her lippe,
    And all her necke was snowe.

Sir Gawaine kiss'd that lady faire,
    Lying upon the sheete:
And swore, as he was a true knighte,
    The spice was never soe sweete.

Sir Gawaine kiss'd that lady brighte,
    Lying there by his side:
"The fairest flower is not soe faire:
    Thou never can'st bee my bride."

I am thy bride, mine owne deare lorde,
    The same whiche thou didst knowe,
That was soe lothlye, and was wont
    Upon the wild more to goe.

The Adventures of Sir Gawain

Nowe, gentle Gawaine, chuse, quoth shee,
    And make thy choice with care;
Whether by night, or else by daye,
    Shall I be foule or faire?

"To have thee foule still in the night,
    When I with thee should playe!
I had rather farre, my lady deare,
    To have thee foule by daye."

What when gaye ladyes goe with their lordes
    To drinke the ale and wine;
Alas! then I must hide myself,
    I must not goe with mine?

"My faire ladyè, sir Gawaine sayd,
    I yield me to thy skille;
Because thou art mine owne ladyè
    Thou shalt have all thy wille."

Nowe blessed be thou, sweete Gawàine,
    And the daye that I thee see;
For as thou seest mee at this time,
    Soe shall I ever bee.

My father was an aged knighte,
    And yet it chanced soe,
He tooke to wife a false ladyè,
    Whiche broughte me to this woe.

She witch'd mee, being a faire yonge maide,
    In the greene forèst to dwelle;
And there to abide in lothlye shape,
    Most like a fiend of helle.

The Adventures of Sir Gawain

Midst mores and mosses; woods, and wilds;
   To lead a lonesome life:
Till some yong faire and courtlye knighte
   Wolde marrye me to his wife:

Nor fully to gaine mine owne trewe shape,
   Such was her devilish skille;
Until he wolde yielde to be rul'd by mee,
   And let mee have all my wille.

She witchd my brother to a carlish boore,
   And made him stiffe and stronge;
And built him a bowre on magicke grounde,
   To live by rapine and wronge.

But now the spelle is broken throughe,
   And wronge is turnde to righte;
Henceforth I shall bee a faire ladyè,
   And hee be a gentle knighte.

The Last Love of Gawaine

You will betray me – oh, deny it not!
What right have I, alas, to say you nay?
I, traitor of ten loves, what shall I say
To plead with you that I be not forgot?
My love has not been squandered jot by jot
In little loves that perish with the day.
My treason has been ever to the sway
Of queens; my faith has known no petty blot.
You will betray me, as I have betrayed,
And I shall kiss the hand that does me wrong.
And oh, not pardon – I need pardon more –
But in proud torment, grim and unafraid,
Burn in my hell nor cease the bitter song
Your beauty triumphs in forevermore.

Of Sir Gawaine's Hatred, and the War with Sir Lancelot

King Arthur, in the hall of his palace in London, walked quickly up and down, thinking in great grief of the death of his queen. A group of pages stood quietly in the shadow by the door, and two or three knights gazed silently at the moody king.

Suddenly there came the sound of running footsteps; a man dashed into the hall, and threw himself at the feet of the king. It was a squire of Sir Mordred's, and he craved leave to speak. 'Say on,' said the king.

'My lord,' said the man, 'Sir Lancelot hath rescued the queen from the fire and hath slain some thirty of your knights, and he and his kin have taken the queen among them away to some hiding-place.'

King Arthur stood for a little while dumb for pure sorrow; then, turning away, he wrung his hands and cried with a voice whose sadness pierced every heart:

'Alas, that ever I bare a crown, for now is the fairest fellowship of knights that ever the world held, scattered and broken.'

'Further, my lord,' went on the man, as others came into the hall, 'Sir Lancelot hath slain the brethren of Sir Gawaine, and they are Sir Gaheris and Sir Gareth.'

The king looked from the man to the knights that now surrounded him, as if that which he heard was past all belief.

'Is this truth?' he asked them, and all were moved at the sorrow on his face and in his voice.

'Yea, lord,' said they.

'Then, fair fellows,' he said, very heavily, 'I charge you that no man tell Sir Gawaine of the death of his two brothers; for I am sure that when he heareth that his loved younger brother, Sir Gareth, is slain, he will nigh go out of his mind for sorrow and anger.'

The king strode up and down the chamber, wringing his hands in the grief he could not utter.

'Why, oh why, did he slay them?' he cried out at length. 'He himself knighted Sir Gareth when he went to fight the oppressor of the Lady Lyones, and Sir Gareth loved him above all others.'

The Adventures of Sir Gawain

'That is truth,' said some of the knights, and could not keep from tears to see the king's grief, 'but they were slain in the hurtling together of the knights, as Sir Lancelot dashed in the thick of the press. He wist not whom he smote, so blind was his rage to get to the queen at the stake.'

'Alas! alas!' said the king. 'The death of them will cause the greatest woful war that ever was in this fair realm. I see ruin before us all—rent and ruined shall we be, and all peace for ever at an end.'

Though the king had forbidden any of his knights to tell Sir Gawaine of the death of his two brothers, Sir Mordred called his squire aside, and bade him go and let Sir Gawaine know all that had happened.

'Do you see to it,' he told the man, 'that thou dost inflame his mind against Sir Lancelot.'

The knave went to Sir Gawaine, and found him walking on the terrace of the palace overlooking the broad quiet Thames, where the small trading ships sailed up and down the river on their ways to and from Gaul and the ports of the Kentish coast.

'Sir,' said the squire, doffing his cap and bowing, 'great and woful deeds have been toward this day. The queen hath been rescued by Sir Lancelot and his kin, and some thirty knights were slain in the melée about the stake.'

'Heaven defend my brethren,' said Sir Gawaine, 'for they went unarmed. But as for Sir Lancelot, I guessed he would try a rescue, and I had deemed him no man of knightly worship if he had not. But, tell me, how are my brethren. Where be they?'

'Alas, sir,' said the man, 'they be slain.'

The grim face of Sir Gawaine went pale, and with an iron hand he seized the shoulder of the squire and shook him in his rage.

'Have a care, thou limb of Mordred's, if thou speakest lies,' he said. 'I would not have them dead for all this realm and its riches. Where is my young brother, Sir Gareth?'

'Sir, I tell ye truth,' said the man, 'for I know how heavy would be your anger if I lied in this. Sir Gareth and Sir Gaheris are slain, and all good knights are mourning them, and in especial the king our master.'

Sir Gawaine took a step backwards and his face went pale and then it darkened with rage.

'Tell me who slew them?' he thundered.

'Sir,' replied the man, 'Sir Lancelot slew them both.'

'False knave!' cried Sir Gawaine, 'I knew thou didst lie.'

The Adventures of Sir Gawain

He struck the man a great buffet on the head, so that he fell half dazed to the ground.

'Ha! ha! thou lying talebearer!' laughed Sir Gawaine, half relieved of his fears, yet still half doubtful. 'To tell me that Sir Lancelot slew them! Why, man, knowest thou of whom thou pratest? Sir Lancelot to slay my dear young brother Gareth! Why, man, Gareth loved Sir Lancelot as he loved me—not more than he loved me, but near as much; and Sir Lancelot was ever proud of him. 'Twas he that knighted my young brother Gareth, brave and hearty, noble of mind and goodly of look! He would have stood with Lancelot against the king himself, so greatly he loved him. And thou—thou foul-mouth!—thou tellest me that Lancelot hath slain him! Begone from my sight, thou split-tongue!'

'Nevertheless, Sir Gawaine,' said the man, rising, 'Sir Lancelot slew them both in his rage. As he would—saving your presence—have slain you had you stood between him and the queen at the stake.'

At these words, stubbornly spoken in spite of the furious looks of Sir Gawaine, the knight realised that the man was speaking the truth.

His look was fixed on the face of the knave, and rage and grief filled his eyes as he grasped the fact that his beloved brother was really slain. Then the blood surged into his face, and he dashed away.

Men started to see the wild figure of Sir Gawaine rushing through the passages, his eyes bloodshot, his face white. At length he dashed into the presence of the king. Arthur stood sorrowing amidst his knights, but Sir Gawaine rushed through them and faced the king.

'Ha! King Arthur!' he cried, half breathless, but in a great wild voice, 'my good brother, Sir Gareth, is slain, and also Sir Gaheris! I cannot bear the thought of them slain. It cannot be true! I cannot believe it!'

'Nay, nor can any think upon it,' said the king, 'and keep from weeping.'

'Ay, ay,' said Sir Gawaine in a terrible voice, 'there shall be weeping, I trow, and that erelong. Sir, I will go see my dead brothers. I would kiss them ere they be laid in earth.'

'Nay, that may not be,' said the king gently. 'I knew how great would be thy sorrow, and that sight of them would drive thee mad. And I have caused them to be interred instantly.'

'Tell me,' said Gawaine, and men marvelled to see the wild look in his eyes and to hear the fierce voice, 'is it truth that Sir Lancelot slew them both?'

'It is thus told me,' said the King, 'that in his fury Sir Lancelot knew not whom he smote.'

'But, man,' thundered Sir Gawaine, 'they bare no arms against him! Their hearts were with him, and young Gareth loved him as if—as if Lancelot was his own brother.'

'I know it, I know it,' replied King Arthur. 'But men say they were mingled in the thick press of the fight, and Lancelot knew not friend from foe, but struck down all that stood between him and the queen.'

For a space Sir Gawaine was silent, and men looked upon him with awe and compassion. His mane of hair, grizzled and wild, was thrown back upon his shoulders, and his eyes flamed with a glowing light as of fire. Suddenly he stepped up to the king, and lifting his right hand said, in a voice that trembled With rage:

'My lord, my king, and mine uncle, wit you well that now I make oath by my knighthood, that from this day I will seek Sir Lancelot and never rest till he be slain or he slay me. Therefore, my lord king, and you, my fellow knights and lords, I require you all to prepare yourselves for war; for, know you, though I ravage this land and all the lands of Christendom, I will not rest me nor slake my revenge until I come up to Lancelot and drive my sword into his evil heart.'

With that Sir Gawaine strode from the room, and for a space all men were silent, so fierce and full of hatred had been his words.

'I see well,' said the king, 'that the death of these twain knights will cause the deadliest war that hath ever raged, and never shall we have rest until Gawaine do slay Lancelot or is slain by him. O Lancelot! Lancelot! my peerless knight, that ever thou shouldst be the cause of the ruin of this my fair kingdom!'

None that heard the king could keep from tears; and many felt that in this quarrel the king's heart was not set, except for the sake of Sir Gawaine, his nephew, and all his kin.

Then there were made great preparations in London and all the lands south of Trent, with sharpening of swords and spears, making of harness and beating of smiths' hammers on anvils.

Men's minds were in sore distress, and the faces of the citizens were long and white with dismay. Daily the quarrel caused other quarrels. Many a group of knights came to high words, some taking the side of Lancelot and the queen, and others that of the king and Sir Gawaine. Often they came to blows, and one or other of their number would be left writhing and groaning on the ground.

Families broke up in bad blood by reason of it, for the sons would avow their intent to go and enlist with Lancelot, while the fathers, in high anger at such disloyalty to Arthur, would send their tall sons away, bidding them never to look upon their faces again.

Women sorrowed and wept, for whichever side they took, it meant that one or other of their dear ones was opposed to them, and would go to battle, fighting against those of their own kin and of their own hearths.

Towards midsummer the host was ready, and took the road to the north. The quarrel had been noised abroad throughout Britain, and many kings, dukes and barons came to the help of Arthur, so that his army was a great multitude. Yet many others had gone to Lancelot, where he lay in his castle of Joyous Gard, not far from Carlisle.

Thither, in the month of July, when the husbandmen were looking to their ripening fields and thinking of harvest, King Arthur and Sir Gawaine drew with their army and laid a siege against the castle of Joyous Gard, and against the walled town which it protected. But for all their engines of war, catapults which threw great stones, and ramming irons which battered the walls, they could not make a way into the place, and so lay about it until harvest time.

One day, as Queen Gwenevere stood at a window of the castle, she looked down at the tents of the besieging host, and her gaze lingered on the purple tent of King Arthur, with the banner of the red dragon on the pole above it. As she looked, she saw her husband issue from the tent and begin to walk up and down alone in a place apart. Very moody did he seem, as he strode to and fro with bent head. Sometimes he looked towards Joyous Gard, and then his face had a sad expression upon it which went to the queen's heart.

She went to Sir Lancelot, and said:

'Sir Lancelot, I would that this dreadful war were done, and that thou wert again friends and in peace with my dear lord. Something tells me that he sorrows to be at enmity with thee. Thou wert his most famous knight and brought most worship to the fellowship of the Round Table. Wilt thou not try to speak to my lord? Tell him how evil were the false reports of the conspiracy against him, and that we are innocent of any treason against him and this dear land.'

116

The Adventures of Sir Gawain

'Lady,' said Sir Lancelot, 'on my knighthood I will try to accord with my lord. If our enemies have not quite poisoned his thoughts of us, he may listen and believe.'

Thereupon Sir Lancelot caused his trumpeter to sound from the walls, and ask that King Arthur would hold a parley with him. This was done, and Sir Pentred, a knight of King Arthur's, took the message to the king.

In a little while King Arthur, with Sir Gawaine and a company of his counsellors and knights, came beneath the walls, and the trumpeters blew a truce, and the bowmen ceased from letting fly their arrows and the men-at-arms from throwing spears.

Then Sir Lancelot came down to a narrow window in the gate-tower, and cried out to the king:

'Most noble king, I think that neither of us may get honour from this war. Cannot we make an end of it?'

'Ay,' cried Sir Gawaine, his face red with anger, and shaking his mailed fist at Lancelot, 'come thou forth, thou traitor, and we will make an end of thee.'

'Come forth,' said the king, 'and I will meet thee on the field. Thou hast slain thirty of my good knights, taken my queen from me, and plunged this realm in ruin.'

'Nay, lord, it was not I that caused this war,' said Sir Lancelot. 'I had been but a base knight to have suffered the noble lady my queen to be burned at the stake. And it passes me, my lord king, how thou couldst ever think to suffer her to be burned.'

'She was charged with poisoning a knight who slandered her,' said the king. 'I must see justice done on high and low, and though it grieved me to condemn her, I could do naught else. Moreover, if Sir Pinel spoke true, both you and she were conspiring to slay me and to rule this kingdom in my stead.'

'A foul lie, a black calumny!' cried Sir Lancelot fiercely. 'And I would answer for it with the strength which God might give me on any six of your knights that may say I am so black a traitor. I tell you, my lord king, and I swear it on my knighthood, and may death strike me now if I lie, that neither I nor the queen have ever had evil thoughts against your person, nor had designs upon your crown.'

At so solemn an oath men stood still and waited, for few doubted in those days that if a man who took so great an oath was speaking falsely, fire from heaven would instantly descend and consume him.

The moments passed and nothing happened, and men breathed again.

Sir Lancelot looked at the face of King Arthur, and saw by the light upon it that the king believed him; and Sir Lancelot rejoiced in his heart.

He saw the king turn to Sir Gawaine with a questioning air, as if he would ask what more his nephew wanted. But next moment, with a harsh laugh, Sir Gawaine spoke.

'Hark ye, Sir Lancelot, thou mayest swear to Heaven as to some things, and there are those that may be moved by thy round oaths. But this I charge upon thee, thou false, proud knight, that thou didst slay two unarmed men—men that loved thee and worshipped thee! Forsooth, thou boastful braggart and mouthing hero, thou wilt not dare to deny it!'

Sad was the face and voice of Sir Lancelot as he made reply.

'I cannot hope to find excuse from you,' he said, 'for I cannot and never will forgive myself. I would as lief have slain my nephew, Sir Bors, as slay young Sir Gareth whom I loved, and Gaheris his brother. Sorrow is on me for that! I was mad in my rage and did not see them. Only I knew that many knights stood between me and the queen, and I slew all that seemed to bar my passage.'

'Thou liest, false, recreant knight!' cried Sir Gawaine, whose grief by now had made him mad with the lust for revenge; 'thou slewest them in thy pride, to despite me and the king, because we had permitted the queen to go to the stake. Thou coward and traitor! Therefore, wit thee well, Sir Lancelot, I will not quit this quest until I feel my sword thrusting into thy evil heart.'

'Sorrow is on me,' said Sir Lancelot, 'to know that thou dost so hatefully pursue me. If thou didst not, I think my lord the king would give me his good grace again, and receive back his queen and believe us innocent.'

'I believe it well, false, recreant knight!' cried Sir Gawaine, full of rage to know that the king verily wished to have peace; 'but know ye that while I live, my good uncle will make war upon thee, and at last we will have thee in spite of thy castle walls and thy skill in battle. And then I will have thy head.'

'I trust ye for that,' said Sir Lancelot, 'for I see that thy hatred hath crazed thee. So, if ye may get me, I shall expect no mercy.'

Then, seeing how useless it was to keep up the parley any longer, Sir Lancelot withdrew. Next day spies brought in word to Sir Lancelot that, at a council of his chief men, the king had said he would take back his queen and make peace with Sir Lancelot; but that Sir Gawaine had fiercely told him that if he did not keep up the war until Sir Lancelot was taken or slain, he and all the kin of Lot would break away from the realm and their allegiance. Indeed, it was rumoured that Sir Gawaine would have made the king prisoner had he not yielded; and so powerful was Sir Gawaine and the lords that followed him, that none could have been strong enough to withstand them.

Sir Gawaine, yearning, by reason of his hatred, to get Sir Lancelot out of his castle to fight with him, now sent knights to cry out shame upon him under his walls. Thus they marched up and down, calling out insulting names and charging him with dishonourable deeds.

Until at length the very men-at-arms that kept watch upon Sir Lancelot's walls reddened for shame, and hurled down spears and stones at the foul mouths. Sir Bors, Sir Ector de Maris and Sir Lionel, they also heard the words, and going to the other knights of Sir Lancelot, took counsel with them, and decided that this could no longer be suffered.

Together they went to Sir Lancelot and said to him:

'Wit ye well, my lord, that we feel great scorn of the evil words which Sir Gawaine spoke unto you when that ye parleyed with him, and also of these shameful names which men call upon ye for all the citizens to hear. Wherefore, we charge you and beseech you, if ye will to keep our service, hold us no longer behind these walls, but let us out, in the name of Heaven and your fair name, and have at these rascals.'

'Fair friends,' replied Sir Lancelot, 'I am full loth to fight against my dear lord, King Arthur.'

'But if ye will not,' said Sir Lionel, his brother, 'all men will say ye fear to stir from these walls, and hearing the shameful words they cry, will say that there must be truth in them if ye seek not to silence them.'

They spoke long with Sir Lancelot, and at length he was persuaded; and he sent a message to the king telling him that he would come out and do battle; but that, for the love he bore the king, he prayed he would not expose his person in the fight.

But Sir Gawaine returned answer that this was the king's quarrel, and that the king would fight against a traitor knight with all his power.

On the morrow, at nine in the morning, King Arthur drew forth his host, and Sir Lancelot brought forth his array. When they stood facing each other, Sir Lancelot addressed his men and charged all his knights to save King Arthur from death or wounds, and for the sake of their old friendship with Sir Gawaine, to avoid battle with him also.

Then, with a great hurtling and crashing, the knights ran together, and much people were there slain. The knights of Sir Lancelot did great damage among the king's people, for they were fierce knights, and burned to revenge themselves for the evil names they had heard.

Sir Gawaine raged like a lion through the field, seeking Sir Lancelot, and many knights did he slay or overthrow. Once, indeed, King Arthur, dashing through the fight, came upon Sir Lancelot.

'Now, Sir Lancelot,' he cried, 'defend thee, for thou art the causer of this civil war.'

At these words he struck at Sir Lancelot with his sword; but Sir Lancelot took no means to defend himself, and put down his own sword and shield, as if he could not put up arms against his king. At this the king was abashed and put down his sword, and looked sorrowfully upon Sir Lancelot.

Then the surging tide of battle poured between them and separated them, until it happened that Sir Bors saw King Arthur at a little distance. With a spear the knight rushed at the king, and so fierce was his stroke and hardy his blow that the king was stricken to the ground.

Whereupon Sir Bors leapt from his horse and drew his sword and ran towards the king. But some one called upon him, and looking up he saw Sir Lancelot riding swiftly towards him.

Sir Bors held the king down upon the ground by the nose-piece of his helm, and in his other hand he held his naked sword.

Looking up to Sir Lancelot, he cried in a fierce voice:

'Cousin, shall I make an end of this war? 'Twere easy done.'

He meant that, if the king were slain, Sir Gawaine would lose half his forces, and could not hope to keep up the war against Sir Lancelot singlehanded.

'Nay, nay,' said Sir Lancelot, 'on peril of thy head touch not the king. Let him rise, man. I will not see that most noble king, who made me knight and once loved me, either slain or shamed.'

Sir Lancelot, leaping from his horse, went and raised the king, and held the stirrup of his horse while the king mounted again.

'My lord Arthur,' said Lancelot, looking up at the king, 'I would in the name of Heaven that ye cause this war to cease, for none of us shall get honour by it. And though I forbear to strike you and I try to avoid my former brothers and friends of the Round Table, they do continually seek to slay me and will not avoid me.'

The Adventures of Sir Gawain

King Arthur looked upon Lancelot, and thought how nobly courteous was he more than any other knight. The tears burst from the king's eyes and he could not speak, and sorrowfully he rode away and would fight no more, but commanded the trumpets to cease battle. Whereupon Sir Lancelot also drew off his forces, and the dead were buried and the wounded were tended.

Next morning the battle was joined again. Very fiercely fought the king's party, for Sir Gawaine had commanded that no quarter should be given, and that whoever slew a knight of Sir Lancelot's should have his helm filled with gold. Sir Gawaine himself raged like a lion about the field, his spear in rest. He sought for Sir Lancelot; but that knight always avoided him, and great was Gawaine's rage and scorn.

At length Sir Bors saw Sir Gawaine from afar, and spurred across the field towards him.

'Ha! Sir Bors,' cried the other mockingly, 'if ye will find that cowardly cousin of thine, and bring him here to face me, I will love thee.'

''Twere well I should not take thy words seriously,' mocked Sir Bors in his turn. 'For if I were to bring him to thee, thou wouldst sure repent it. Never yet hath he failed to give thee thy fall, for all thy pride and fierceness.'

This was truth. Often in the jousting of earlier days, when Sir Lancelot had come in disguise and had been compelled to fight Sir Gawaine, the latter had had the worst. But Sir Lancelot, loving his old brother-in-arms as he did, had in later years avoided the assault with Sir Gawaine; yet the greater prowess and skill of Sir Lancelot were doubted by none.

Sir Gawaine raged greatly at the words of Sir Bors, for he knew they were true, though he had wished they were not.

'Thy vaunting of thy recreant kinsman's might will not avail thee,' he cried furiously. 'Defend thyself!'

'I came to have to do with thee,' replied Sir Bors fiercely. 'Yesterday thou didst slay my cousin Lionel. To-day, if God wills it, thou thyself shall have a fall.'

Then they set spurs to their horses and met together so furiously that the lance of either bore a great hole in the other's armour, and both were borne backwards off their horses, sorely wounded. Their friends came and took them up and tended them, but for many days neither of the knights could move from their beds.

The Adventures of Sir Gawain

When the knights of Sir Lancelot saw that Sir Bors was grievously wounded, they were wroth with their leader. Going to him, they charged him with injuring his own cause.

'You will not exert yourself to slay these braggart foes of yours,' they said to him. 'What does it profit us that you avoid slaying knights because, though they are now your bitter foes, they were once brothers of the Round Table? Do they avoid ye, and seek not to slay you and us your kindred and friends? Sir Lionel is dead, and he is your brother; and Sir Galk, Sir Griffith, Sir Saffre and Sir Conan—all good and mighty knights—are wounded sorely. Ye were ever courteous and kindly, Sir Lancelot,' they ended, 'but have a care lest now your courtesy ruin not your cause and us.'

Seeing by these words that he was like to chill the hearts of his friends if he continued to avoid slaying his enemies, Sir Lancelot sorrowfully promised that henceforth he would not stay his hand. After that he avoided none that came against him, though for very sorrow he could have wept when some knight, with whom in happier times he had drunk wine and jested at the board in Camelot, rushed at him with shrewd strokes to slay him.

As the fight went on, the lust of battle grew in Sir Lancelot's heart, and manfully he fought, and with all his strength and skill he lay about him. By the time of evensong his party stood very well, and the king's side seemed dispirited and as if they would avoid the fierce rushes with which Sir Lancelot's knights attacked them.

Staying his horse, Sir Lancelot looked over the field, and sorrowed to see how many dead there were—dead of whom many may have been slain by their own kindred. He saw how the horses of his knights were splashed with the blood that lay in pools here and there, and grief was heavy upon him.

Sir Palom, a very valiant knight, came up to him.

'See, lord,' he cried, 'how our foes flinch from the fierce hurtling of our knights. They are dispirited by the wounding of Sir Gawaine. Sir Kay is also wounded, and Sir Torre is slain. Now, if ye will take my advice, this day should cease this war once for all. Do ye gather all your forces, lord, and I think with one great dash together ye should scatter their wavering knights, and this field would be won.'

'Alas!' said Sir Lancelot, 'I would not have it so. It cuts me to my heart to war as I do against my lord Arthur, and to trample him and his people in the mire of defeat—nay, I should suffer remorse till my last day.'

'My lord,' said Sir Palom, 'I think ye are unwise. Ye spare them thus to come again against ye. They will give ye no thanks, and if they could get you and yours at so great a disadvantage, wit you well they would not spare you.'

But Sir Lancelot would not be moved, and in pity he ordered the trumpeters to sound the retreat. King Arthur did likewise, and each party retired in the twilight from the field, where the wounded lay groaning till death or succour came; and the dead lay still and pale, until the kindly earth was thrown over them.

Some weeks passed in which the armies did not meet; for the host of King Arthur was not now so proud as they had been, seeing that they had lost many good knights; and Sir Lancelot would not of his own will sally out from his castle to fall upon the king.

But ever Sir Gawaine tried to inflame the mind of King Arthur and his kinsmen against Sir Lancelot, and he advised them to join battle with their enemy. Moreover, from the lands of his kingdom of Lothian, of which Sir Gawaine was now king in the place of his dead father, King Lot, a great body of young knights and men-at-arms came; and the king's party began to recover their courage.

Many began daily to ride to the walls of Joyous Gard, and by insult and evil names endeavoured to tempt forth the men of Sir Lancelot. Soon the young knights clamoured to King Arthur and Sir Gawaine to permit them to attack the walls, and reluctantly the king consented to call his council for next day to devise some means of breaking down the castle.

Headstrong was the counsel given by the young knights at that meeting, and greatly did King Arthur sorrow to feel that, for love of his nephew, Sir Gawaine, he would be compelled to yield to their wild demands for further battle.

Suddenly the door of the hall where sate the council was opened, and the porter of the gate appeared and approached the king.

'My lord,' he said, 'the holy Bishop of London and King Geraint of Devon crave audience of you.'

Some of the fierce young knights scowled at the names and uttered cries of disgust.

The king's face brightened, and before any could advise him against his will, he said:

'Bid them enter instantly.'

The Adventures of Sir Gawain

'The meddling priest and the petty king that knoweth not his mind!' sneered Sir Gawaine, looking fiercely about the room. 'I pray thee, uncle,' he said to the king, 'listen not to their womanish persuasions, if thou lovest me.'

King Arthur did not answer, but looked towards the door impatiently.

Through this there came first three priests and three armed men, and behind them stepped an old and reverend man, the hair beside his tonsure white as driven snow, and falling over his white robe edged with red, that showed his rank as bishop. Then, towering above him, a noble knightly figure, came Geraint of Devon, grown nobler still since those noble days when he had proved himself to be a strong leader indeed, while men had thought him soft and foolish.

All rose to their feet in reverence to the bishop, and fondly did King Arthur welcome Geraint, for this wise knight had from the first opposed Sir Gawaine in this war, and had refused to fight against Sir Lancelot and the queen, though he abated not his service to the king.

Dark was the look which Gawaine darted at Geraint, but quiet yet fearless was Geraint's answering gaze.

'What ye have to say,' said Gawaine angrily, 'say it quickly and begone. If ye are still of two minds, there seems no need to speak, and there is no need to bring a bishop to your aid.'

'Gawaine,' said King Geraint, and his voice was quiet, yet with a ring of menace in it, 'I think grief hath made you a little mad. Let the bishop speak, I pray ye. He hath a message for the king.'

'My lord,' said the bishop, 'I come from his Holiness the Pope.'

At these words Sir Gawaine started forward, his hand upon his sword, as if he would willingly in his madness slay the holy priest.

'And,' went on the bishop, his grave voice and his quiet look not bating for all the wrathful fire in Sir Gawaine's eyes, 'I bear with me the bull of his Holiness—see, here it is—by which his Highness doth charge King Arthur of Britain, as he is a Christian king, to take back Queen Gwenevere unto his love and worship, and to make peace with Sir Lancelot.'

The murmurs of the wild young knights rose in a sudden storm, while Sir Gawaine glared with looks of hatred at King Geraint and the bishop.

'And if ye do not this command,' rang out the voice of the bishop (and there was sorrow in its tone, and silence sank on all), 'if ye do not, then will his Holiness excommunicate this land. None of ye here have seen so terrible a thing as a land laid under the interdict of the Holy Church, and rarely doth she find her children so stubbornly evil as to merit it. But the Father of the Church, seeing how this land is torn and rent by this bitter war between brothers, and fearful lest, while ye tear at each others' lives, the fierce and evil pagan will gain upon ye and beat the lives from both of ye, and possess this fair island and drive Christ and His religion from it utterly—seeing all this, his Holiness would pronounce the doom if ye are too stiffnecked to obey him. Then will ye see this land lie as if a curse were upon it. Your churches will be shut, and the relics of the holy saints will be laid in ashes, the priests will not give prayers nor the Church its holy offices; and the dead shall lie uncoffined, for no prayers may be said over them. Say, then, King Arthur of Britain, what shall be the answer to the command of his Holiness which here I lay before thee.'

With these words the bishop held a parchment rolled out between his hands before the eyes of the king. Men craned forward and saw the black writing on the white skin, and the great seals, or bulls, hanging from it whereon those who could read saw the device of the Pope of Rome.

'Say, is this thy doing?' cried Sir Gawaine fiercely, looking at King Geraint. 'Didst thou send this meddling priest to Rome to get this?'

'That did I,' replied Geraint.

'Then now I make this vow,' thundered Sir Gawaine, 'that though thou hast balked me of my vengeance now, I will mark thee, thou king of two minds, and be thou sure that erelong I will avenge me of this treachery, and that upon thy body and in thy blood.'

'I mark thy words, Sir Gawaine,' said Geraint, whose eyes flashed fiercely, though his voice was calm, 'and I say again thou art mad. I will tell thee and the king, our lord and master, why I did advise the holy bishop to go to Rome and get the Pope's command. First, as ye all know, I did think this war a wicked one beyond all measure, and ever have I raised my voice against it. And what I foresaw has come to pass. As the good priest saith, while ye tore at each other's throats here in the furthest marches of the north, the sly, fierce pagan, learning how all the land was rent and weakened by this evil war, has crept up in his longships, he has landed at many solitary places on the coast, and has spread far and wide throughout the land, burning and slaughtering. The long files of his captives, our kinsmen, go day by day, even as ye fight here, brother with brother, down to the black ships, and ye do naught to save them or avenge them. Already have I, in my office as Count of the Saxon Shore, battered them back to their ships at Lemanis, Llongporth and Rutupiæ; but here in the north, for all that the old lion, Uriens of Reged, worn with war and full of age, hath taken the field against them, here, behind your backs as ye battle, kin with kin, a great and a stubborn pagan, whom men call Hyring the Land-waster, hath entered the land and still prevails. Crafty he is and strong, for he hath made treaties with some of our weaker kin, and their women he hath taken in marriage for his leaders, and thus in our very midst there is treachery, hand-in-hand with the brutal invaders. Yet still you, Gawaine, are so mad, so lost to all care for your nation's weal, that you would see your people ruined and your land possessed by the savage boars of Saxons, while ye slake your vengeance for a private wrong. If still you so would do, I call you traitor, and, by the grace of God, I will make good my words upon your body, when we have thrust the pagan from the land and peace is within our borders once again.'

While the thunder of his noble anger still rolled through the wide hall, King Arthur arose, and men marked the resolution in his eyes.

'I will that there be no more war,' he said, and he looked sternly at Gawaine. 'Geraint hath spoken the truth, and the truth shall prevail. I repent me that I have so long forgotten the needs of my kingdom. Do thou now, good bishop, go to Sir Lancelot, tell him that I will make peace with him and that I will receive back my queen. And do thou, good Geraint, fare south again. I thank thee from my heart for what thou hast done. Would to Heaven that all my knights were as clean-souled and as single-minded in devotion unto me as thou art. Do thou go and fulfil thy great office. Watch thou the coasts as hitherto thou hast watched them; and soon I will follow to aid thee, should the foul and savage pagans strive again to break into my realm.'

But, after all, Sir Gawaine had his way in part. The bishop took the king's assurance, sealed with his great seal, whereby he promised Sir Lancelot that he should come and go safe from murder or sudden onset, and desiring him to bring the queen to the king at his hall at Carlisle. But in that parchment was no word of reconciliation with Sir Lancelot. Sir Gawaine fiercely told the king that the day on which he, the king, should clasp the hand of Lancelot in friendship, he, Sir Gawaine, with all his vassals and his men, would leave the kingdom. So deep and burning was the hatred which Gawaine bore Sir Lancelot that he even threatened that, if his will was not granted, he would join the pagans and fight against the king.

The Adventures of Sir Gawain

So shamed and saddened was the king at these words that, to put an end to his nephew's rage, he consented to do as he desired. Therefore, though the bishop strove to persuade the king to make his peace with Sir Lancelot, Sir Gawaine's will was done, and the bishop went sadly to Joyous Gard.

He showed his writings to Sir Lancelot and the queen, and both were sorrowful in that no word of reconciliation was said.

'I will do my lord's desire,' said the knight, 'but I see that Sir Gawaine's hatred of me is in no way abated. Nevertheless, do thou ride, my lord bishop, to the king. Commend me unto his good grace, and say to him that in five days I will myself bring my lady, Queen Gwenevere, unto him as he doth desire.'

On the day appointed, as the king sat in hall at Carlisle, surrounded by his knights and their ladies, with Sir Gawaine standing on the high seat beside him, there came the beat of many hoofs, and into the town rode Sir Lancelot with the queen, knights and squires accompanying them. They reined up at the wide door of the hall, and Sir Lancelot alighted, and having helped the queen to dismount, he took her hand, and led her through the ranks of knights and ladies to where sat King Arthur.

Sir Lancelot kneeled upon the edge of the dais, and the queen with him; and to see so noble a knight and so beautiful a lady, sad of countenance as they were, forced many a tear to the eyes of the knights and dames who looked on. Then, rising, and taking up the queen, Sir Lancelot spoke:

'My most redoubted lord,' he said, 'you shall understand that by the pope's commandment and yours I have brought unto you my lady your queen, as right requireth; and if there be any knight here, of any degree, who shall say that she or I have ever thought to plot treason against your person or your crown, or the peace of this realm, then do I say here and now that I, Lancelot du Lake, will make it good upon his body, that he lies. And, my gracious lord, if this is all that there is between you, my king, and myself, there need be naught of ill thought between us, but only peace and goodwill. But I wist well that one that hates me will not suffer ye to do what is in your good and kingly heart.'

Sternly did Sir Lancelot look at Sir Gawaine, while the tears gushed from King Arthur's eyes, and from the eyes of many that heard Sir Lancelot's sad words.

Fierce and dark was the look which Sir Gawaine returned to Sir Lancelot.

The Adventures of Sir Gawain

'The king may do as he will,' he said harshly and in a loud voice, 'but wit thou well, Sir Lancelot, thou and I shall never be at peace till one of us be slain; for thou didst slay my twain brothers, though they bore no harness against thee nor any ill will. Yet traitorously thou didst slay them!'

'Alas, my lord,' said Sir Lancelot, and the tears bedewed his face, 'I cannot ask you for your forgiveness for that deed, unwitting though it was done and in my madness. Would to Heaven they had worn harness! Wit you well that ever will I bewail the death of my dear friend, Sir Gareth. 'Twas I that made him knight, and ever did I delight to see him, to hear his manly laugh ring out, and to see the light in his brave eyes that never suffered a mean or evil action. I wot he loved me above all other knights, and there was none of my kinsmen that I loved so much as I loved him. Ever will the sorrow of the death of thy brethren lie upon my soul; and to make some small amends I will, if my lord will suffer it and it will please you, Sir Gawaine, I will walk in my shirt and barefoot from Lemanis even unto this town, and at every ten miles I will found a holy house, and endow it with monks to pray for the souls of Sir Gareth and Sir Gaheris. Surely, Sir Gawaine, that will do more good unto their souls than that my most noble lord and you should war on me.'

Every cheek was wet and the tears of the king fell from his eyes, yet made he no effort to restrain or hide them.

'Out upon such monkish deeds!' cried Sir Gawaine, and his scornful eyes surveyed the weeping knights and dames. 'Know thee, once for all, that never shalt thou wipe away the treacherous murder of my brothers but by thy blood. Ye are safe now for a season, for the pope hath given you safety, but in this land—whatever comes of it I care not—thou shalt not abide above fifteen days, or else I shall have thy head. So make ye no more ado; but deliver the queen from thee, and get thee quickly out of this court and out of this realm.'

'Well,' said Sir Lancelot, and laughed grimly, 'if I had known I should have so short an answer to my proffers of peace, I had thought twice ere I had come hither. But now, madam,' he said, turning to the weeping queen beside him, 'I must say farewell to ye, for now do I depart from this noble fellowship and this dear realm for ever. Pray for me, and send me word if any lying tongues speak evil of you, and if any knight's hand may deliver you by battle, believe me mine shall so deliver you.'

With these words Sir Lancelot bent and kissed the queen's hand, and so turned away and departed. There was neither king, baron, knight nor squire of all that great company who did not weep, nor think that Sir Gawaine had been of most evil mind to refuse the noble proffers of Sir Lancelot.

Heavy was King Arthur ever thereafter, and never might man see his face brighten nor hear his laugh; and the better of his knights sorrowed with him, and knew what was in his heart.

'In this realm will be no more quiet,' said Sir Owen of the Fountain to his fellows as they stood upon the walls of Carlisle and saw the band of Sir Lancelot riding southwards, the sunlight flashing from their helms and armour. 'The pagans have gathered strength daily while we have fought with each other, and that which would have given us the strength and the union which would hurl them from our coasts is shattered and broken. By the noble fellowship of the Round Table was King Arthur and his realm borne up, and by their nobleness the king and all his realm was in quietness and in peace. And a great part,' he ended, 'was because of the noble nature of Sir Lancelot, whom Sir Gawaine's mad rage hath driven from the kingdom. Nor is all the evil ended yet.'

Castle Orguellous

For seven full days King Arthur and his men journeyed, and passed through many a forest ere they came into the open land and saw before their eyes the rich Castle Orguellous, the which they had greatly desired to behold. They who had gone ahead had already pitched the king's pavilion in a fair meadow nigh unto a grove of branching olive trees, very fair and full of leaf. There the king, and they who were with him, dismounted gladly; they might go no further, since 'twas well known in the land that they came to make war on the castle.

They had made no long abiding when they heard a great bell toll—no man had ever heard a greater—five leagues around might the sound be heard, and all the earth trembled. Then the king asked of him who knew the customs of the castle wherefore the bell tolled thus.

Quoth Bran de Lis, "Of a truth, 'tis that all the country round may know that the castle is besieged, till that the bell be tolled nor shield nor spear may be set on the walls, the towers, or battlements." As he spake thus they saw to the right more than five thousand banners wave from the walls, the towers, and donjon, and as many shields hung forth from the battlements. Then they saw issue forth from the forest on to the plain knights mounted on palfreys and war-horses, who made their way by many roads to the castles; right gladly did the king and his comrades behold them.

I will not devise unto ye all the fashion of the castle, I must needs spend overmuch time thereon, but since the birth of Christ no man ever saw one more fairly placed, nor richer, nor better garnished with tall towers and donjon.

Now was meat made ready in the king's tent, and all sat them down to supper in right merry mood; they said among themselves that enough knights were entered into the castle to give work to each and all. Thus they spake and made sport concerning those within.

So soon as the king had sat him down Lucains the butler poured the wine into a golden cup, and spake unto the king, "I pray the right of the first joust that be ridden to-morrow morn, for it pertaineth unto mine office!" Quoth the king, "I were loth to refuse the first gift prayed of me here in this land." "'Tis well said," quoth the lord of Lys. And the king said to the butler, "Go, eat with my nephew," and he did so right gladly.

The Adventures of Sir Gawain

So soon as supper was done, and they had washed, swiftly they commanded their arms to be brought, nor will I lie to ye; thereafter might ye have seen a great testing, many greaves of iron laced on, limbs outstretched, feet bent; squires were bidden don the hauberks that they might look well to them, and add straps or take away—all were fain to see that naught was lacking, but all in fair and knightly order. Ye never saw a folk thus busy themselves. They made merry with the king the while, and prayed of him in sport to say the day he would allot to each, that their pain might be the sooner ended. "Nay, lords," quoth Arthur, "I would fain keep ye the longer in dread." Thus when they had made sport enow, and it was nightfall, they drank, and betook them to rest.

On the morrow, without delay, they arose at sunrise, and betook them to a chapel in a wood, nigh to a meadow where were buried all the good knights slain before the castle, whether strangers or men of the land. And so soon as the priest had said the Mass of the Holy Ghost, and the service was ended, they turned them again, and made ready for meat in the king's pavilion, and the king and all his knights ate together right joyfully. When they had eaten they arose, and armed Lucains the butler well and courteously. The vest he ware under his hauberk was of purple broidered with gold. Then they brought him his horse and his shield, and he mounted right glad and joyful, and they brought unto him his pennon. Thus he departed from the king and his comrades, and set spurs to his steed, and stayed not till he came unto the field of battle, whither they betook them and demanded joust of those of the castle.

Masters, at the four corners of the meadow were planted four olive trees, to show the bounds of the field, and he was held for vanquished who should first pass the boundary of the olives. Since he had come thither armed, it befell not Lucains to await long, but short space after he had entered the field he saw ride proudly forth from the castle a great knight, mounted on a roan steed, right well appointed of arms and accoutrements. He came at full speed to the meadow, and swiftly, as befitted, each lowered his lance, and set spurs to his steed, and rode the one against the other. Great blows they dealt on each other's shield, and the knight smote Lucains so fiercely that he brake his lance all to shivers, and the butler smote back in such wise that he bare him out of the saddle on to the ground. Then he took the steed, and turned him, leaving his foeman afoot, and came gladly and blithely again to the pavilion. Quoth Bran de Lis, "Certes, butler, the siege had been raised had ye brought yon knight captive, nor would ye have had further travail, for the quest on which ye came hither had been achieved, and ere nightfall Sir Giflet had been delivered up, for yonder is so good a knight they had gladly made the exchange!"

When the butler heard this he was ill-pleased, and he tarried no longer at the pavilion, but leaving the steed gat him back to the meadow, nor turned again for the king, who many a time called upon him. Then from the gateway rode forth a great knight bearing his pennon, and came spurring into the meadow, and when the butler saw him he rode against him, and smote him so fiercely on the shield that the shaft of apple-wood brake, and the knight smote him back with so strong a lance that he bare him to the ground. Lucains sprang up swiftly, and thought to take the splinters from his arm without delaying, but the knight ran upon him fiercely, and he defended himself as best he might, though wounded, but since the blade was yet in him, whether he would or no, he must needs yield himself prisoner, as one who might do no more. Thus he yielded up his sword to the knight, who led him with him to the castle, but first he drew out the blade carefully, stanching the blood, and binding up the wound.

Very wrathful was the king when he saw his butler thus led thence; then quoth Sir Gawain, "Certes, an Lucains were whole I should rejoice in that he is captive, for now will our comrade Giflet, the brave and valiant, who hath been there in durance four years, learn such tidings of us as shall make him glad and joyful. The butler is a right gallant knight, and it may chance to any that he be overthrown and wounded. I have no mind to blame him for such ill hap." Sir Bran de Lis answered, "Fair Sir, an God help me, he hath overthrown one of their men, and I know no better among their ten thousand knights." So spake Sir Bran de Lis, but for all that was he somewhat vexed concerning the butler, in that he had reproached him for not having taken the knight captive, for he thought in his heart that for these words of his, and for naught else, had Lucains been taken.

Then he came unto the king, and besought him for the great love he bare him to grant him the morrow's joust; but though he prayed him straitly the king was loth to yield, but answered that in no wise would he grant his request save that he was fain not to anger him by reason of the true faith that he bare unto him. "So God help me, fair friend; I have it in my mind that I were but ill sped did I chance to lose ye!"

"Sire, think not of that; 'tis ill done to summon evil, an God will this shall not befall so long as I live; doubt ye not, Sire, but grant me the fight freely, ere others ask it!"

Then the king quoth, "Have your desire, since ye so will." With that they gat them to meat in the tent, but that day a butler was lacking to them.

Into that selfsame chamber where that good knight, Giflet fis Do, had long lain, they led Lucains prisoner, and Giflet when he beheld him failed not to know him, but sprang up, and embraced him, and asked straightway, "Tell me, gentle friend, in what land were ye made captive?" Then Lucains told him the truth from beginning to end, how the king had set siege to the castle, and was lodged without, "And he hath sworn he will not depart hence, nor lift the siege, till that he hath freed ye." Giflet was right joyful when he heard this, and he spake again, "Sir Lucains, greatly do I desire to hear from ye tidings of the best knights in the world, even the companions of the Round Table; 'tis over long since I saw them, or heard speak of them." And the butler made answer, "Sir, by all the Saints in the calendar, such an one is dead, such an one made captive, this and that knight are hale and whole, and to the places of the dead many a good knight and true hath been elect." And Giflet cried, "Ah, God, how minished is that goodly company; I know not the half of them who yet live!"

Quoth Lucains, "Know of a truth that all greatly desire to have ye again, nor will they know joy in their hearts till that ye be once more of their fellowship."

At these words they brought them food, and they washed, and ate, and when 'twas time they gat them to rest, and passed the night in great joy of each other's company. But the night was short, since Pentecost was past, and the feast of S. John, when the days are the longest in the year.

On the morrow the sun rose fine and fair, for the weather was calm and clear, and the king arose betimes with his comrades. First they gat them to the chapel and heard Mass, and then dinner was made ready, since to eat ere noon is healthful for the brain. The dinner was rich and plentiful, they sat them down gaily and ate with speed, they had larded venison (for of deer was there no lack), and so soon as they had dined the chamberlain armed the lord of Lys right richly, on a fair flowered carpet, and the king himself laced his helmet. Then Sir Bran de Lis mounted and hung the shield about his neck, and took his lance whereon was a pennon, and spurred straight for the meadow, which he knew full well.

Then from the gates of the castle he beheld issue forth a knight on a gallant steed, right fittingly armed, who rode at full speed to the meadow where Sir Bran de Lis awaited his coming. And so soon as each beheld the other they spurred swiftly forward, and I tell ye of a truth that they smote each other on the shield so that their lances brake, and they came together with such force that they hurled each other to the ground; but they lay not there for long, but sprang up anon, and laid to with their swords, dealing each other mighty blows on the gleaming helmets, for the worser of the twain was a gallant knight. But he of the castle was sore vexed, in that he was wounded while Bran de Lis was yet whole, and passing light on his feet, so that he pressed him sore, in so much that he might not abide in any place. By force Sir Bran de Lis brought his foeman to his knees, and ere he might rise he must perforce yield himself captive. Thus he led him to the pavilion, and made gift of him to Arthur, who received him well, and thanked the lord of Lis right heartily.

Then the king bade them make a lodge of boughs, with curtains round about, whereto they led the wounded knight to rest, for much need had he of repose. King Arthur and his men disarmed Sir Bran de Lis gaily, and he washed himself, and they made great sport all day long. And when it came to the freshness of the evening they went forth to disport themselves; many a valiant knight sat there, round about the king, in the shade of an olive tree.

Then they heard the sound of those who blew loudly on the horn and played upon the flageolet; there was no instrument befitting a watch the music of which was not to be heard within the castle, and much joy they made therein. The king was the more wakeful by night in that he took pleasure in the fair melody which the watchmen who sounded the horn made in answering the one the other.

Beside the lord of Lys sat Kay, who hearkened to the music, nor might he long keep silence, but must needs speak his mind. "Sire," quoth he, "by Saint Denis, meseemeth the joust be forgotten, for this eve none hath demanded it; the king hath neither companion nor peer who hath so far prayed it, I wot none be desirous thereof!"

"Kay," quoth the King, "I grant thee the joust."

"Sire," quoth Kay, "by Saint Martin, I were liever to handle a spit than a spear to-morrow; I thank ye for naught! Nevertheless, Sire, an such be your pleasure I will do it, by the faith I owe to my lord Sir Gawain." Then all laughed at Kay's words, and when they had made sport enow of him they gat them back to the tent.

Thus the night passed, and on the morrow at dawn, ere prime had rung, the king hearkened Mass, and when they had dined they armed the seneschal, and he mounted, and took his shield, and departed from them swiftly. No sooner had he come to the meadow when a knight, right well armed, came forth from the castle, and rode on to the field. They smote each other on the shields so that they fell to the ground, and springing up lightly they fell to with their sharp swords; right dourly they pressed on each other, and smote sounding blows on the helms. He of the castle struck wrathfully at Kay, and the seneschal caught the blow, and the knight smote again on the boss of the shield so that the blade brake, notwithstanding he had so pressed on the seneschal that he made him by force to pass the boundary of the four olives, which stood at the corners of the field.

There the knight stayed him, and turned him back to his steed which was in the midst of the meadow, and remounted, and took Kay's horse, for he saw well 'twas a good steed, and led it away, none gainsaying him. Kay went his way back, and knew not that he had been deceived, but deemed he had won the day, though in sooth he was vanquished.

Then the knights spake unto the king, "Sire, let us go to meet Kay, and make merry over him; 'twill be rare sport to mislead him!" The king was right willing, so they went in company towards the seneschal.

The king went ahead, as one wise and courteous, and spake gently, "Kay, hast thou come from far? Has mischance befallen thee?" and Kay, who was ever sharp and ready of tongue, answered, "Sire, let me be; ye have naught wherewith to reproach me. I have vanquished one of their knights, but he hath taken my horse; the field is mine, for I have conquered it; and he who hath ridden hence hath the worse!" All held their peace, and laughed not.

"Sir, are ye in need of help?" quoth Tor fis Ares. And then the others spake; "Seneschal, are ye wounded?" "Methinks ye limp somewhat," quoth Sir Gawain.

"Kay, hand me your shield," said Sir Ywain. "Right valiantly have ye approved yourself, marvellous were the blows I saw ye deal! God be thanked that ye did thus well!" With that he took the shield, and hung it around his own neck. Each joined in the sport as best he might, and Kay was right well aware thereof.

The Adventures of Sir Gawain

Then he spake to Sir Ywain, "Sir, I will grant ye to-morrow so much as I have won to-day, the joust and the field shall ye have in exchange for my shield which ye bear. Ye can do well, an ye will, and I were fain to repay ye in such wise as I may."

Those who heard might not refrain their mirth, and in merry mood they led him to the tent, and disarmed him, and the lord of Lys said, "Sir Kay, ye passed the boundary of the four olive trees, and he who first passes betwixt them is held for vanquished." And Kay answered, "May be, Sir, by the faith I owe the King of Heaven an ye know the differ 'twixt entry and exit 'tis more than I may do; sure, 'tis all one, for there where one cometh in the other goeth out!"

Suddenly there rang forth from the castle and the minster a peal so great and glad that ye might scarce hear God thunder, and the king asked wherefore the bells rang thus.

Then Bran de Lis spake, "I will tell ye, Sire: 'tis Saturday to-day, and now that noon be past they within will do naught against ye, come what may. In this land is the Mother of God more honoured than elsewhere in Christendom; know of a truth that ye shall presently see knights and ladies, burgesses and other folk, clad in their best, betake them to the minster; they go to hear Vespers, and do honour to Our Lady. Thus it is from noon on Saturday till Tierce on Monday, when Mass is sung, and the bells chimed throughout the burg, then they get them to their tasks again; the minstrels and other folk. I tell ye without fail till then shall no joust be ridden; to-morrow, an ye will, ye may go forth to hunt in the forest."

The king praised the custom much, and spent the night with a light heart until the morn, when he arose, and with his knights betook him to the woods, and all day long the forest rang to the sound of the huntsman's horn.

Now it chanced that Sir Gawain beheld a great stag, which two of his hounds had severed from the rest of the herd, and he followed hard after the chase till that the quarry was pulled down in a clearing. There he slew and quartered it, and gave their portion to the dogs, but would take with him naught save the back and sides. So he rode on fairly, and without annoy, the hounds running ahead, till, as he went his way, he heard nigh at hand a hawk cry loudly. Then he turned him quickly towards the sound, and came on to a wide and dusky path, and followed it speedily to a dwelling, the fairest he had found in any land wherein he had sojourned.

The Adventures of Sir Gawain

'Twas set in the midst of a clearing, and no wish or thought of man might devise aught that was lacking unto it. There was a fair hall and a strong tower, 'twas set round about with palisades, and there was a good drawbridge over the moat, which was wide enow, and full of running water. At the entry of the bridge was a pine-tree, and beneath, on a fair carpet, sat a knight; never had ye seen one so tall, or so proud of bearing.

Sir Gawain rode straight and fast to him, but he stirred no whit for his coming, but sat still, frowning and thoughtful. Sir Gawain marvelled at his stature, and spake very courteously, "Sir, God save ye!" But the stranger answered nor loud nor low, having no mind for speech. Thrice Sir Gawain greeted him, but he answered not, and the good knight stayed his steed full before him, but he made no semblance of seeing him.

Quoth Sir Gawain, "Ha, God, who hath made man with Thine own hand, wherefore didst Thou make this man so fair if he be deaf and dumb? So tall is he, and so well fashioned he is like unto a giant. An I had a comrade with me I would lead him hence, even unto the king; methinks he would thank me well, for he would look on him as a marvel!" And he bethought him that he would even bear the knight hence with him on his steed. Thus he laid his venison beneath a tree, and bent him downwards from his saddlebow, and took the other by the shoulders, and raised him a little.

Then the knight clapped hand to his side, but his sword was lacking, and he cried, "Who may ye be? It lacked but little and I had slain ye with my fist, since ye have snatched me from death; had I my sword here 'twere red with your blood! Get ye hence, vassal, and leave me to my death."

Then he sat him again under the tree, and fell a-musing, even as when Sir Gawain found him. And that good knight, without more ado, reloaded his venison and turned him back, leaving the knight sad and sorrowful.

Scarce had Sir Gawain ridden half a league when he saw coming towards him a maiden, fair and courteous, on a great Norman palfrey; nor king nor count had been better horsed. The bridle, the harness, the trappings of her steed were beyond price, nor might I tell ye how richly the maiden was clad. Her vesture was of cloth of gold, the buttons of Moorish work, wrought in silk with golden pendants. The lady smote her steed oft and again, and rode past Sir Gawain with never a word of greeting.

Sir Gawain marvelled much at her haste, and that she had failed to speak with him, and he turned him about, and rode after, crying "Stay a little, Lady!" but she answered not, but made the more haste.

Then Sir Gawain overtook her, and rode alongside, saying, "Lady, stay, and tell me whither ye be bound." Then she made answer, "Sir, for God's sake, hinder me not, for an ye do I tell ye of a truth I shall have slain the best and the fairest knight in any castle of Christendom!"

"What," quoth Sir Gawain, "have ye slain him with your own hands?"

"I, sir? God forbid, but I made covenant with him yesterday that I would be with him ere noon, and now have I failed of my compact. He awaiteth me at a tower near by, mine own true love, the best knight in the world!"

"Certes, Lady, he is yet alive, of that am I true witness; 'twas but now he well nigh dealt me a buffet with his fist! Make not such haste!"

"Fair sir, are ye sure and certain?"

"Yea, Lady, but he was sore bemused."

"Then know of a truth, Sir Knight, that he may no longer be alive, and I may not tarry." With that she struck her steed and rode off apace. Sir Gawain gazed after her, and it vexed him much that he had not asked more concerning the knight, whence he came, his land and his name, but knew neither beginning nor end of his story.

Thus he went on his way, and came again to the pavilion where his companions awaited him, sore perplexed at his delay, and were right joyful when they beheld him. Then straightway he told them the adventure, even as it had chanced, and when the lord of Lys heard it he said unto the King, "Sire, the knight is the Rich Soudoier, he who maintaineth all this goodly following and seignorie; and so much doth he love the maiden whom he calleth his lady and his love, that all men say he will die an he win her not."

As he spake they beheld a great cloud of dust arise toward the forest, and there rode past so great a company of folk there cannot have been less than twenty thousand; there was left in the city not a soul who might well stir thence who went not forth of right good will toward the forest. 'Twas nigh unto nightfall ere all had entered therein.

Then the king asked whither all this folk were bound, and Bran de Lis answered, "Sire, they go to meet their lord, and to do him honour, for never before this hath he led his lady hither. I tell ye of a truth that each one of his barons will dub three new knights, to honour and pleasure him, for so have they sworn, and for that doth he owe them right good will."

What more may I tell ye? All night they held great feast through the city, with many lights in castle, tower, and hall. They blazed upon the walls, the trees, and round about the meadows, till that the great burg seemed all aflame, and all night long they heard the sound of song and loud rejoicing.

Then the king betook him to rest, and at dawn Sir Ywain prayed as gift the joust which Kay had given unto him. The king made no gainsaying, but after meat they armed their comrade well and fittingly, and he mounted quickly, and took shield and lance; nor did he long await a foe, for there rode forth from the castle one well armed, on a strong and swift steed, and spurred upon Sir Ywain. He smote him so that his lance brake, and Sir Ywain smote him again with such force that he bare him to earth ere that his lance failed. Then he rode upon him with unsheathed sword, and by weight of his steed bare him to earth when he had fain arisen, and trod him underfoot so hardly that, whether he would or no, he must needs yield. Then Sir Ywain took his pledge, and led him without more ado to the pavilion, and delivered him to the king.

Such was the day's gain, but know that 'twas one of the new made knights, not of the mesnie of the Rich Soudoier. And when he was disarmed the king spake unto him in the hearing of all his men, and said, "Fair friend, whence do ye come, and of what land may ye be?"

Then he answered, "Sire, I am of Ireland, and son to the Count Brangelis, and ever have I served the lady of the Rich Soudoier. She bade me carve before her, and my lord for love of her yestermorn made me knight, and as guerdon for my service they granted me the joust; yet, but for my lady who prayed for me this grace, they had not given it to me, since within the walls there be many a good man and true who was sore vexed thereat."

"Friend," quoth Sir Gawain, "know ye, perchance, the which of them shall joust on the morrow?"

"Certes, Sir, I should know right well; 'tis the lord of the castle himself who shall be first on the field, and I will tell ye how I know this. 'Tis the custom therein that each morn the maidens mount the walls, and she who first beholds the armed knight take the field, 'tis her knight who shall ride forth against him. Yestereven my lady assembled all the maidens and prayed of them that they would let her alone mount the wall—thus shall the joust be as I tell ye."

Straightway Sir Gawain sprang to his feet, and went before the king, and demanded the joust, but Arthur forbade him saying, "Fair nephew, ye shall not go to-morrow, but later, ere it be my turn, 'tis for us twain to ride the last jousts; ye shall have it when all save I have proved themselves."

The Adventures of Sir Gawain

"Sire, Sire, I shall be sore shamed an ye deny me this gift; never more shall I be joyful, nor will I ride joust in this land, but will get me hence alone!"

Quoth the king, "An it be thus ye may have it." And Sir Gawain answered, "I thank ye, Sire."

Thus they passed the night, and at daybreak, when the dew lay thick upon the grass, Sir Gawain arose, and Sir Ywain with him. Know that the morning was so fine, so fair and clear, as if 'twere made to be gazed on. Then he who was no coward washed face and hands and feet in the dew, and gat him back to the pavilion. There they brought him a wadded vest, of purple, bordered with samite, and he donned it, and fastened on his armlets deftly.

And ere he was fully armed the king his uncle had risen, and they gat them to Mass, and when Mass was said, to meat. When they had well dined they bade bring thither the armour, and Sir Gawain sat him on a rich carpet, spread on the ground in the midst of the tent, and there was never a knight but stood around uncovered, till that he had armed him at his leisure with all that pertaineth to assault and defence, so that he had naught to do save but to set forth.

Then they led unto him his steed, all covered with a rich trapping, and he mounted, and sat thereon, so goodly to look upon that never might ye hear speak of a fairer knight. Excalibur, his good sword, did King Arthur hand to him, and he girt it round him as he sat on the saddle, lightly, so that it vexed him not. Then he took shield and lance, and departed from them, making great speed for the meadow.

Now the adventure telleth that he had been there but short space when from the master tower of the castle a horn was sounded long and clear, so that for a league around the earth quivered by reason of the echo of the blast, and Sir Bran de Lis spake to the king, "Sire, in short space shall ye see the Rich Soudoier come forth armed on his steed, for they sound not the horn thus save for his arming. I know well by the long blast that he laceth on his spurs."

Then the horn sounded a second time, and he said, "By my faith, now hath he donned and laced his greaves."

For a long space there was silence, and again the horn rang forth so loudly that all the castle re-echoed, and the lord of Lys said, "Sire, now hath he donned his hauberk and laced his helm." With that the horn sounded once again, "Now, Sire, he is mounted, and the horn will be blown no more to-day."

This had the good knight told them truly, for the burg was all astir: he who bare lordship therein rode proudly down from the castle, and after him so many of his folk that they of the pavilion heard the sound of their tread, though they might not behold them. Even to the gate they bare him company, and as he issued forth the king's men beheld him covered with a silken robe, even to his spurs, his banner in his hand. Then they saw a great crowd mount to the battlements to watch the combat of the twain; the walls were covered even to the gateways, so that 'twas a marvel to behold.

Thus the lord of the castle came proudly to the meadow where Sir Gawain awaited him, and when he saw him he gripped his shield tightly, and made ready for the onslaught. Then they laid their lances in rest, and shook forth their blazons, and smote their spurs into their steeds; nor did the joust fail, for they came together with such force of steed and shield and body that, an they would or no, both came to the ground in mid meadow and the good steeds fell over them. But the twain were full of valour, and arose up lightly, and drew their swords, and ran boldly on each other. Then might ye behold a dour combat, and a sight for many folk, for with great wrath they dealt each other mighty blows, so that all who beheld were astonied, and the king was in sore dread for his nephew, and they of the castle for their lord.

From either side many a prayer went up to Heaven that their champion might return safe and whole. And the twain spared not themselves, but each with shining blade smote the other, so that their strength waned apace. For know that that day there was so great a heat that never since hath the like been known, and that heat vexed and weakened them sore.

Now know ye of a certain truth that my lord Sir Gawain waxed ever in strength, doubling his force from midnight, and even till noon was past and the day waned did his strength endure, but then he somewhat weakened till 'twas midnight again. This I tell ye of a truth, 'twas early morn that they fought thus in the meadow, and greatly did this gift aid him, and great evil it wrought to the Rich Soudoier. Neither had conquered aught on the other till it waxed high noon. If the one dealt mighty blows the other knew right well how to return them with wrath and vigour; 'twas hard to say the which were the better, and all marvelled much that neither was as yet or slain or put to the worse.

'Twas the Soudoier who first gave ground; by reason of the over great heat so sore a thirst seized him that he might no longer endure the heavy blows, and well nigh fell to the earth. When Sir Gawain felt his foe thus weakening he pressed him the more, till that he staggered on his feet, and Sir Gawain ran on him with such force that both fell to the ground. But the king's nephew sprang to his feet lightly and cried, "Vassal, yield ye prisoner ere I slay ye!" but his foe was so dazed that for a space he might speak no word.

When he gat breath and speech he sighed forth, "Ah, God, who will slay me? Since she be dead I care naught for my life."

Sir Gawain wondered much what the words might mean, and he shook him by the vizor, and when he saw that he took no heed he spake again, "Sir Knight, yield to me!" And he sighed, "Suddenly was she slain who was fairest in the world; I loved her with a passing great love!"

When Sir Gawain saw that he would answer none otherwise, conjure him as he might, he cut the laces of his helmet, and saw that he lay with his eyes closed as one in a swoon; by reason of the great heat and his sore thirst he had lost all colour, and was senseless. Sir Gawain was vexed in that he might not win from him speech, neither by word nor by blow, yet was he loth to slay him; nor would he leave him lying; for he thought an he slew him he might lose all he would gain by his victory, and should he get him back to the pavilion to seek aid to bear his prisoner hence, on his return he would surely find him gone. Thus was he much perplexed in mind. Then he doffed his helm, and sat him down beside the knight, sheathing Excalibur, and taking the sword of his foe. In a short space the Soudoier came again to himself, and seeing him sit thus, asked of him his name. Then he answered straightway, and when the other knew 'twas Gawain, he said, "Sir, now know I for a certainty that ye be the best knight in the world." Then he held his peace, and spake no further, and Sir Gawain looked upon him, and said, "Fair Sir Knight, bear me no ill will for aught ye may have heard me say, but come with me, an ye will, to yonder pavilion, and we will take your pledge."

Then the Rich Soudoier answered, "I have a lady I love more than my life, and if she die then must I needs die too, so soon as I hear tell thereof. I pray ye, sir, for God's sake, for love's sake, for gentleness, for courtesy, save me my love that she die not, by covenant that, whether for right or for wrong, no man of the Castle Orguellous shall henceforth be against ye. Fair sir, an ye will do for me that which I now pray, I will pledge my faith to do all the king's will, nor shall there be therein man of arms whom I will not make swear the same. But an if my lady knew thereof, as God be my witness, she would die straightway, for never would she believe that ye had conquered me; 'tis truth I tell ye! Now of your courtesy, Sir Knight, I pray of ye this great service, that ye come back with me to the castle, that ye there do me honour, and kneeling to my lady declare ye her prisoner; an ye will thus make feint and say I have vanquished ye in fair field, then shall ye save my life, and that of my most sweet lady, and if ye will not do thus, then slay me here and now!"

Then that gentle knight, Sir Gawain, remembered him of how he had found him aforetime in the forest beneath the tower, and how the maiden who rode to keep tryst feared for his life, and he knew that he loved his lady with so great a love that he would die an she knew him to be shamed, and he thought within himself 'twas over much cruelty to slay so good a knight, and he answered. "Fair sir, certes will I go with ye to the Castle Orguellous, and there yield me captive, nor will I forbear for any doubt or misgiving. It might well turn to my shame, but even if I should die thereby, I would not, Sir Knight, that ye or your lady be wronged or aggrieved."

Then the knight spake frankly, "Sir, I am your liege man all the days of my life." And he gave him his hand, and sware straitly that he would do all the king's pleasure. And when Sir Gawain had taken his oath, straightway the two mounted their steeds and betook them to the Castle Orguellous.

Well nigh did King Arthur die of wrath when he saw his nephew ride hence, and he cried, "Now am I indeed bereft if my nephew be led therein; now will they hold him prisoner! Think ye, my lords, that he be of a truth captive?"

"Yea, Sire, of a faith, so it seemeth, yet are we greatly in marvel thereat, for we know certainly that he had vanquished and overthrown his adversary. Never so great an ill hap hath befallen any knight, for ere the knight of the castle rose we said surely that he was conquered!"

The king had no heart to hearken longer, but betook him straightway to his bed; cause enow had he for woe, or so it seemed him!

But they of the castle sped joyously to meet their lord, whom they thought to have lost, and ran to bear the tidings to the lady, who was well nigh distraught with grief, and anger, and they told her that her lord came again. "And he leadeth by the bridle, as one conquered, Sir Gawain!"

The Adventures of Sir Gawain

Even at these words came the knights unto the gateway, and dismounted, and Sir Gawain speedily yielded him prisoner to the maiden, saying, "Lady, take here my sword, and know of a proven truth that this good knight, your true lover, hath vanquished me by force of arms."

Never since the hour ye were born did ye see such rejoicing as the maiden made, and the Rich Soudoier spake, saying, "Ride ye to my castle of Bouvies with five hundred knights, and make ready the chambers. I will be with ye to-morrow, and would fain sojourn there; we will have but few folk with us. Marvel not at this, for to-day have I been over much wearied."

And the maiden answered, "Ye have well said; the castle is very fair and pleasant." With that she was mounted, and the knights set forth to convoy her to the castle. And know ye why he sent her hence? 'Twas that he might tell his men the truth of what had passed.

When the lady had departed 'twas made known throughout the castle how the matter had in very truth fallen out, and the lord bade release the son of Do, and the butler, and they did his bidding. But when Sir Gawain saw Giflet he ran towards him, and kissed him more than a hundred times, and made marvellous great joy of him. Then they sat them down on a bench, side by side, and held converse together. And when the twain who had fought were disarmed they brought for the four very fair robes of rich and royal cloth; never had ye seen such. Then the Soudoier bade saddle four steeds, and they mounted, and rode thus adown the street.

Thus they four alone took their way to the pavilion, and the king's men beheld them, even as they came forth from the castle gateway, and Sir Ywain cried, "By my faith, and no lie, I see four men come hither, and all four be knights, so it seemeth me!" And Kay answered, "I see them too!"

And when they came so near to the pavilion that their faces might be seen, Sir Ywain ran joyfully to the king. "Sire, Sire, an God help me, here cometh Sir Gawain, and with him three others, all hand in hand: there be the son of Do, and Sir Lucains, and for the fourth a great knight!"

The king answered no word, but made semblance as if he heard not, and rose not from his couch, save that he raised himself somewhat higher thereon.

In a little space he spake to his knights, "Be not over dismayed, but make as fair a countenance as ye may; methinks they come thither to bid us return with them to prison, but I go not hence ere that I be vanquished, or have freed my comrades." And all answered, "Well spoken, Sire!"

The Adventures of Sir Gawain

But now had the four come so nigh that they had dismounted, and come before the king; never was seen such rejoicing as his lord made of Giflet, but now was he in sore distress, and, lo! his sorrow was turned to joy! Why should I lie to ye? The Rich Soudoier told him how Sir Gawain had conquered him, and how, by his courtesy, he had given life to him and to his fair lady; and the king hearkened to the tale right willingly.

Now will I leave speaking of them, but this much will I say, that well might the lord of the castle love and cherish him who first overcame him by arms and then did him so great honour as to yield him to his lady so that his life might thereby be saved. So here will I hold my peace, no, nor speak further, save to tell ye that now was the king lord alike of the Castle Orguellous and the lands around; never in all his days did he make so great a conquest, as Bleheris doth witness to us.

Gawayne and the Green Knight: A Fairy Tale

Preface

Arms and the man I sing, – not as of old
The Mantuan bard his mighty verse unrolled,
But in such humbler strains as may beseem
Light changes rung on a fantastic theme.
My tale is ancient, but the sense is new, –
Replete with monstrous fictions, yet half true; –
And, if you'll follow till the story's done,
I promise much instruction, and some fun.

Canto I: The Green Knight

King Arthur and his court were blithe and gay
In high-towered Camelot, on Christmas day,
For all the Table Round were back again,
At peace with God and with their fellow-men
Their shields hung idly on the pictured wall;
Their blood-stained banners decked the festal hall;
Light footsteps, rustling on the rush-strewn floors,
And laughter, rippling down long corridors,
Attested minds at ease and hearts at play, –
Rude Mars unharnessed for love's holiday.
In the great hall the Christmas feast was done.
The level sunbeams from the setting sun
Stretched through the mullioned casements to the wall,
And wove fantastic shadows over all.
The revelry was hushed. In tranquil ease
The warriors grouped themselves by twos and threes
About the dames and damsels of the court,
And chattered careless words of small import;
But in an alcove, unobserved, apart,
Young Gawayne sat with Lady Elfinhart.
In Arthur's court no goodlier knight than he
Wore shirt of mail, or Cupid's panoply;
And Elfinhart, to Gawayne's eager eyes,
Of all heaven's treasures seemed the goodliest prize.
Now daylight faded, and the twilight gloom
Deepened the stillness in the vaulted room,
Save where upon the hearth a fitful glow
Blushed from the embers as the fire burned low.
There is a certain subtle twilight mood,
When two hearts meet in a dim solitude,
That thrills the soul e'en to the finger-tips,
And brings the heart's dear secrets to the lips.
In Gawayne's corner, as the shades grew thicker,
Four eyes waxed brighter, and two pulses quicker;

The Adventures of Sir Gawain

Ten minutes more of quiet talk unbroken,
And heaven alone can tell what might be spoken!
But it was not to be, for fates unequal
Compelled – but this anticipates the sequel.
Just in the nick of time, King Arthur rose
From his sedate post-prandial repose,
And called for lights. Along the shadowy aisles
His pages' footsteps pattered o'er the tiles,
Speeding to do his errand, and at once
Four tapers flickered from each silver sconce.
The scene was changed, the dreamer's dream dispelled,
And what might else have been his fate withheld
From Gawayne's grasp. So may one touch of chance
Shatter the fragile fabric of romance,
And all the heart's desire, – the joy, the trouble, –
Flash to oblivion with the bursting bubble!

But Arthur on his kingly dais-seat,
Felt nothing of the passion and the heat
That fire young blood. He raised his warlike head
And glancing moodily around him, said:
"So have ye feasted well, my knights, this day,
And filled your hearts with revel and with play.
But to my mind that day is basely spent
Which passes by without accomplishment
Of some bright deed of arms or chivalry.
We rust in indolence. As well not be,
As be the minions of an idle court
Where all is gallantry and girlish sport!
Some bold adventure let our thoughts devise,
To stir our courage and to cheer our eyes."
And lo! while yet he spoke, from far away
In the thick shroud of the departed day,
Upon the frosty air of evening borne,
Came the faint challenge of a fairy horn!

King Arthur started up in mild surprise,
While knights and dames looked round with questioning eyes,

The Adventures of Sir Gawain

And each to other spoke some hurried word,
As, "Did you hear it?" – "What was that I heard?"
But well they knew; for you must understand
That Camelot lay close to Fairyland,
And the wild blast of fairy horns, once known,
Is straightway recognized as soon as blown,
Being a sound unique, unearthly, shrill, –
Between a screech-owl and a whip-poor-will.
The mischief is, that no one e'er can tell
Whether such heralding bodes ill or well!

The ladies of the palace looked faint fear,
Dreading some perilous adventure near;
For peril can the bravest spirits move,
When threatening not ourselves, but those we love;
But Lady Elfinhart clapped hands in glee, –
In sooth, no sentimentalist seemed she, –
And cried: "Now, brave Sir Gawayne, – O what fun!
Succor us, save us, else we are undone;
Show us the prowess of your arm this night;
I never saw a tilt by candle-light!"
Gaily she spoke, and seemed all unconcerned;
And yet a curious watcher might have learned
From a slight quaver in her laughter free
To doubt the frankness of her flippancy.
Gawayne, bewildered, looked the other way,
And wondered what she meant; for in that day
The ready wit of man was under muzzle,
And woman's heart was still an unsolved puzzle;
And Gawayne, though in valor next to none,
Wished that her heart had been a tenderer one.
His sword was out for any foe on earth,
And yet to face death for a lady's mirth
Seemed scarce worth while. What honor bade, he'ld do,
But would have liked to see a tear or two.

While thus he pondered, came a sudden burst
Of high-pitched fairy horn-calls, like the first,

The Adventures of Sir Gawain

But nearer, clearer, deadlier than before,
Blown seemingly from just outside the door.
The casements shook, the taper lights all trembled;
The bravest knight's dismay was ill-dissembled;
And as all sprang with one accord to win
Their swords and shields, stern combat to begin,
The great doors shot their bolts, and opened slowly in.
And now my laboring muse is hard beset,
For something followed such as never yet
Was writ or sung, by human voice or hand,
Save those that tell old tales from Fairyland.
"Miracles do not happen:" – 't is plain sense,
If you italicize the present tense;
But in those days, as rare old Chaucer tells,
All Britain was fulfilled of miracles.
So, as I said, the great doors opened wide.
In rushed a blast of winter from outside,
And with it, galloping on the empty air,
A great green giant on a great green mare
Plunged like a tempest-cleaving thunderbolt,
And struck four-footed, with an earthquake's jolt,
Plump on the hearthstone. There the uncouth wight
Sat greenly laughing at the strange affright
That paled all cheeks and opened wide all eyes;
Till after the first shock of quick surprise
The people circled round him, still in awe,
And circling stared; and this is what they saw:
Cassock and hood and hose, of plushy sheen
Like close-cut grass upon a bowling-green,
Covered his stature, from his verdant toes
To the green brows that topped his emerald nose.
His beard was glossy, like unripened corn;
His eyes shot sparklets like the polar morn,
But like in hue unto that deep-sea green
Wherewith must shine those gems of ray serene
The dark, unfathomed caves of ocean bear.
Green was his raiment, green his monstrous mare.
He rode unarmed, uncorsleted, unshielded,

The Adventures of Sir Gawain

Except that in his huge right hand he wielded
A frightful battle-axe, with blade as green
As coppery rust; – but the long edge shone keen.

Such was the stranger, and he turned his head
From one side to the other, and then said,
With gentle voice, most like a summer breeze
That rustles through the leaves of the grren trees:
"So this is Arthur's court! My noble lord,
You said just now you felt a trifle bored,
And wished, instead of dancing, feasting, flirting,
Your gallant warriors might be exerting
Their puissance upon some worthier thing.
The wish, my lord, was worthy of a king!
It pleased me; here I am; and I intend
To serve your fancy as a faithful friend.
I bring adventure, – no hard, tedious quest,
But merely what I call a merry jest.
Let some good knight, the doughtiest of you all,
Swing this my battle-axe, and let it fall
On whatsoever part of me he will;
I will abide the blow, and hold me still;
But let him, just a twelvemonth from this day,
Come to me, if by any means he may,
And let me, if I live, pay back my best,
As he pays me. What think you of the jest?"
He said; and made a courteous bow, – the while
Lighting his features with a bright green smile;
As when June breezes, after rain-clouds pass,
Ripple in sunlight o'er the unmown grass.

The jest seemed fair indeed; but none the less
No knight showed any undue forwardness
To seize the offer. Some with laughter free
Daffed it aside; while others carelessly
Strolled to the farthest corners of the hall
As if they had not heard his words at all,
And whistled with an air of idle ease,

The Adventures of Sir Gawain

Or studied figures in the tapestries.
Not so Sir Gawayne. Vexed in mind he stood
With downcast eyes, and knew not what he would.
Trained in the school of chivalry to prize
His honor as the light of his dear eyes,
He held his life, his fortunes, everything,
In sacred trust for knighthood and his king,
And in the battle-field or tilting-yard
He met his foe full-fronted, and struck hard.
But now it seemed a foolish thing to throw
One's whole life to the fortune of a blow.
True valor breathes not in the braggart vaunt;
True honor takes no shame from idle taunt;
So let this wizard, if he wants to, scoff;
Why should our hero have his head cut off?

While thus Sir Gawayne, wrapped in thought intense,
Debated honor versus common sense,
The stranger knight was casting his green glance
Around the circling throng, – until by chance
He met the eyes of Lady Elfinhart,
And – did she flush? – and did the Green Knight start?
Surely a quiver twinkled in each eye;
But what of that? It need not signify:
Beneath his glance a brave man well might flush;
What wonder then that a fair maid should blush?
And as for him, no man that ever loved
Could look upon her loveliness unmoved.
Could I but picture her – ah, you would deem
My tale the figment of a poet's dream;
And if you saw her, (could such bliss be given),
You'ld think yourself in dreamland – or in heaven,
Not the red rapture of new-wakened roses,
When morning dew their soul of love uncloses,
(Roses that must be wooed, – nor may be won
Save by the prince of lovers, the warm sun),
Not the fair lily, nor the violet shy,
Whose heart's love lurks deep in her still blue eye,

The Adventures of Sir Gawain

Nor any flower, the loveliest and the best,
Can image to you half the charm compressed
In those dear eyes, those lips, – nay, every part
That made that sum of witcheries – Elfinhart.

Her face was a dim dream of shadowy light,
Like misty moonbeams on the fields of night,
And in her voice sweet nature's sweetest tunes
Sang the glad song of twenty cloudless Junes.
Her raiment, – nay; go, reader, if you please,
To some sage Treatise on Antiquities,
Whence writers of historical romances
Cull old embroideries for their new-spun fancies;
I care not for the trivial, nor the fleeting.
Beneath her dress a woman's heart was beating
The rhythm of love's eternal eloquence,
And I confess to you, in confidence,
Though flowers have grown a thousand years above her,
Unseen, unknown, with all my soul I love her.

From these digressions upon love and glory,
'T is time we were returning to our story.
I only meant, in a few words, to tell you
(For fear my heroine's conduct should repel you)
That if she jests, for instance, out of season,
Perhaps there is a good substantial reason.
Sir Gawayne, had he seen the stranger wink
And seen the lady blushing, you may think
Might have been spared a most unhappy lot.
Perhaps you're right; – but peradventure not.
I give you the hint, for half the art
Of narrative is holding back a part,
And if without reserve I gave my best
In the first canto, who would read the rest?

But now Sir Gawayne, with a troubled eye,
Looked up, and saw his lady standing by.
Quoth he: "And if this conjurer unblest

The Adventures of Sir Gawain

Win no acceptance of his bitter jest,
How then in after days shall Arthur's court
Confront the calumny and foul report
Of idle tongues?" The wrath in Gawayne's eyes
Flashed for an instant; then in humbler wise
He spoke on: "Yet God grant I be not blind
Where honor lights the way; for to my mind
True honor bids us shun the devil's den,
To fight God's battles in the world of men.
Who takes this challenge up, I doubt will rue it."
Quoth Elfinhart: "I'ld like to see you do it!"
She laughed a gay laugh, but by hard constraint;
Then turned and hid her face, all pale and faint,
As one might be who stabs and turns the knife
In the warm heart of one more dear than life.
She turned and Gawayne saw not; but he heard,
And felt his heart-strings tighten at her word.
"Nay, lady, if you wish it I will try;
Be your least wish my will, although I die!
Yet one thing, if I may, I fain would ask,
Before I make the venture; – if this task
Prove fateful as it threatens, – do you care?"
"Perhaps," said Elfinhart, "you do not dare!"
Lightly she laughed, and scoffing tossed her head,
Yet spoke as one who knew not what she said,
With random words, and with quick-taken breath;
Then turned again, ere that same look of death
Should steal upon her and betray her heart
Despite all stratagems of woman's art.
And Gawayne heard but saw not; and the night
Descended on him, and his face grew white
With grief and passion. When all else is lost,
The brave man gives life too, nor counts the cost.
"I dreamt," he murmured to himself, "and dreaming
I took for truth what was but sweetest seeming.
My waking eyes find naught in life to keep;
I take the venture, and so back – to sleep."

The Adventures of Sir Gawain

By this, the stranger had at last become
Tired of long waiting, and of sitting dumb
Upon his charger; so with greenest leer
He vented his impatience in a sneer.
"Is this," he said, "the glorious Table Round,
And is its glory naught but empty sound?
Braggarts! I put your bluster to the test,
And find you quail before a merry jest!"
Then the great king himself stood up in ire,
With clenched hand raised, and eyes that gleamed dark fire,
And fronting the Green Knight he cried: "Forbear!
For by my sword Excalibur I swear,
Whate'er thou be, thou shall not carry hence
Unscathed the memory of thine insolence.
Such jests as thine please not; yet even so
I take thine axe; kneel down, and take my blow."

Across the Green Knight's features there was seen
To pass a fleeting shade of deeper green,
Whether of disappointment or resentment
None knew; but straight a smile of bright contentment
Followed, as through the throng of dazed beholders
He saw Sir Gawayne thrust his sturdy shoulders.
The stranger winked at Elfinhart once more,
Well pleased, and Gawayne knelt down on the floor.
"A boon," he cried, "a boon, my lord and king!
If ever yet in any little thing
These hands have served thee, hear my last request:
Let me adventure this mad monster's jest!"
King Arthur shook his head in dumb denial,
Loth to withdraw his own hand from the trial,
And leave the vengeance that himself had vowed;
But all the people called to him aloud,
"Sir Gawayne! let Sir Gawayne strike the blow!"
And Guinevere, the queen, besought him low
To leave this venture to the lesser man.
He yielded, and the merry jest began.

The Adventures of Sir Gawain

The visitor, dismounting, made a bow
To Arthur, then to all the court. "And now,"
Said he to Gawayne, "wheresoe'er you choose
To strike your blow, strike on; I'll not refuse;
Head, shoulders, chest, or waist, I little reck;
Where shall it be?" Quoth Gawayne, "In the neck!"

So Gawayne took the axe. The stranger knelt
Before him on the hearth and loosed his belt,
And threw back his green cassock and his hood,
To give his foe the fairest mark he could.
Then thus to Gawayne: "Ready! But remember
To come the twenty-fifth of next December,
And take from me the self-same stroke again!"
"And where," asked Gawayne, "may I find you then?"
"We'll speak of that, please, when you've struck your blow;
For if I can't speak, then you need not go!"
He chuckled softly to himself; then turned
And waited for the blow, all unconcerned.
Not so the knights and ladies of the court;
They pushed and craned their necks to see the sport;
Not from the lust of blood, for few expected
To see blood shed, or the Green Knight dissected,
But knowing that some marvel was in store
Unparalleled in all Arthurian lore,
And fairly filled with wide-eyed wonderment.
But Lady Elfinhart stayed not. She went
Into the alcove where we saw her first
And laid her sweet face in her arms, and burst
Into – but none could tell, unless by peeping,
Whether she shook with laughter or with weeping.

And Gawayne rubbed his arms, his chest he beat,
Then grasped the battle-axe and braced his feet,
And swung the ponderous weapon high in air,
And brought it down like lightening, fair and square
Upon the stranger's neck. The axe flashed through,
Cutting the Green Knight cleanly right in two,

The Adventures of Sir Gawain

And split the hard stone floor like kindling wood.
The head dropped off; out gushed the thick, hot blood
Like – I can't find the simile I want,
But let us say a flood of crême de menthe!
And then the warriors standing round about
Sent up from fifty throats a mighty shout,
As when o'er blood-sprent fields the long cheers roll
Cacophonous, for him who kicks a goal.
"O Gawayne! Well done, Gawayne!" they all cried;
But straight the tumult and the shouting died,
And deadly pallor overspread each face,
For the knight's body stood up in its place
And stepping nimbly forward seized the head
That lay still on the hearth-stone, seeming dead;
Then vaulted lightly, with a careless air,
Back to the saddle of his grass-green mare.
He held the head up, and behold! it spoke.
"My best congratulations on that stroke,
Sir Gawayne; it was delicately done!
Our merry little jest is well begun,
But look you fail me not this day next year!
At the Green Chapel by the Murmuring Mere
I will await you when the sun sinks low,
And pay you back full measure, blow for blow!"
He wheeled about, the doors flew wide once more,
The mare's hoofs struck green sparkles from the floor,
And with a whirring flash of emerald light
Both horse and rider vanished in the night.

Then all the lords and ladies rubbed their eyes
And slowly roused themselves from dumb surprise.
The great hall echoed once more with the clatter
Of laughing men's and frightened women's chatter;
But Gawayne, with the axe in hand, stood still,
Heedless of what was passing, with no will
For life or death, for all that made life dear
Was fled like summer when the leaves fall sere.
And Arthur spoke, misreading Gawayne's thought:

The Adventures of Sir Gawain

"Heaven send we have not all too dearly bought
Our evening's pastime, Gawayne. You have done
As fits a fearless knight, and nobly won
Our thanks in equal measure with our praise.
Be both remembered in the after days!"

So spoke the king, and, to confirm his word,
From far away in the deep night was heard
Once more the fairy horn-call, clear and shrill;
It died upon the wind, and all was still.
The hour was late. King Arthur, rising, said
Good-night to all the court, and went to bed.

Canto II: Elfinhart

In Canto I. I followed the old rule
We learned from Horace when we went to school,
And took a headlong plunge in medias res,
As Maro did, and blind Mæonides;
And now, still following in the ancient mode,
I come to the time-honored "episode,"
Retrace my way some twenty years or more,
And tell you what I should have told before.
It seems an awkward method, but it's art; –
Besides, it brings us back to Elfinhart.
In those dark days before King Arthur came,
When Britain was laid waste with sword and flame,
When cut-throats lurked behind the blossoming thorn,
And young maids cursed the day when they were born,
A lady, widowed in one hideous night,
Fled over hearth and hill, and in her flight
Came to the magic willow-woods that stand
Beside the Murmuring Mere, in Fairyland;
And there, untimely, by the forest-side,
Clasping her infant in her arms, she died.
Yet not all friendless, – for such mortal throes
Pass not unpitied, though no mortal knows; –

The Adventures of Sir Gawain

The spirits that infest the clearer air
Looked down upon the innocent lady there,
While troops of fairies smoothed her mossy bed
And with sweet balsam pillowed her fair head.
Her dim eyes could not see them, but she guessed
Whose gentle ministrations thus had blessed
Her travail; and when pitying fairies laid
Upon her heart the child, – a blue-eyed maid, –
Ere yet her troubled spirit might depart,
With one last word she named her "Elfinhart."

So with new-quickened love the fairy elves
Took the forlorn child-maiden to themselves
And reared her in the wildwood, where no jar
Of alien discord, echoing from afar,
Broke the sweet forest murmur, long years round.
Her ears, attuned to every woodland sound,
Translated to her soul the great world's voice,
And the world-spirit made her heart rejoice.
And love was hers, – perennial, intense, –
The love that wells from joy and innocence
And sanctifies the cloistered heart of youth, –
The love of love, of beauty, and of truth.

So Elfinhart grew up. Each passing year
Of forest life beside the Murmuring Mere
Enriched tenfold the natural dower of grace
That shone from the pure spirit in her face.
I cannot tell why each revolving season
Enhanced her beauty thus. Some say the reason
Was in the stars; I think those luminaries
Had less to do with it than had the fairies!
The more they found of grace in her, the more
Their silent influence added to her store;
For they were always with her; they and she
Still bore each other loving company.
And yet one further virtue, – not the least
Of those that make life lovable, – increased

159

The Adventures of Sir Gawain

In Elfinhart's sweet nature from her birth
By fairy tutelage; and that was mirth.
For fairy natures are compounded all
Of whimsies and of freaks fantastical,
And what the best of fairies loves the best
(Except pure kindness) is an artless jest.
And so wise men have argued, on the whole,
That the misguided creatures have no soul;
But as for me, if the bright fairy elf
Has none, I'll get along without, myself!
These fairies laughed and danced and sang sweet songs,
And did all else that to their craft belongs, –
All tricks and pranks of whole-souled jollity
That makes life merry 'neath the greenwood tree.
The youngest of them childishly beguiled
The time when Elfinhart was still a child;
They pinched her fingers, and they pulled her ears,
Or sometimes, when her blue eyes dreamed of tears,
Half smothered her with showers of four-leafed clover, –
Then fled for refuge to some sweet-fern cover;
But she pursued them through their tangled lair
And caught them, and put fire-flies in their hair;
And then they all joined hands, and round and round
They danced a morris on the moonlit ground.

The years went by, and Elfinhart outgrew
The madcap antics of the younger crew,
(For fairies age but slowly: don't forget
That at two hundred they are children yet!)
But still she frolicked with them, though scarce of them,
And learned each year more tenderly to love them.
But most of all she loved with all her heart
On quiet summer nights to walk apart
And hold close converse with the fairies' queen, –
A radiant maiden princess who had seen
Some twenty centuries of revolving suns
Pass over Fairyland, – all golden ones!
Sometimes they sat still in the mild moon's light,

The Adventures of Sir Gawain

Where chestnut blooms made sweet the breath of night,
And talked of the great world beyond the wood, –
Of death, or sin, or sorrow, understood
Of neither, – till the twinkling stars were gone,
And bustling Chanticleer proclaimed the dawn.
And Elfinhart grew wise in fairy learning;
But by degrees a half unconscious yearning
For humankind stirred in her gentle heart,
And woke a deep desire to bear her part
Of love and sorrow in the larger life
As sister, helper, – nay, perhaps as wife; –
For such vague instincts, after all, are human,
And Elfinhart herself was but a woman.
And yet, for all this new desire, I doubt
If Elfinhart would e'er have spoken out,
And told the fairies of her wish to leave them,
(A wish her conscious heart well knew would grieve them),
If in the ripening of her silent thought
A still voice had not whispered that she ought
To leave that world of love and mirth and beauty,
To share man's burden in this world of duty.
(There's anticlimax for you! Most provoking,
Just when you thought that I was only joking,
Or idly fingering the poet's laurel,
To find my story threatens to be moral!
But as for morals, though in verse we scout them,
In life we somehow can't get on without them;
So if I don't insert a moral distich
Once in a while, I can't be realistic; –
And in this tale, I solemnly aver,
My one wish is to tell things as they were!
But not all things; time flies, and art is long,
And I must hurry onward with my song.)
How Elfinhart at last told what she wanted,
And what the fairies said, please take for granted.
She prayed, they yielded; Elfinhart full loth
To leave, as they to let her go, but both
Agreeing that this bitter thing must be;

161

The Adventures of Sir Gawain

For they were fairies, and a mortal she.
But ere they yielded, they made imposition
Of what then seemed to her a light condition.
'T was done in kindness, be it understood,
With fairy foresight for the maiden's good.
The elf-queen spoke for all: "Dear Elfinhart,
We bind you to one promise ere we part.
We fear naught from men's malice; hate and wrath
And every evil thing will shun your path,
And sunshine will go with you when you move;
The only danger that we dread is love.
If in the after days, when suitors woo you,
Your heart makes choice of one, as dearest to you,
Before you put your hand in his and own
The sacred trust reserved for him alone,
Let us make trial of him, and approve
His virtue, and his manhood, and his love.
Send him to us; and if he bears the test,
And if we find him worthy to be blest
With love like yours, be sure we will befriend him;
And may a life-long happiness attend him!
But if he prove a traitor, or faint-hearted,
Or if his love and he are lightly parted,
In the deep willow-woods he shall remain,
And never look upon your face again!"
The maiden, fancy-free, was well content,
And with light laughter gave her full consent;
For when maids think of love (as maidens do)
It seems a far-off thing; and well she knew
Her lover, if she loved, would be both brave and true!
Not long thereafter came an errant band
Riding along the edge of Fairyland, –
Stout men-at-arms, without reproach or spot,
And in the lead the bold Sir Launcelot.
He, riding on ahead, silent, alone,
Was stopped by a beseeching ancient crone
Who hobbled to his side, as if in pain,
And clutched with palsied fingers at his rein.

162

The Adventures of Sir Gawain

And there behind her, from the leafage green,
The sweetest eyes his eyes had ever seen
Were gazing at him with wide wonderment,
Not bold or fearful; innocence unshent
Shone from their blue depths, and old dreams awoke
In Launcelot's breast, while thus the beldame spoke:
"A boon, a boon, Sir Launcelot of the Lake!
I pray you of your courtesy to take
This damsel to the King. Her enemies
Have spoiled her of her birthright, and she flees
An innocent outcast from her wasted lands,
To lay her life and fortune in his hands."
She spoke, and vanished in the woodland shade.

Then Launcelot, leaning over, helped the maid
To mount behind, and at an easy trot
They and the troop rode on to Camelot.
He asked no questions, for some fairy spell
Made light his heart, and told him all was well;
And as these two rode through the land together,
By dappled greenwood shade and sunlit heather,
Her soft voice in his ears, the innocent charm
Of her light, steady touch upon his arm,
Wrought magic in his soul. That day, I ween,
Sir Launcelot well-nigh forgot his queen.
And Elfinhart (you knew those eyes were hers!)
Laughed with the silvery jingle of his spurs,
And from her heart the new world's rapture drove
All thought of Fairyland – excepting love.

And so to high-towered Camelot they came,
The golden city, – now a shadowy name;
For over heath-clad hills the wild winds blow
Where Arthur's halls, a thousand years ago,
Bright with all far-fetched gems of curious art,
Shone brighter with the eyes of Elfinhart.
She came to Camelot; the king receives her;
And there for five glad years my story leaves her.

The Adventures of Sir Gawain

Five glad years, and this "episode" is done,
And we are back again at Canto I.
I write of merry jest and greenwood shade,
But tales of chivalry are not my trade;
So if you wish to read that five years' story
Of lady-love, romance, and martial glory, –
The mighty feats of arms that Gawayne did, –
The ever ripening love that Gawayne hid
Five long years in his breast, biding his time, –
Go seek it in some abler poet's rime.
My tale begins with the young knight's brave soul
All Elfinhart's. She thinks herself heart-whole.

But at that Christmas feast, in Arthur's hall,
With night's soft mantle folded over all,
The magic influence of the evening tide
Stole on their two hearts beating side by side.
And Gawayne talked of troubles long ago,
When each man's neighbour was his dearest foe,
And of the trials he himself had passed,
And the high purpose that from first to last
Had been his stay and spur, he scarce knew how,
Since on Excalibur he took the vow.
He told of his own hopes for future days,
And how he wrought and fought not for men's praise,
(Though like all good men Gawayne held that dear),
Yet trusting, when men laid him on his bier,
They might remember, as they gathered round it,
"He left this good world better than he found it."
He talked as true men seldom talk, unless
Swayed utterly by some pure passion's stress,
And ever gently, though with heart on fire,
Still hovered nearer to his soul's desire.
And Elfinhart in gravest silence listened,
But her sweet heart beat high, her blue eyes glistened;
For as he bared his soul to her she dreamed
A day-dream strange and new, wherein it seemed
That in that soul's clear depth she saw her own,

164

The Adventures of Sir Gawain

And his most secret thought (till then unknown)
Seemed hers eternally. He spoke of death,
And then her heart shrank, and she drew deep breath.
Suddenly, ere she understood it all
What new life dawned before her, came the call
Of fairy horns; and so the Green Knight burst
Upon the scene, as told in Canto First.

One jarring note, the tuneful chords among,
May make mad discord of the sweetest song.
E'en so with dissonant clamor through the breast
Of Gawayne rang the Green Knight's merry jest;
But what wild meaning must it not impart
To the vague fears of gentle Elfinhart?
For she had heard in the first trumpet-blast
A signal to her from the far-gone past;
And now, of all the strange things that had been,
Her half forgotten compact with the queen
Flushed through her memory, and a swift thought came
Like sudden fear, a thought without a name,
An unvoiced question and a blind alarm;
And in sheer helplessness she reached an arm
Toward Gawayne, scarcely knowing what she would;
Her eyes beheld him, and she understood.
And is it Gawayne? He? Yes, Elfinhart,
The hour has come, and you must play your part.

So now it's all explained; and I intend
To go straight onward to the story's end.
Sir Gawayne had cut off the Green Knight's head,
And Arthur and his court had gone to bed;
In the great hall the dying embers shone
With a faint ghostly gleam, and there, alone,
While all the rest of Camelot was sleeping,
In the dark alcove Elfinhart lay weeping.
But as she lay there, all about her head
There fell a checkered beam of moonlight, shed
Through the barred casement; and she faintly stirred,

165

The Adventures of Sir Gawain

For in her troubled soul it seemed she heard
Vague music from some region far away.
She raised her head and, turning where she lay,
Saw in the silver moonlight the serene
And tranquil beauty of the fairy queen!

"We sent before you called us, Elfinhart,
For love lent keener magic to our art,
And warned us of the thoughts that in your breast
Awoke new rapture, trembling unconfessed."
And Elfinhart moved closer to her knees
And hid her face in the white draperies
That veiled the fairy form, till, nestling there,
Her heart recovered from that blank despair,
And whispered her that whatsoe'er befell
Love ruled the world, and all would yet be well.
And the good fairy stroked the maiden's head
And kissed her tear-starred eyes, and smiling said:
"Fie on you women's hearts! Consistency
Hides her shamed head where mortal women be!
True love breeds faith and trust, it makes hearts strong;
The heart's anointed king can do no wrong!
And yet you weep as if you feared to prove him; –
Upon my word, I don't believe you love him!"
And Elfinhart replied: "Laugh if you will,
My queen, but let me be a woman still.
You fairies love where love is wise and just;
We mortal women love because we must:
And if I feared to prove him, I confess
I fear I still must love him none the less."
She paused, for once again her eyes grew dim:
"Think you I love his virtues? I love him!
But yet you judged me wrongly, for believe me,
(And then laugh once again, and so forgive me),
If at the first I feared what you might do,
My doubts were not of Gawayne, but of you!"
And so both laughed, and for a little space
Folded each other in a glad embrace;

The Adventures of Sir Gawain

(For fairies, bathed the whole year round in bliss,
May yet be gladdened by a fair maid's kiss);
And Elfinhart spoke on: "Do what you will,
I trust you with my all, and fear no ill.
But oh, my friend, to wait the long, long year, –
To keep my heart in silence, not to hear
The words my whole soul hungers for, nor say
One syllable to brighten his dark day!
Must it be so, my queen? And how shall I
School eyes and lips to act this year-long lie?
From the dear teacher-guardian of my youth
The only ways I learned were ways of truth!
I tried my skill this night, and learned to know
That there are deeps below the deeps of woe;
Hearts may be bruised and broken, yet still live; –
The wounds that kill us are the wounds we give!"

And so these two talked on, until the night
Began to shiver with the gray dawn's light,
And in the deep-dyed casement they might see
New life flush through old dreams of chivalry.
And then they parted. What the queen had said
I know not, but the lady, comforted,
Bade farewell with calm voice and tranquil eyes,
And saw with new-born strength the new sun rise.
Perhaps in Fairyland there chanced to be
For them that grieve some sovereign alchemy
To turn the worst to best, and the good queen
Applied this soothing balm. Such things have been;
But yet I doubt if any fairy art
Was needed in the case of Elfinhart;
The medicine that charmed away her dole
Nature had planted in her own sweet soul.
Of all sure things, this thing I'm surest of, –
That the best cure for love's own ills is love.

The Adventures of Sir Gawain

Canto III: Gawayne

O Muse! – But no: heaven knows I need a muse;
But which of all the nine, pray, should I choose?
Thalia, Clio, and Melpomene,
I love them all, but none, alas, loves me;
For if you want a muse to take your part
You must be solely hers with all your heart;
And I have mingled since my earliest youth
My smiles and tears, my fictions and my truth;
Nay, in this very tale, scarce yet half done,
I've courted all the nine, and so won none!
Not for me, therefore, the Parnassian lyre,
Or winged war-horse shod with heavenly fire;
Harsh numbers flow from throats whose thirst has been
A whole life long unslaked of Hippocrene;
But I will e'en go on as best I can
And let the story end as it began, –
A plain, straightforward man's unvarnished word,
Part sad, part sweet, – and part of it absurd.

A year passed by, as years are wont to do,
Winter and spring, summer and autumn too,
Till mid-December's flaw-blown flakes of snow
Warned Gawayne that the time was come to go
To the Green Chapel by the Murmuring Mere,
And take again the blow he gave last year.
In the great court his charger stamped the ground,
While knights and weeping ladies thronged around
To arm him (as the custom was of yore)
And bid him sad farewell for evermore.
One face alone in all that bustling throng
Our hero's eyes sought eagerly, and long
Sought vainly; for the lady Elfinhart,
Debating with herself, stood yet apart;
But as Sir Gawayne gathered up his reins
And bade the draw-bridge warden loose the chains,

168

The Adventures of Sir Gawain

Suddenly Elfinhart stood by his side,
Her fair face flushed with love, and joy, and pride.
She plucked a sprig of holly from her gown
And looked up, questioning; and he leaned down,
And so she placed it in his helm. No word
Might Gawayne's lips then utter, but he heard
The voice that was his music, and could feel
The touch of gentle fingers through the steel.
"Wear this, Sir Gawayne, for a loyal friend
Whose hopes and prayers go with you to the end."
And, staying not for answer, she withdrew,
And in the throng was lost to Gawayne's view.
He roused himself, and waving high his hand,
Struck spur, and so rode off to Fairyland.

Long time he traveled by an unknown way,
Unhoused at night, companionless by day.
The cold sleet stung him through his shirt of mail,
But, underneath, his stout heart would not fail,
But beat full measure through the fiercest storm,
And kept his head clear and his brave soul warm.
No need to tell the perils that he passed;
He conquered all, and came unscathed at last
To where a high-embattled castle stood
Deep in the heart of a dense willow-wood.
And Gawayne called aloud, and to the gate
A smiling porter came, who opened straight,
And bade him enter in and take his rest;
And Gawayne entered, and the people pressed
About him with fair speeches; and he laid
His armor off, and gave it them, and prayed
That they would take his message to their lord, –
A prayer for friendly shelter, bed and board.
He told them whence he was, his birth and name;
And the bold baron of the castle came,
A mighty man, huge-limbed, with flashing eyes,
And welcomed him with old-time courtesies;
For manners, in those days, were held of worth,

The Adventures of Sir Gawain

And gentle breeding went with gentle birth.
He heartily was glad his guest had come,
And made Sir Gawayne feel himself at home;
And as they walked in, side by side, each knew
The other for an honest man and true.

That night our hero and the baron ate
A sumptuous dinner in the hall of state,
And all the household, ranged along the board,
Made good cheer with Sir Gawayne and their lord,
And passed the brimming bowl right merrily
With friendly banter and quick repartee.
And Gawayne asked if they had chanced to hear
Of a Green Chapel by a Murmuring Mere,
And straightway all grew grave. Within his breast
Sir Gawayne felt a tremor of unrest,
But told his story with a gay outside,
And asked for some good man to be his guide
To find his foe. "I promise him," said he,
"No golden guerdon; – his reward shall be
The consciousness that unto him 't was given
To show a parting soul the way to heaven!"

Up jumped his host. "My friend, I like your attitude,
And know no surer way to win heaven's gratitude
Than sending thither just such men as you;
I'll be your guide. But since you are not due
At the Green Chapel till three nights from now,
And since the way is short, I'll tell you how
The interim may be disposed of best: –
In short, let me propose a merry jest!"
At this Sir Gawayne gave a sudden start,
For some old memory seemed to clutch his heart,
And in the baron's eyes he seemed to see
A twinkling gleam of green benignity
Not wholly strange; but like a flash 't was gone.
Gawayne sank back, and his good host went on:
"Two days you sojourn here, and while I take

170

The Adventures of Sir Gawain

My daily hunting in the wood, you make
My house and castle yours; and then, each night,
We'll meet together here at candle-light,
And all my winnings in the wood, and all
That comes to you at home, whate'er befall,
We'll give each other in exchange; in fine,
My fortune shall be yours, and yours be mine."
To Gawayne this seemed generous indeed.
And with most cordial laughter he agreed.
They clasped hands o'er the bargain with good zest,
And then all said good-night, and went to rest.

Next morning Gawayne was awakened early
From a deep slumber by the hurly-burly
Of footman, horseman, seneschal, and groom,
Bustling beneath the windows of his room.
He rose and looked out, just in time to see
The baron and a goodly company
Of huntsmen, armed with cross-bow, axe, and spear,
Ride through the castle gate and disappear.
And then, while Gawayne dressed, there came a knock
Upon his chamber door. He threw the lock,
And a boy page brought robes of ermine fur
And Tarsic silk, – black, white and lavender, –
For his array, and with them a kind message,
Which the good knight received with no ill presage:
"Will brave Sir Gawayne spare an idle hour
For quiet converse in my lady's bower?"
The boy led on, and Gawayne followed him
Through crooked corridors and archways dim,
Along low galleries echoing from afar,
And down a winding stair; then "Here we are!"
The page cried cheerily, and paused before
The massive carvings of an antique door.
This he swung open; and the knight passed through
Into a garden, fresh with summer dew!
A lady's bower in Fairyland! What pen
Could make that strange enchantment live again?

The Adventures of Sir Gawain

Not he who drew Acrasia's Bower of Bliss
And Phædria's happy isle could picture this.
That sweet-souled Puritan discerned too well
The serpent's coil behind the witch's spell;
And he who saw – when the dark veil was torn –
The rose of Paradise without the thorn,
(Sublimest prophet, whose immortal verse
Lent mightier thunders to the primal curse),
Even he too sternly, in the soul's defense,
Repressed the still importunate cries of sense.
Bid me not, therefore, task my feebler pen
With dreams beyond the limits of their ken;
The phantom conjurings of the magic hour
That Gawayne passed in that enchanted bower
Must be from mortal eyes forever hid.
But yet some part of what he felt and did
These lines must needs disclose. As he stood there,
Breathing soft odors from the mellow air,
All hopes, all aims of noble knighthood seemed
Like the dim yesterdays of one who dreamed,
In starless caves of memory sunken deep,
And, like lost music, folded in strange sleep.

"How long, O mortal man, wilt thou give heed
To the world's phantom voices? The hours speed,
And fame and fortune yield to moth and rust,
And good and evil crumble into dust.
Even now the sands are running in the glass;
Set not your heart upon vain things that pass;
Ambitions, honors, toils, are but the snare
Where lurks for aye the blind old world's despair.
Nay, quiet the bootless striving in your breast
And let your tired heart here at last find rest.
In vain have joy, love, beauty, struck deep root
In your heart's heart, unless you pluck the fruit;
Then put away the cheating soul's pretense,
Heap high the press, fill full the cup of sense;
Shatter the idols of blind yesterday,

The Adventures of Sir Gawain

And let love, joy, and beauty reign alway!"

Such thoughts as these, confused and unexpressed,
Flooded the silence in Sir Gawayne's breast.
Meanwhile a brasier filled the scented air
With wreaths of magic mist, and he was ware
That the mist drew together like a shroud;
And then the veil was rent, and in the cloud
Stood one who seemed, in features, form, and dress,
The perfect image of all loveliness.

The wonders of that vision none could tell
Save one whose heart had felt the mystic spell.
Once and once only, in the golden days
When youth made melody for love's sweet lays,
In two dark eyes (yet oh, how bright, how bright!)
I saw the wakening rapture of love's light,
And, in the hush of that still dawning, heard
From two sweet trembling lips love's whispered word.
The twilight deepens when the sun has set;
In memory golden glories linger yet;
But these avail not. Though my soul lay bare,
With all those memories sanctuaried there,
That spell was human. But the unseen power
That wove the witchery of this fairy bower,
In Gawayne's heart such subtle magic wrought
That past and future were well-nigh forgot,
And all that earth holds else, or heaven above,
Seemed naught worth keeping, save this dream of love.

And now, as the strange cloud of incense broke,
The vision, if it were a vision, spoke, –
If it were speech that filled the quivering air
With low harmonious music. Let none dare
In the rude jargons of this world to fashion
That sweet, wild anthem of unearthly passion.
Could I from the broad-billowing ocean borrow
Of Tristan's love and of Isolde's sorrow,

The Adventures of Sir Gawain

The flood of those world-darkening surges, wrought
With thoughts that lie beyond the reach of thought,
Might bring me succor where weak words must fail.
But Gawayne saw and heard, and passion-pale
Shrank back, and made a darkness of his face;
(As though the unplumbed deeps of starless space
Could quench those lustrous eyes, or close his ears
To the eternal music of love's spheres!)
But the voice changed, and Gawayne, listening there,
Heard now a heart's low cry of wild despair.
He turned again, and lo! the vision knelt
And drew a jeweled poniard from her belt,
To arm herself against her own dear life;
But as she bared her white breast to the knife
He started quickly forward, and he grasped
The hand that held the hilt; and then she clasped
Her soft arms round his neck, and as their lips
Met in the shadowing fold of love's eclipse,
All earth, all heaven, all knightly hopes of grace,
Died in the darkness of one blind embrace.

Died? Nay; for Gawayne, ere the moment passed,
Broke from the arms that strove to bind him fast,
And turned away once more; and, as he pressed
A trembling hand against his throbbing breast,
His aimless fingers touched a treasured part
Of the green holly-branch of Elfinhart,
Laid in his breast when he put off his arms.
What perils now are left in fairy charms?
For poets fable when they call love blind;
Love's habitation is the purer mind,
Whence with his keen eyes he may penetrate
All mists and fogs that baser spells create.
Love? What is love? Not the wild feverish thrill,
When heart to heart the thronging pulses fill,
And lips that close in parching kisses find
No speech but those; – the best remains behind.
The tranquil spirit – the divine assurance

The Adventures of Sir Gawain

That this life's seemings have a high endurance –
Thoughts that allay this restless striving, calm
The passionate heart, and fill old wounds with balm; –
These are the choirs invisible that move
In white processionals up the aisles of love.

Such love was Gawayne's, – love that sanctifies
The heart's most secret altar; and his eyes
Were opened, and his pulses beat once more
Their old true rhythm. And so the strife was o'er,
And all the perilous wiles of magic art
Were foiled by Gawayne – and by Elfinhart.

But time flies, and 't were tedious to delay
My song for all the trials of that day.
Light summer breezes, skurrying o'er the deep,
Ripple and foam and flash, – then sink to sleep;
But underneath, serene and changing never,
The mighty heart of ocean beats forever,
And his deep streams renew from pole to pole
The living world's indomitable soul.
Enough, then, of the spells that vexed the brain
Of Gawayne; love and knighthood made all vain.
And in the afternoon, when Gawayne learned
That his good host, the baron, had returned,
He met him in the hall at candle-light,
According to his promise of last night.
And then the baron motioned to a page,
And straightway six tall men, of lusty age
And mighty sinews, entered the great door,
Bearing the carcass of a huge wild boar,
In all its uncouth ugliness complete,
And dropped it quivering at our hero's feet.
"What do you say to that, Sir Gawayne?" cried
The baron, swelling with true sportman's pride
"But come: your promise, now, of yester-eve;
'T is blesseder to give than to receive!
Though I'll be sworn you'll find it hard to pay

The Adventures of Sir Gawain

Full value for the winnings of this day."
"Not so," said Gawayne; "you will rest my debtor;
Your gift is good, but mine will be far better."
And then he strode with solemn steps along
The echoing hall, and through the listening throng,
And with the words, "My noble lord, take this!"
He gave the baron a resounding kiss.
The baron jumped up in ecstatic glee.
"Now by my great-great-grandsire's beard," quoth he,
"Better than all dead boars in Christendom
Is one sweet loving kiss! – Whence did it come?"
"Nay, there," Sir Gawayne said, "you step beyond
The terms we stipulated in our bond.
Take you my kiss in peace, as I your boar;
Be glad; give thanks; – and seek to know no more."
Loud laughter made the baron's eyes grow bright
And glitter with green sparkles of delight;
And then he chuckled: "Sir, I'm proud of you;
I drink your best of health; I think you'll do!"

And now the board was laid and dressed, and all
Sat down to dinner at the baron's call;
And Gawayne looked along the room askance,
Seeking the lady; and he caught one glance
Of laughing eyes – then looked away in haste,
But turned again, and wondered why his taste
Had erred so strangely, for the lady seemed
Not fairer now than others. Had he dreamed?
He rubbed his eyes and pondered, – though in sooth
Without one glimmering presage of the truth, –
Till all passed lightly from his puzzled mind,
Leaving contentment and good cheer behind.
So all the company feasted well, and sped
The flying hours, till it was time for bed.

One whole day longer must our hero rest
Within doors, to fulfill the merry jest.
So when, next morning, Gawayne once more heard

The Adventures of Sir Gawain

The hunt's-up in the court, he never stirred,
But let the merry horsemen ride away
While he slept soundly well into the day.
Later he rose, and strolled from room to room,
Through vaulted twilights of ancestral gloom,
Until, descending a long stair, he found
The dim-lit castle crypt, deep under ground,
Where sculptured effigies forever kept
Their long last marble silence as they slept,
And iron sentinels, on bended knees,
Held eyeless vigil in old panoplies.

Sir Gawayne, wandering on in aimless mood,
Pondered the tomb-stone legends, quaint and rude,
Wherein the pensive dreamer might divine
A tragic history in every line;
For so does fate, with bitterest irony,
Epitomize fame's immortality,
Perpetuating for all after days
Mute lamentations and unnoted praise.
And Gawayne, reading here and there the story
Of fame obscure and unremembered glory,
Found on a tablet these words: "Where he lies,
The gray wave breaks and the wild sea-mew flies:
If any be that loved him, seek not here,
But in the lone hills by the Murmuring Mere."
A nameless cenotaph! perhaps of one
Like Gawayne's self deluded and undone
By the green stranger; and the legend brought
A tide of passion flooding Gawayne's thought;
A flood-tide, not of fear, – for Gawayne's breast
Shrank never at the perilous behest
Of noble knighthood, – but the love of life,
Compassion, and soul-sickness of the strife.
"If any be that loved him!" Oh, to die
Far from green-swarded Camelot, and lie
Among these bleak and barren hills alone,
His end unwept for and his grave unknown, –

177

The Adventures of Sir Gawain

Never again to see the glad sunrise
That brightened all his world in those dear eyes!

Half suffocating in the charneled air
Of that low vault, he staggered up the stair,
Out of the dim-lit halls of silent death
Into the living light, and drew quick breath
Where, through a casement-arch of ivied stone,
Bright from the clear blue sky the warm sun shone.
The whole of life's glad rapture thrilled his heart;
Till a quick step behind him made him start,
And there, deep-veiled, in muffling cloak and hood,
Once more the lady of the castle stood.

Low-voiced she spoke, as if with studied care
Weighing the syllables of her parting prayer.
"Sir Gawayne – nay, I pray you, turn not yet,
But hear me; – though my heart may not forget
That once, for one sweet moment, you were kind,
I come not to recall that to your mind; –
Between us two be love's words aye unspoken!
Yet ere you go, I pray you, leave some token
That in the long, long years may comfort me
For the dear face I nevermore shall see."
"Nay, lady," said the knight, "I have no gifts
To give you. Errant knighthood ever drifts
From shore to shore, by wandering breezes blown,
With naught save its good name to call its own.
In friendship, then, I pray you keep for me
My name untarnished in your memory."
"Ah, sir," she said, "my memory bears that name
Burnt in with characters of living flame.
But though you give me naught, I pray you take
This girdle from me; – wear it for my sake;
Nay, but refuse me not; you little know
Its magic power. I had it long ago
From Fairyland; and its encircling charm
Keeps scathless him who wears it from all harm;

178

No evil thing can touch him. Gird it on,
If but to ease my heart when you are gone."

She held a plain green girdle in her hand,
In outward seeming just a narrow band
Of silk, with silver clasps; but in those days
The strangest things were wrought in simplest ways,
As Gawayne knew full well; and he could see
That all the lady said was verity.
He took the girdle, held it, fingered it,
Then clasped it round his waist to try the fit,
Irresolutely dallying with temptation,
Till conscience grew too weak for inclination;
For at the last he threw one wandering glance
Out at the casement, and the merry dance
Of sparkling sunbeams on the fields of snow
Wrought havoc in his wavering heart; and so,
Repeating to himself one word: "Life, life!"
He took the token from the baron's wife.

That evening, when the baron and our knight
Met to exchange their gifts at candle-light,
The baron, looking graver than before,
Said: "Sir, my luck has left me; not a boar
Did we get wind of, all this blessed day.
I come with empty hands, only to pray
Your pardon. What good fortune do you bring?"
And Gawayne answered firmly: "Not a thing!"

Canto IV: Conclusion

By noon the next day, Gawayne and his host
Rode side by side along the perilous coast
Of the gray Mere, from whose unquiet sleep
Reverberating murmurs of the deep
Startled the still December's listening air.
The baron, shuddering, pointed seaward. "There,"

179

The Adventures of Sir Gawain

He said, "year in, year out, these voices haunt
That fearful water; heaven knows what they want!
Men tell me – and I have no doubt it's true –
They are knights-errant whom the Green Knight slew!
Woe unto him, the over-bold, who dares
Adventure near that uncouth monster's snares!"
Quoth Gawayne: "How have you escaped the net?"
The baron answered: "I? We never met!
When I'm about, he seems to shun the place,
And where he is, I never show my face;
But if we did meet, 't would be safe to say
Not more than one of us would get away!"

And then the baron told tales by the score
About the Green Knight's quenchless thirst for gore,
And kept repeating that no magic charm
Was proof against the prowess of his arm;
At his first blow each vain defense must fall,
For he was arch-magician over all.
And as from tale to tale the baron ran,
Sir Gawayne, had he been another man,
Would certainly have felt his heart's blood curdle,
Despite his secret wearing of the girdle;
But when the baron finally suggested
Abandoning the venture, and protested
That the whole monstrous business was absurd,
Sir Gawayne simply said: "I gave my word.
And when the baron saw he would not bend,
He seemed to lose all patience. "Well, my friend,
I'll go no further with you. On your head
Shall be your own mad blood when you are dead.
Yonder your two roads fork; pause there, I pray,
And ponder well before you choose your way.
One takes the hills, one winds along the wave;
To Camelot this, – the other to your grave!
Choose the high road, Sir Gawayne; shun the danger!
Say you were misdirected by a stranger; –
I swear by all that's sacred, I'll not tell

The Adventures of Sir Gawain

One syllable to a soul: – and so farewell!"
He galloped off without another word,
And vanished where the road turned. Gawayne heard,
Long after he had disappeared, the sound
Of iron hoof-beats on the frozen ground,
Till all had died into silence, save those drear
And hollow voices from the Murmuring Mere.

But Gawayne chose the lower road, and passed
Along the desolate shore. The die was cast.
The western skies, as the red sun sank low,
Cast purple shades across the drifted snow,
And Gawayne knew that the dread hour was come
For the fulfillment of his martyrdom.
And now, from just beyond a jutting hill,
Came hideous sounds, as of a giant mill
That hisses, roars, and sputters, clicks and clacks; –
It was the Green Knight sharpening his axe!
And Gawayne, coming past the corner, found him,
With ghastly mouldering skulls and bones strewn round him,
In joyous fury urging the keen steel
Against the surface of his grinding wheel.
The place was a wild hollow, circled round
With barren hills, and on the bottom ground
Stood the Green Chapel, moss-grown, solitary; –
In sooth, it seemed the devil's mortuary!
The Green Knight's back was turned, and he stirred not
Till Gawayne hailed him sharply; then he shot
One glance – as when, o'erhead, a living wire
Startles the night with flashes of green fire; –
Then hurried forward, bland as bland could be,
And greeted Gawayne with green courtesy.
"Dear sir, I ask a thousand pardons; pray
Forgive me. You are punctual to the day;
That's good! Of course I knew you would not fail.
How do you do? You look a trifle pale;
I trust, with all my heart, you are not ill?
Just the cold air? It does blow rather chill!

The Adventures of Sir Gawain

What can I do to cheer you? Let me see; –
Suppose I brew a cup of hot green tea?
You'ld rather not? You're pressed for time? Of course,
I understand; then just get off your horse,
And I'll do all I can to expedite
Our little business for you. There, that's right;
And now your helmet? Thanks; and if you please
Perhaps you'll kindly kneel down on your knees,
As I did when I came to Camelot; So!
Are you all ready? Will you bide the blow?"
And Gawayne said "I will," in such soft notes
As happy bridegrooms utter, when their throats
Are paralyzed with blest anticipation; –
(What Gawayne looked for was decapitation!)
And then the Green Knight swung his axe in air
With a loud whirr; and Gawayne, kneeling there,
Shrank back an inch; and the green giant stayed
His threatening hand, and with a cold sneer said:
"You shrink, sir, from the axe; I can't hit true
Unles you hold still, as I did for you."
"Your pardon," Gawayne said, with bated breath;
"This time I swear to hold as still as death."
He did so, and the Green Knight swung again
His axe, and whirled it round his head, and then,
Pausing a second time, said: "Very good!
You're holding quite still now; I knew you would!"
Gawayne, in anger, said: "Jest, if you like,
After the blow; tarry no longer; strike!"
So once again the ponderous axe was raised;
But this time down it came, and lightly grazed
Sir Gawayne's neck. He felt the hot blood flow,
And saw red drops that sank into the snow,
And then he jumped up, faced his foe, and cried:
"Enough: you owed me one blow, though I died;
But be you man or beast or devil abhorred,
I yield no further; with my mortal sword
I do defy you; and if mortal man
May hope against". . .

The Adventures of Sir Gawain

But the Green Knight began
A low melodious laugh, like running brooks
Whose pebbly babble fills the shadowy nooks
Of green-aisled woodlands, when the winds are still.
"My friend, we bear each other no ill will.
When first I swung my axe, you showed some fear;
I owed you that much for your blow last year.
The second time I swung, – yet spared your life, –
That paid you for the kiss you gave my wife!"
"Your wife!" "My wife, Sir Gawayne; 't was my word;
And when I swung my weapon for the third
And last time, then I made the red blood spirt
For that green girdle underneath your shirt!
You played me false, my friend!"
                              And Gawayne knelt
Once more, and casting off the magic belt,
In bitter broken words confessed his shame,
And begged the Green Knight to avenge the name
Of injured knighthood, and with one last blow
To end his guilty life. "Nay, nay, not so,"
The other softly said. "Be of good cheer;
Your fault was small, for all men hold life dear.
We tempted you, my friend, with all our might,
And proved you in good sooth a noble knight;
A veritable Joseph, sir, you are!"
Quoth Gawayne drily, "Thanks, Lord Potiphar!
But may I ask you why you played this part?"
The other said: "Ask Lady Elfinhart!"

He smiled, and from his smile a genial glow
Of green mid-summer seemed to overflow,
Filling with verdure all that barren place.
The warm red blood rushed to Sir Gawayne's face;
He caught his breath, and in his eager eyes
There shone a sudden flash of dark surmise,
And then he stood a long time pondering;
But in his breast his heart began to sing

The Adventures of Sir Gawain

The old, old music whose still echoes roll
Forever voiceless through the listening soul.
He said farewell to his good fairy friend
As in a dream, where real and unreal blend
In phantom unison, and with the light
Of love to lead him home, rode through the night,
Beside the tranquil murmurs of the Mere,
And through the silence of the passing year;
And earth and sea and starlit sky took part
In the still exaltation of his heart,
While all but love and wonder was forgot,
Until he came to high-towered Camelot.

To Camelot he came, and there he found
The good King Arthur and his Table Round
Awaiting his return in anxious doubt;
But ere he passed the gates a mighty shout
Rose from the watchmen on the outward wall
And bore the tidings to the inmost hall.
From every window flaunting flags were flung;
From the high battlements brass trumpets sung;
And great bells, chiming in the topmost tower,
Pealed salutation to the joyous hour,
As Gawayne, riding through the cullis-port,
Faced the glad throng that filled the palace court.

And with this tribute paid to knightly glory
It seems most fitting to conclude my story.
Entreat me not, dear reader, to impart
Further of Gawayne, or of Elfinhart.
Let your own fancy round the story out
Whatever way you please; I cannot doubt
The sequel; but when I, in silent thought,
Had brought Sir Gawayne back to her, and sought
With hand profane to lift the veil, behind
Whose secret shelter their two hearts enshrined
The mutual covenant of love's mystery,
That pure fane would not desecrated be.

The Adventures of Sir Gawain

But this alone I know: the power that wove
Through human lives the warp and woof of love
Wrought not in darkness, nor with hand unsure; –
His fabric must forevermore endure.
And hence I doubt not that these two were blest
As none may be, save they who have confessed
Allegiance to that mighty spirit's law,
And trod his holy ground with reverent awe.

www.ingramcontent.com/pod-product-compliance
Lightning Source LLC
Chambersburg PA
CBHW031350170626
46807CB00002B/909